The Bastard Heir

The Gilded West (book 2)

Harper St. George

Contents

The Bastard Heir

by Harper St. George

A fake engagement between an unconventional heiress and the outlaw she blackmails leads to a high-stakes game of love neither saw coming in this novel from Harper St. George's **The Gilded West** series.

Consumed by vengeance and on the trail of the murderer who killed his grandfather, Castillo Jameson has no room in his life for love. Until a chance encounter on a train throws a beautiful heiress in the crossfire of his revenge, where they share a stolen kiss, never expecting to see each other again.

Caroline Hartford has aspirations that don't include settling down into a loveless, society marriage. Her dream is to become a physician, but her parents demand she marry first. Then the dangerous outlaw from the train arrives at the wedding she's attending, and Caroline knows she's found the answer to her problem. She'll keep his real identity a secret, if he'll pretend to be her fiancé.

Against the backdrop of America's Gilded West, Castillo's enemies threaten to bring their precarious alliance crumbling down around them. Torn between duty and a love that could shatter them both, he'll have to decide if he can let go of the past to embrace a future with the woman he loves.

The Gilded West

Author Note

One of the reasons I love writing about the Wild West is because it was a time of change. Towns sprang up overnight, and they could become ghost towns just as quickly. Fortunes were made and lost at the turn of a card, or with a stroke of luck in a mine. Back East people were divided by social structures and class. While that existed to an extent in the West, the barriers to moving up in the world were far easier to overcome. When it came to battling Mother Nature and outlaws, people were more likely to judge a man by his character than his bank account. The same was true for women. Necessity opened up professional opportunity that might have been closed off to women in more established cities.

That's why I loved writing Caroline's story. It was a great opportunity to dive into a character who had to overcome rather strict social and cultural mores to fulfill her dreams. I also loved the idea of Caroline having to find the one man who would support her. Who better than the outlaw Castillo, who'd had to overcome his own share of bias and hardships, to support her in reaching her dream?

If you'd like to learn more about the obstacles women had to overcome in the past, research Elizabeth Blackwell (1821-1910). She is the first recognized female doctor in the United States. A great online resource is American Memory from the Library of Congress. It devotes a section of its website to Women's History.

I hope you enjoy Castillo and Caroline's story. Please connect with me on Facebook or visit my website at www.harperstg eorge.com to sign up for my newsletter for sneak peeks and exclusive contests.

For Kathryn Cheshire. Thank you for your insightful feedback and all that you've done to help me grow as a writer.

Chapter One

The problem with having two identities was that someone would eventually figure them both out. Castillo's grandfather had told him that with a frown when he'd learned that Castillo had started running cattle. It had been about five years ago, but it looked as if the prediction had finally come to pass.

Castillo Jameson, aka Reyes, leader of the notorious Reyes Brothers, lowered the brim of his hat to shadow his face. It was too late, though. The man at the other end of the train car had already recognized him as the leader of the gang of outlaws, wanted for crimes committed much further south than Montana Territory. Castillo could tell it from the stiff set of the man's shoulders and the way the man's left hand had shifted to the armrest, holding it in a white-knuckled grip. He tried to keep his attention focused on the scenery out the window, but his eyes twitched back toward Castillo in a nervous glance.

"Damn." Castillo stretched his leg out and tapped the boot of his friend, Zane Pierce, who sat facing him. Zane glanced up from the drawing he'd been sketching, but once his dark eyes got a look at Castillo's face he flipped his sketchbook shut and tucked it into the breast pocket of his coat. Visible holsters weren't allowed on the train, but Castillo had a knife in his boot and a small-frame Smith & Wesson tucked into his coat. The problem would be confronting the man on a crowded train. Nearly every row was filled with people—many of them women and children—traveling west.

He waited for the man to pretend to look out the window again before nodding to Zane, who glanced over to set eyes on the man before leaning back in his seat. "Son of a bitch," Zane said with a grin. "We've spent years hunting for Derringer. Never thought his son would show up when we weren't looking."

Castillo stared at the man from beneath the brim of his hat. He was too wary from years of getting close to his prey, only to face disappointment, to allow himself to hope now.

Zane's words released the grip Castillo held on his control. His heart pounded like it was trying to beat its way out of his chest, and his fists clenched. Years of searching and they'd never been this close. Not once. His skin tightened like it was suddenly a size too small, but he forced himself to appear calm. "You sure that's him?"

"Hell, yeah, I'm sure. That's Bennett Derringer, Buck's son. That little son of a bitch gave me this." Zane raised his hand to indicate a pink scar that ran through his eyebrow and down his cheek, narrowly missing his eye. "I'll never forget him."

Castillo had met Buck Derringer and his family when the man had partnered with his grandfather. Before everything had gone to hell and Derringer had killed Castillo's grandfather. Bennett, Derringer's son, had been a teenager then. This man was young, maybe in his early twenties, with a full beard.

When Derringer killed Castillo's grandfather and ran off with the money his grandfather had invested in their partnership, the Derringer family had disappeared, leading Castillo to think they'd changed their name. Castillo and his gang had heard tales of sightings, but those sightings had been from disreputable people and led to dead ends. The trail had long gone cold.

Castillo and the rest of the gang had taken a break from tracking him long enough to take Castillo's younger brother, Miguel, to university back East. Miguel hadn't wanted to go, but after they'd nearly lost him just a couple of months earlier, when he'd been kidnapped by Ship Campbell, one of the many enemies Castillo had made in his line of work as an outlaw, he'd seen no other choice. He didn't want Miguel to follow in his footsteps, but what else had he expected? Castillo was the boy's only living relative, it was inevitable that Miguel would idolize the gang.

What were the odds that they'd find their first solid clue to Derringer's whereabouts on a train from Boston?

"He's made us," Castillo said, mentally tallying the number of people on the car. Too damn many.

"Doesn't matter. He won't do anything here. We just keep an eye on him and follow him when he gets off," Zane said.

Castillo wasn't so sure. The man looked twitchy. Castillo wasn't close enough to tell, but he'd swear the way Bennett was tugging on his collar that a bead of sweat had broken out on his brow. Dammit, if only he'd seen Bennett first. They could've kept out of sight and followed him without him even knowing it.

"Mierda! He's on the move." Bennett had risen and turned to jiggle the door that led to the next car, on his way toward the back of the train.

"Where the hell is he going? It's a damn train." Zane asked, rising to his feet just after Castillo did.

Castillo shook his head, trying to keep his composure so no one in the car would be alerted. He nodded his head in greeting as they passed the curious gazes of the other passengers. This could get ugly real quick.

He reached the door Bennett had passed through, just in time to see him jiggling the handle of the door to the next car in the line. It was a passenger car, like the one they'd occupied, but the two after that were cars with private compartments. Things could get difficult if Bennett got far enough ahead to disappear into one of them. No way in hell did Castillo plan to let him hide, but they'd have a lot of explaining to do, knocking on all of those doors. It'd be best to catch him before he could disappear.

Damn, he was supposed to be Castillo Jameson on this trip. He and Zane were headed to the Jameson Ranch just outside Helena, far away from Texas where the Reyes Brothers were known. They weren't the Reyes Brothers right now, but it looked like they didn't have a choice. Trouble had come to them anyway.

***

Dear Caroline,

Your father and I would see you married this year. Your place in this world is to be a wife and mother first, and a physician second.

I've not changed my position on furthering your medical education. With many reservations, I grant you permission, but only with the caveat that you're wed. If your husband agrees with your education, then go with our blessing.

Your father and I have discussed this. The decision has been made. You are to come home after the wedding and meet the young man I have in mind for you.

With a little luck, we'll begin to plan your own

wedding.

Your loving mother

Caroline Hartford stared at the rumpled letter in her hand. She'd had it for days now, and every time she read the thing it managed to make her chest feel heavy and hollow at the same time. The message had come on the morning before they'd left her aunt's home in Boston to begin their trip west, a special delivery by courier from her mother who was visiting New York City with friends. What had been a joyous morning of packing and anticipation had quickly soured, those happy feelings replaced with dread and bitter betrayal.

Betrayal. There. She'd finally thought it after all this time trying to name it something else. Her fingers clenched around the thick, creamy paper, but she stopped herself from crumpling it again. Placing the sheet on her knee, she painstakingly ran a finger over each of the creases to smooth them out again and then adjusted her spectacles on her nose.

It had become a ritual. Read it, become angry, crumple it, read it again, take a deep breath and smooth it out. All of that just to put it away and repeat the process when the urge became too overwhelming to resist.

"Oh, for heaven's sake. That thing again?" Her aunt snatched the paper away and stuffed it into her reticule before Caroline could stop her. "I've sat here and watched you look at that horrible communication for the better part of a week. Enough, already. You'll deal with your mother later and that's that."

"But Aunt Prudie—" When the woman held up her hand and looked out the train's window, Caroline realized she sounded like a petulant child and took a deep breath. "I feel betrayed," she tried again. "Father was so excited when I was accepted into the program." She could see him now, smiling at the dinner table and talking to whomever they'd happened to have over that evening about how she'd be among the first women accepted into the Boston University School of Medicine. He'd taught her everything she knew and was proud she'd be following in his footsteps. She'd trailed him around in his practice ever since she'd been tall enough to see over the tabletops.

"He's still very excited." Prudie turned and ran her fingers over a strand of Caroline's hair that had fallen free of the pins. "But you know your mother. She's never approved of your choice."

It was true. Her mother had never understood the sense of fulfillment Caroline felt when she helped a patient. Caroline suspected that her mother didn't care, because it wasn't part of the plan she had for her only child. Perhaps if Caroline had had siblings things would be different, but she didn't, so all her mother's hopes of a society marriage rested on Caroline's shoulders. "No, she hasn't, and she's never kept a secret of that. I suppose I thought he would make her see reason. Why didn't he mention anything to me before the letter?"

"In a way, he has made her see reason," Prudie said. "She's not saying you can't go. Merely that you need to have a husband. And I suspect your mother wanted to send you a letter so you'd have a little time to come to terms with it before seeing her later this week."

Caroline leaned back against the plush seat and folded her arms over her chest. "It feels a lot like extortion. What husband is going to be happy to marry me and then lose me to medical school come autumn? He'll be far more likely to forbid me to go. For that matter, I don't even know of anyone I'd want to marry. I can't even fathom the 'young man' she has in mind. So you see, this is all an attempt to keep me from going."

Aunt Prudie clicked her tongue and ran her hand over Caroline's shoulder. "We'll figure out something. Remember, your father is very much on your side in this. In the meantime, let's enjoy the trip as we'd planned. It's your first time out West and you're missing how beautiful it is. Just look at those mountains. Have you ever seen anything so green in your life?"

Caroline glanced back toward the window. The sun was just starting to set, painting the mountains in the distance with a burnished glow, setting off the deep green of the shadows. "I'm sorry I'm being so gloomy." Aunt Prudie was right. There was no reason to allow her troubles at home to interfere with their adventure.

"Don't be sorry, child. No one wants a marriage forced on them." The haunted look in her eye made Caroline think that

Prudie knew better than most. Her aunt's marriage hadn't been the happiest. "I make you this promise right now. You'll go to medical school come September. I'll see to it myself."

Caroline smiled and gave the woman a hug. "I don't know what I'd do without you. Thank you for putting up with me."

"Yes, you're a terrible burden," Aunt Prudie teased. "Now, go to the dining car and fetch me another scone before they put them away for the night. Fetch your father back, too. He's probably fallen asleep over the newspaper again."

Laughing, Caroline rose and paused at the door of their private compartment to look back at her aunt. When her mother hadn't understood her ambitions, her father's sister had. People said that she favored the woman more than her own mother. They both possessed the same blond hair and blue eyes that ran in her father's side of the family. Aunt Prudie was like her second mother. This trip out West for a family wedding was supposed to be their last holiday together before Caroline went to school and then—hopefully—began taking on more patients in her father's practice or possibly even the hospital. She'd be foolish to allow a letter to ruin it.

She unlatched the door and made sure it clicked shut behind her before making her way down the dimly lit hallway to the next car. Her low heels barely made a sound on the dark red carpet. The dining car was four cars ahead, but she didn't mind the walk after being cooped up in that compartment all afternoon. The sway of the train was making her tired, and she stifled a yawn as she jiggled the handle of the stubborn door that led to the next car.

The door flew open unexpectedly, pushing her backward into the paneled wall and knocking her off balance. A bearded man with a crazed look in his eye nearly ran her over in his haste to come inside. She tried to jump back out of his way, but he grabbed her. Before she realized his intention, he'd covered her mouth with his large hand and was pulling her awkwardly with him on his way down the hallway. She clawed at his arm and kicked her feet out, trying to find some purchase on the floor or wall, but he was abnormally strong, or at least, that's how it felt. She'd never actually been manhandled before.

The man kept looking back over his shoulder, and finally she looked that way, too. Two men had just made their way through the door.

"Hell," the bigger one said when he saw her.

"Let her go, Bennett," the calmer one spoke. "This is between us." His hat was pulled too low for her to see his face, but he spoke with an accent, the vowels elongated a bit.

The man—Bennett, apparently—didn't slow down at all. He tightened his hand when she tried to scream and pulled her flush against his chest. Something cold jammed against her neck, but for the life of her she couldn't tell if it was a knife or a gun. She held her breath, so she wouldn't move and find out. Her entire body had gone cold, like she'd stepped outside in December without her coat, and she realized it was best not to scream so she wouldn't draw Aunt Prudie from her compartment. She glanced to the door of her aunt's compartment, willing the woman to stay inside

Please don't let Aunt Prudie open the door. The plea repeated itself in her mind as he kept walking backward, pulling her along with him. The two men kept walking toward them very slowly. For all she knew they were bad men, too, but right now they were the only potential saviors she had.

Before she realized what had happened, Bennett twisted her around so that she was pressed flush against the door leading to the caboose. "Open the damn door." He spoke the words rough, yet low, against her hair, and she heard the unmistakable click of a gun being cocked. She glanced over to see the glint of metal in the lamplight as he trained the gun on the men. "Do it!" he said in an even rougher voice.

Caroline was too terrified to do anything other than what he ordered and struggled to keep a hold on the handle. Between her sweating palms, the swaying of the train and the slightly rusted metal, she had a difficult time getting the handle to turn. When she finally did, she pushed the door open only to feel the cool, outside air rushing past her. There was no railing, nothing to keep her inside, and dizziness overcame her as the ground rushed past. Bennett grabbed her tight, and he switched their positions so that she was once again between him and the two men chasing him.

"Stay away from me, Reyes, or I'll shoot her. Just try me if you don't believe me."

The calm man in front held up his hands as a sign of peace. The big man behind him didn't budge, he just stared at them with his dark eyes and twitching jaw. Now that a bit of the late afternoon sunlight was filtering into the hallway through the open door, she could see the lower half of Reyes' face. He had a strong, clean-shaven jaw, and his skin was dark, more olive than tan.

"You won't shoot her," Reyes said, his deep voice still calm in the face of the madman. "There's no need for her death."

"Her life's in your hands." Bennett tightened his grip on her and started moving them backward onto the platform. She had no idea what he intended but she didn't intend to die today, and she didn't intend to make any of this easy for him. She refused to stay still and suffer whatever he planned, so she twisted and tried to loosen his hold, her hands grasping at the wood-paneled wall so that he couldn't pull her out the door with him.

"We only want your father. Tell us where he is and you're free to go."

Bennett's laughter vibrated through her chest, they were so close. "Tell that to your friend with the scar. I bet he'd like to get back at me for that."

The big man didn't respond except to clench his jaw even tighter and square his shoulders. The light moved over his face and she noticed the scar. It looked as if something had sliced clean through his skin, narrowly missing his eye, and the wound hadn't been stitched shut properly. The scar was too broad and jagged to have healed neatly.

Before Reyes could respond, the brakes on the train screeched as it began the long process of slowing down. They were due to make one more stop, though she couldn't remember the name of the town, before pulling into Helena in the morning. Bennett planted his feet, jerking them back against the change in momentum that pulled them forward and causing them to sway dangerously toward the open door.

From the corner of her eye, she saw a flash of movement. Both men moved forward, but Bennett saw it, too. She had no time to react before he was pushing her toward them. Reyes reached out and caught her before she could stumble to the ground. One arm held her tight against his chest, while the other braced against the wall, his legs planted wide to take the brunt of the impact.

She grabbed onto his broad shoulders as if her life depended on it and squeezed her eyes shut, expecting gunfire to erupt. But it didn't. Her savior's arm held her tight against his chest, and the pounding of his heart was the only sound that registered. The big one pushed her even further against Reyes as he rushed past them to try to catch Bennett. Though she didn't know where the man had disappeared to. The door was open but she couldn't see him.

Her skin prickled hot and then cold as blood whooshed in her ears. She could've been killed. That wild-eyed man could've put a bullet through her body just as easily as he'd tossed her away. Or, just as horrifying, he could have flung her out the open door of the train, leaving her crumpled and broken on the ground or pulled beneath the wheels. The awareness of how easily things could have gone differently left her shaking, her knees threatening to buckle beneath her.

She pressed her face against Reyes' coat and took in a deep, calming breath. Oh. He smelled good. She took another breath to get more of his scent. It was clean and masculine with a hint of bay rum. His big hand moved up and down her back in a soothing caress. She let out a long, slow breath, savoring the calming motion.

Nothing horrible was happening. Pushing back a little, she stared into a pair of the most gorgeous eyes she'd ever seen. They were a vivid green, but lit with gold around the pupils and rimmed with dark lashes.

"Are you hurt?" His deep voice rumbled through her, softened with that hint of an accent she'd noticed earlier. Despite what had happened, he was still calm and unhurried, as if her well-being meant more to him than chasing down that madman.

Was she hurt? She did a mental inventory and everything seemed to be in order. "No, I'm not hurt."

"The bastard jumped." The big one had been standing there, staring out the open door, but he paced back toward them. He ran a hand through his dark mass of unruly, shoulder-length hair and looked as if he'd just barely stopped himself from punching the wall. "Unbelievable."

The train was slowing, but it was still going too fast for any sane person to risk jumping. She didn't want to believe it, but where else could he have gone?

"We'll find him," Reyes said, again the voice of reason. "He didn't fall into our laps for us to lose him. If he jumped, then he's hurt and we can track him this far from town." The big one nodded and headed back to the open door to secure it, casting a last longing glance outside before he did.

Now that her heartbeat had slowed a little, Caroline realized that her palms had flattened themselves against the hard chest of the man holding her. His strong hands had moved to grip her waist as he held her steady. As strange as it seemed, she felt safe and reassured in his arms. He wouldn't let any harm come to her. She was aware that she should move away, yet her body refused to give him up. It craved the closeness he offered. She'd never quite had such a visceral reaction to a man before. And she'd never been held so closely against one. He was hard everywhere, as though his muscles were carved from granite. His fingers flexed into her, and instinctively hers did the same, giving the muscles beneath her fingers a gentle squeeze.

"I'm sorry," he said, his voice low and a little husky. The r sound rolled off his tongue.

Something powerful moved between them, so unexpected that she couldn't even name it. It was almost like familiarity and excitement rolled into one, but that couldn't be. She'd never met him.

"It's not your fault. I stepped out at the wrong time." She offered a smile, and he did, too. It was a quick flash of white in the dim light of the hallway, but it was beautiful. His mouth curved up in a flawless crescent that centered her gaze on his perfectly formed lips, the bottom one just a bit fuller than the top one.

She'd just had a brush with death and here she was standing with a stranger and flirting. It must be the shock. Her father had taught her that people sometimes exhibited strange behavior after experiencing a trauma. That was the only explanation for her conduct.

A shadow loomed over them, drawing her attention to the big man. He didn't seem pleased with the moment they were sharing and raised a brow at her with some sort of implied censure. Then he handed her a pair of folded spectacles, their gold rims glinting in the lamplight, and the action was enough to jolt her back to reality. She hadn't even realized they'd fallen off in the commotion. She accepted them and stepped back. The man called Reyes dropped his hands from her waist. He didn't appear as chastened as she felt, though. What was she thinking, standing here with a possible criminal and smiling? She'd come within an inch of getting killed.

He hadn't looked away from her, either. Even as he spoke, he kept his gaze on her. "Go arrange for our luggage. We'll be the first off at the station."

The big man said something in agreement—she could hardly pay attention to him—before he moved between them and made his way through the door to the next train car. Then they were alone and the air thickened with awareness. It sizzled down her spine and feathered out along her nerve endings until her entire body was alive with it.

She'd been kissed before, once or twice at the annual fundraiser galas her family participated in, but they'd been flirty and hasty, nothing bordering even remotely on the intensity gaining momentum between her and this stranger. Except he hadn't kissed her. Not in the way she wanted. Dear God, she wanted this stranger to kiss her. What the devil was wrong with her?

Still keeping a firm hold on her gaze, he caught her fingers in his and raised them. His hands were broad and slightly calloused and his skin was dark against her pale fingers. His lips brushed the back of her hand in a feather-light caress, not even leaving a hint of moisture behind. "Safe travels, mi corazón."

He dropped her hand and followed his friend. She opened her mouth to call to him, but then stopped when she realized there was nothing to say. Would she ask him to call on her in Boston? Give him—a stranger who'd been chasing an obvious criminal—her name?

There was nothing to do but watch him go. When he'd disappeared through the door, she walked to the door of the compartment she shared with her aunt and paused. She took some breaths and waited for her fingers to stop shaking before she went inside, forgetting all about the scones and her father in the dining car.

Chapter Two

Castillo tensed when the study door opened. He was expecting his brother Hunter to join him, but he was always on alert when at the Jameson Ranch. He didn't belong here, and no amount of familiarity with the place would change that. His blood might be that of a Jameson, but his heart and soul would always be that of a Reyes, his mother's family, the people who'd raised him when his father had abandoned them. He belonged in Texas at the Reyes hacienda, not here.

"I didn't mean to pull you from supper." Castillo looked over at Hunter and threw back the last of his whiskey. Setting his tumbler on the mantel, he turned from the low-burning fire and crossed the room to pull him into a hug. Even after having known his half-brother for the better part of five years, Castillo sometimes couldn't believe how similar they were. Where Castillo was dark, Hunter was light, but their frames, strong jaws and green eyes had all been inherited from their father.

"We just sat down," Hunter said, as if he wasn't bothered. "Why don't you join us? You must be starving."

Hunter's wedding was only a week away and guests had already begun to arrive. Castillo had only just arrived at sunset, tired and irritable from tracking Bennett Derringer in what had been a fruitless effort. It was as if the man had jumped from the train and vanished. Castillo and Zane had found the place they'd thought he landed, and a few footprints leading east, but Bennett had walked on the tracks to hide his path and there'd been no sightings of him in any of the towns farther along the line. The thought of socializing with strangers and making pleasant conversation wasn't appealing to Castillo. Instead, he'd had a bath and come straight to the study.

"I'm not fit for company," he muttered and fell into one of the overstuffed chairs before the fireplace.

Hunter poured himself a whiskey and refilled his brother's tumbler, handing it to him before taking a seat in the other chair. "What happened? Your telegram was vague." He looked around the room. "Where's Zane?"

The telegram had only stated that he and Zane had been detained with a possible lead. It would've been foolish to say more in a communication that was impossible to keep secret.

"Zane stayed in town at Glory's." Castillo had been tempted

to stay at Victoria House, the brothel, and avoid the houseful of people a little longer, but he couldn't put off this conversation with his brother. Not with the possibility of Derringer nearby posing a threat. "We saw Buck Derringer's son on the train. Or, rather, he saw us. He recognized us and ran."

"Ran? On a train?" Hunter smiled, sitting forward at the prospect of an exciting story.

Castillo shrugged and took a sip of the twelve-year-old aged whiskey he liked. It sat warm on his tongue before going down to heat his belly and ease his tired muscles. "He tried. Ended up jumping off when we were just outside Moreland. We got off at the station and followed the tracks, but we never found him. I know he must've been hurt from the fall, but he just disappeared. Like his father."

Hunter frowned into his own tumbler. "You don't think it was coincidence that he was on the train?"

"It was an accident that we saw him, but he didn't just happen to be on that train. What are the odds that when Derringer ran away with my grandfather's money he'd settle here?"

"Zero. We would've heard about him moving here." The Jamesons knew everyone in the area, especially if they were throwing around money.

Castillo nodded. "He'd have been looking to get far away from Texas, but all the signs pointed to California."

"So, he's heard we've been looking for him and he's come to find us first?" Hunter said.

"Could be. There aren't many people left who knew Tanner Jameson when he married my mother. Those who did either died in the war or moved on after it was over. But it's possible Derringer made the connection and figured out I'm his son. Since he couldn't find me in Texas, he could be sniffing around up here."

"Then the ass should know we're ready for him." Hunter tossed back the rest of his whiskey and stood up, pacing with excited energy at the prospect of finally catching the man they'd been chasing for the past few years.

"No, Hunter. I won't have you involved. Your wedding is in a week. Zane and I will go and that will lead him away, if he's even here. I don't want to put Emmaline and her sisters at risk. And the guests..." Castillo ran a hand over his head. He hadn't even thought about all the guests who were due to arrive and the nightmare of protecting them from possible attacks by Derringer and any hired guns the man might've brought with him.

"Are you kidding me? It's my wedding." Hunter paused in his pacing and held his arms out wide. "You're my brother. I want you here."

Castillo sighed and rubbed the back of his neck. He didn't want to miss the wedding, but honestly, avoiding an awkward confrontation with their father held its own special appeal. "I want to be here, too, but not if it's safer for everyone if I'm not."

"It's not safer. If Derringer knows you're a Jameson then he knows I'm your brother. I imagine he'd be happy to take us all out, because he knows if anything happens to you, Zane and I won't stop hunting him until he's dead."

It had been over three years since Derringer had murdered his grandfather. Hunter had been riding with him ever since to track the killer down. It had made them closer than most brothers, with a loyalty that ran deeper than blood.

But, still, Castillo felt like an outsider in his father's home, especially now that Hunter was getting married and had his own family to consider. "I don't want you putting your family at risk for me."

"Brother?" Hunter waited for Castillo to look at him before finishing. "I never would've met Emmy if it hadn't been for you. You, Zane and Emmy are my family. We stand together to take this man down. Besides, Buck Derringer may not even be here. You only saw Bennett."

Castillo rose to his feet. "But this isn't what you meant when you pledged to help me find Derringer. We never meant for the fight to end up on your doorstep. It already came far too close when Ship Campbell and his gang found their way here just a couple months ago."

"That was my fight, too. It wasn't just yours. That was about saving Emmy from them as much as it was about getting Miguel back. We fought together then and we'll fight together now."

"Together," Castillo said, grasping his brother's arm. Perhaps this was ideal. Between the ranch hands and the men in the gang, they'd have enough to take Derringer down. "I promise you, Hunter, I'll make sure Derringer doesn't get anywhere close to Emmy."

Hunter nodded. "We'll take precautions, but Derringer won't attack with so many guests here. My mother's invited her family from Boston, so there'll be a few arriving every day. Derringer will stay hidden, and in the meantime we'll quietly figure out where he's hiding."

"I already spoke with Glory. She claimed to know nothing, but that's one reason Zane's stayed behind. Someone at the brothel will know something...if Derringer is here."

"Damn right. I bet we find Derringer before he knows what hit him."

Castillo laughed, his mood improving for the first time since losing Bennett on the train.

"Come on. Let's get you fed." Hunter slapped him on the back and led the way toward the dining room.

Castillo followed, his belly grumbling as he anticipated Willy's famous biscuits with the buffalo-berry jam she made to go with them. He'd been hooked on them ever since the housekeeper made them for him the first time he'd come home with Hunter. They'd make suffering through useless conversation with a few guests worth it.

Hunter put his hand on the crystal doorknob but paused before opening the door to the dining room. "The old man's inside."

Castillo took in a sharp breath through his nose. He hadn't seen his father since his first visit after his mother's death. Her last request had been for Castillo to go meet his father, so he'd gone to honor her, but Castillo had had nothing to say to the man who'd abandoned him and his mother. Though he'd known it was inevitable that he'd see Tanner Jameson this week, he'd managed to push the reality of that aside. Now it was time to face it.

He let the breath out slowly, forcing the tension in his shoulders away. Be civil. Avoid him. Hunter deserved that much from Castillo. "Let's get it over with."

Hunter smiled and opened the door.

The candlelight from the large chandelier overhead wrapped the room in a warm glow. He'd eaten meals here many times when Tanner had been out of town but had never seen the room like this. Several candelabras sat at intervals down the middle of the table, light from the candles flickering off the pristine white tablecloth and glinting off the silverware. The candles created an intimacy that hadn't existed before. Or perhaps it was that the table was large enough for twelve but only set for five people. They were all gathered at one end.

Tanner sat at the head, in the middle of telling one of his elaborate stories, but paused when he caught sight of Castillo. His mouth hung open, a momentary lapse in composure, before he pushed back his chair and rose to his feet. "Castillo. What a pleasant surprise."

Emmy sat to his right, with Hunter's place vacant beside her. Two blond women sat across from them, one of them a bit older, but Castillo didn't pay them much attention. He opened his mouth to reply, but he'd never called the man Father and wouldn't start now. However, calling him Tanner might seem rude with guests present. Damn, he probably should've thought this through. "Sorry if I'm interrupting. I offered to wait, but Hunter insisted."

Tanner started to wave off his concern, but Hunter interrupted. "Ladies, you'll have to forgive our provincial ways. This is my brother, Castillo. He's just returned from Boston and we've missed him. I didn't think you'd mind if he joined us."

"Why, of course not." The older woman seated at his father's left pushed back from the table and rose to greet him. "I've been anxious to meet your brother. Besides, we're only on the second course." She laughed as she offered her hand to Castillo. She had golden hair streaked with gray at the temples, but was still very pretty with vivid blue eyes.

"This is Prudence Hartford Williams, my mother's first cousin," Hunter said, an obvious fondness for the woman in his voice.

"Your father has told us many good things about you, dear. I've been looking forward to meeting you." Prudence's smile brightened when Castillo took her fingers in his hand. If he wasn't mistaken, her sharp gaze took in his shoulders with some appreciation. He couldn't help but smile back at her.

He was shocked that she'd stood to greet him and that Tanner had spoken of him to her.

"This is Caroline Hartford, her niece." Hunter's voice lowered conspiratorially and he smirked, winking at the women. "They were the only ones of the whole Hartford lot I could stomach during my years in Boston."

"One would like to think he's exaggerating, but he's not. It's going to be a long week." Prudence smiled.

Hunter threw back his head and laughed. Castillo smiled, having heard from Hunter how much he disdained his mother's side of the family. Hunter had been all but disowned by them when he'd chosen to stay out West with his father, who was already estranged from the Hartfords. They'd wanted him to become civilized and live in Boston with his mother. It was heartening to know that some of his mother's family could appreciate him.

The niece moved, coming to her feet, as well. She had the exact shade of golden-blond hair as the woman he'd saved on the train. And there'd been a woman passing by on the street in Helena who'd had similar blue eyes. It was funny how often he'd thought about her since that strange encounter. There had been something about her, some look in her eye that had drawn him in. Some instinct within him that had recognized a part of himself in her. It sounded crazy, but when he'd walked away it had been with a deep regret and an acknowledgment that he was leaving something important behind.

When the niece turned to face him all the air was sucked from his lungs.

It was her. She wasn't smiling at him, like her aunt had, but staring at him with wide blue eyes. Eyes that recognized him as the man—Reyes—she'd met on the train who'd been chasing a man with a gun. Eyes that now knew him as Castillo Jameson.

Mierda. She knew who he was. Aside from the gang and Emmy, no one else here knew about his double identity as leader of the Reyes Brothers. Her knowledge could ruin everything. Hell, not only could it ruin everything, it could get them all thrown in jail or killed. His skin tightened as though he was about to spring out of his own body as his heart tried to pound its way out of his chest.

Her lips trembled, and she parted them twice before finally speaking. His next moments, hell, his entire future hinged on the words she would say. Her voice was clear and strong. "It's a pleasure to meet you, Mr. Jameson." She watched him carefully, her gaze holding fast to his, and he couldn't look away.

At least she hadn't called him Reyes. He took her offered hand, and that same jolt he'd experienced on the train moved up his arm to settle in his belly. She was wearing her spectacles this time, the thin gold rims perched high on her nose, making her look more prim and ordered than she had then. Her eyes weren't wild from excitement, her cheeks weren't flushed and her lips weren't parted and gasping for air as they had been when he'd held her in his arms.

As if she was remembering the same thing, her lips did part and she took in a shaky breath. His gaze honed in on those perfectly formed lips the same way he stared a man down when looking for weakness. Only he wasn't looking for weakness in her. He breathed in deep through his nose, breathing in the lavender scent he remembered from the train. His gaze dropped to the pulse fluttering beneath the pale skin of her neck.

She appeared off balance, just like she had then. Real. He didn't like prim and proper on her, though she wore it well. She was elegant, with her hair tied up intricately, shining gold in the candlelight. The gown she wore fell just off her shoulders, the tastefully low cut of her neckline revealing just enough pale skin and shadows to draw his gaze to the hint of her breasts. She breathed in and they swelled beneath the pale pink silk. Elegant suited her, but he preferred her real and flushed, like on the train. The strange mix of emotions from that day came flooding back.

He forced himself to blink, hoping to break her spell. Now was not the time to notice her as a woman, as she could easily become an adversary. The silence had begun to drag out noticeably, so he brought her fingers to his lips. "The pleasure is mine, Miss Hartford."

She took in a sharp breath and stared down at her fingers as if she was afraid she might not get them back. Good. She should be afraid of him. That edge of fear was the only certainty he had that she'd keep quiet for now. It was a fine line. Too much fear could make her reckless. He'd have to play her carefully.

Castillo dropped her hand because Emmy had come around the table to embrace him.

"Welcome back," she said. "How was your trip? Did you get to see any sights?"

He gave the standard answers: the trip was fine, the food on the train was awful, and yes, he'd gone to a play at the Bijou Theater. The whole time he spoke, he was taking in the reactions around him. He'd had too much practice having to be constantly aware of the mood in the room.

Hunter had noticed that something transpired between him and Caroline Hartford. His shoulders straightened and the smile fell from his lips as he put a hand at Emmy's waist and pulled her close.

Prudence had noticed, too, though her response was very different. She didn't know about his other identity and their constant need to be vigilant of danger. She only knew that her niece had reacted to him, and she watched them both now with a gleam in her eye, looking back and forth between them as if she'd had the thought to play matchmaker. He'd have to figure out a way to get Caroline alone before she could talk to anyone. She needed to know what was at risk before she inadvertently revealed the Jamesons were the Reyes Brothers.

Tanner indicated that they needed another place set at the table. A maid who'd been standing at attention along the wall, sprang into action, taking a place setting from the glass-faced cabinet at the end of the room. Hunter led Emmy back around to their side of the table.

"Put him there, next to Caroline." Prudence smiled, already meddling. "I'd love to hear more of what you thought about Boston, Castillo. Caroline loves the theater. We'll take you next time you visit."

The woman wasn't subtle. "That was my first and only visit, senora." Castillo waited for the women to sit, before daring a glance at his father and taking his own seat. Tanner didn't seem to notice that Caroline had had a reaction to him. His brow was furrowed, but his thoughts seemed to be turned inward. Castillo wasn't looking forward to the after-dinner confrontation they were certain to have. He hadn't seen Tanner in years. The man would certainly want to speak to him.

"Welcome home, Mr. Jameson." The maid murmured near his ear as she leaned forward to place a glass of wine on the table for him.

He nearly smiled but only inclined his head. "Mary." Most of the time the household ran with a skeleton staff, but she must've been brought from town due to the extra guests. She usually worked for Glory at Victoria House, not in the brothel upstairs, but serving drinks and beefsteaks downstairs in the various dining rooms. Though she'd made it clear to him several times that she'd be willing to make herself available for more. What would the uptight guests from Boston think if they knew a serving girl from a brothel was serving them their dinner?

She stepped back and a bowl of pea soup was placed in front of him. He'd been starving, but now he felt too damned tired and anxious to eat. His shoulders were tight, and he was on edge, so attuned to Caroline Hartford at his side that he was aware of every breath she took. Every time she gathered one in, he tensed, knowing that this time she'd tell everyone at the table what she knew. It wasn't until she resumed eating her half-finished bowl of soup that he relaxed enough to pick up his own spoon.

Caroline. The name didn't suit the woman he'd held on the train. She'd been bold and only barely fazed by the ordeal. This woman was a little afraid, but not subdued. Her brow was furrowed and her shoulders tense. She was quiet because she was plotting. He could practically hear her thoughts churning. It was an unpredictable combination that kept him worried.

"May I ask what took you to Boston?" Prudence asked.

"I escorted my younger brother, Miguel. He starts university there in autumn." Castillo inwardly cringed at the explanation. There was no way to adequately explain Miguel's existence without labeling either Hunter or Castillo a bastard and Tanner a man with two wives. This was one reason he avoided social interactions with the Jamesons.

Tanner had grown up in Texas and married Castillo's mother shortly after being injured in the war. It had been a simple ceremony in a chapel on Castillo's grandfather's property. But after Castillo had been born, Tanner had been lured to Montana Territory by the promise of wealth in the mines, and he'd forgotten about his first family. He'd soon married Isabelle Hartford, daughter of the wealthy Hartford family from Boston. Unlike with Tanner's first wedding, however, all the appropriate papers had been filed to prove the marriage was legal and binding. Castillo's mother had been heartbroken at the abandonment, but she'd eventually moved on and Miguel had been born from a new marriage.

The only hint Prudence gave that she thought the fact he had a younger brother named Miguel odd was when she paused with her spoon halfway to her mouth. She was so poised, with her back ramrod straight, that she didn't spill a drop. "How wonderful. You'll have a Harvard boy at your table before long," she finally said, and carried on as if Castillo hadn't laid one of Tanner's biggest scandals at her feet.

"We're very proud of the boy," Tanner said. Castillo couldn't help but glance at him in surprise, but the man's gaze was on Prudence. Tanner had had enough practice playing the politician in Washington as he fought for statehood that he easily wrangled any awkwardness out of a conversation and smoothed it out. "He's sharp as they come, if a bit wild from living his life out West. Boston will civilize him."

"I've no doubt of that, but let's hope he keeps some of that wildness about him. Too much polish dulls the edges. We could use more men in the world like your sons." She winked across the table at Hunter, who threw his head back and laughed.

"I've missed you, Aunt Prudie. Never change."

"Oh, posh, you can't have missed me too much. Seems you've kept yourself occupied." She smiled at Emmy and brought her wine glass up in a toast before taking a dainty sip, causing Emmy to blush.

Castillo couldn't help but smile and took a drink from his own glass. Red wine wasn't his first choice, but it went down smooth.

Hunter smiled at Emmy, and Castillo wasn't certain his brother was aware of the naked love and adoration on his face for everyone to see. Emmy practically glowed beneath the power of his gaze. Castillo had to look away from their obvious happiness. He didn't begrudge them their love, but jealousy tore at him, digging its claws in deep.

It wasn't that he wanted Emmy for himself; it was that he wanted a wife. He wanted a family, love, devotion, the satisfaction of building a life together. All of that was supposed to have been his before his grandfather had been murdered and his home burned to the ground. In the years since, Castillo hadn't been able to do anything more than fight to get back what was his. Looking for a wife wasn't something he could consider right now. Especially when he only had danger and instability to offer her.

Tanner cleared his throat. "Tell us more about your trip, Castillo. How were the Andersons?"

For the first time, Caroline broke her silence. As soon as she opened her mouth, Castillo tensed, prepared to cover her mouth and drag her away from the table if he had to. "Yes, Mr. Jameson, I'd love to hear all about your trip." She took a sip of her wine and shot him a challenging glance over the edge of her glass.

That glance landed like a punch to his gut. Her eyes shone up at him like sapphires, and he wasn't sure why she was taunting him, but something in him liked it. A lot. Taking a breath, Castillo launched into a general retelling of his trip to Boston. The tale had the benefit of allowing him to control the conversation, so he didn't mind, but he kept an eye on Caroline. She made sure her comments were benign, but her eyes snapped at him. She was planning something, but he didn't know what.

"Did you take the train out?" she asked when he'd finished. Mary had just cleared their plates from the table, and Willy had given them bowls of hothouse strawberries with clotted cream. "Aunt Prudie and I took the number two train. You weren't on that train, by chance? How serendipitous it would've been."

Castillo clenched his jaw so tightly he nearly saw stars. She was playing with fire, and she damn well knew it judging from the glint in her eye. He shook his head but was saved from responding by Prudence.

"Oh, that would've been lovely. It was a beautiful trip." She described the scenery they'd passed, leaving Castillo to glare at her niece. Caroline merely glared back.

Dessert was mercifully short, and then Emmy suggested they all retire to the front porch for brandy. Castillo gritted his teeth as he wondered how to get Caroline alone. He couldn't let her out of his sight until he'd somehow garnered her cooperation.

"That sounds lovely, but I'm afraid that I must go upstairs and check on my father," Caroline said, placing her linen napkin on the table and pushing her chair back to rise to her feet.

Castillo immediately rose and gripped her chair to assist her. "Your father?" How many potential allies did she have?

"Yes, he doesn't travel well, I'm afraid," Caroline explained.

"You'll meet him tomorrow, dear." Prudence rose. "My brother is a brilliant man, but he's never taken to travel, and he suffered a brain attack two years ago that only exacerbated the issue. Go on up and check on him, Caro, but then come out and join us. It's a beautiful night."

Caroline cast him a glance that had him thinking she intended to go directly to her father and confess everything. For the first time that night, Castillo's palms began to sweat. He had to talk to her before she saw her father. Desperate to stop her, he grabbed his wine glass and intentionally fumbled it, spilling the expensive Bordeaux across the tablecloth and down her skirt.

She gasped and jumped away from the table, but the damage had been done. The room erupted in a flurry of activity as napkins were gathered to blot the liquid, and the women crooned over the loss of the silk. Caroline's eyes flashed with fire as they met his.

"I'm sorry," he said. Prudence was quick to reassure him, but Caroline recognized it as the token apology it was. Her jaw clenched and she didn't look away from him. She knew he'd done it intentionally.

Castillo caught Hunter's attention, and gave a brief nod of his head toward Caroline. Hunter had no idea Castillo had met her on the train, but he knew that look and moved to get closer to her. He would be vigilant and stop her before she could say too much. Castillo turned and made his way upstairs to figure out which bedroom was hers. When she retreated to it to change her gown, he'd be waiting.

Chapter Three

The housekeeper, a no-nonsense woman named Wilhelmina, or Willy for short, appeared to join the legions of hands blotting at Caroline's stained gown. "Let's get you out of this gown. I'll need to get some soap and vinegar on it before that stain sets in."

In the day and a half she'd been at the ranch, Caroline had come to admire the woman. If anyone could get the wine out, Willy could. Not that Caroline cared overly much about the gown. She needed to get to her room and think about what to do. She'd never thought to meet the strangely appealing man from the train again, and not under a new identity. What did it mean? Who was he, really? Ever since he walked in, he'd looked at her differently than he had on the train. There was suspicion and caution in his eyes, and she didn't like the change.

Over the heads of Willy and the maid, who were inspecting the stain, Caroline met Hunter's gaze. He watched her with narrowed eyes, some new awareness there that hadn't been present until now. Did he know about his brother's other identity as Reyes?

"Mary, go help her out of her gown and bring it to me straightaway." The young maid murmured her understanding of Willy's command, and together Caroline and Mary made their way up the stairs. Caroline looked for Reyes' dark head the entire way, but she didn't see him. He'd slipped out during the ruckus, which was worrisome because she had no idea what he intended.

Did these people know about the man they welcomed into their home? As Mary pushed her up the stairs, Caroline darted a glance at Emmy, who was standing next to Hunter in the wide hallway outside the dining room and smiling at something Aunt Prudie had said. Emmaline seemed oblivious, perhaps too deliriously happy in the days leading up to her wedding to even know that she'd embraced someone dangerous. Or did she, too, know about Castillo Jameson's double identity? Caroline was so confused, she hardly knew what to think.

Was he dangerous? Caroline took in a deep breath and tried to think through the facts. The only thing she really knew from the incident on the train was that he and his friend had been chasing a madman who'd had a gun and had tried to take her hostage. The man was obviously dangerous and a criminal to stoop to such actions. But Reyes, or Castillo Jameson as he was known here, hadn't even had a gun, as far as she knew. It was entirely possible that the madman had stolen from him or slighted him in some way, and that was the reason they'd followed him.

The only problem with that theory was that the madman had known them. He'd mentioned giving the big one that horrible scar and had referred to Castillo as Reyes. Law-abiding men didn't go by two names. Caroline hadn't reported the incident because when they got to the station there had been no mention of a man jumping from the train, and she hadn't seen the point of involving their family name in a scandal and upsetting Aunt Prudie. But, at dinner, Castillo Jameson had clearly been worried that she would mention their encounter. Every time she'd opened her mouth, he'd tensed. And she knew that he'd spilled the wine intentionally as soon as she'd mentioned leaving and going to see her father.

Had she made a mistake keeping quiet? Was he trying to get her alone?

After making their way up the wide staircase, Caroline and Mary reached her room at the end of the long hallway and rushed inside. Caroline half expected to find the man waiting for her, but the room was vacant. She closed her eyes in relief and nearly smiled at her own ridiculous notion. Mary was with her, and he wouldn't risk approaching her with someone around.

She hoped.

The maid closed the door behind them. "Here, miss, turn around and I'll help you out of this."

"Thank you, Mary," Caroline said, and faced the leaded glass door that led out to the second-floor wraparound balcony as the maid unfastened the row of tiny buttons along her spine. The door was framed by windows covered with blue velvet drapes. She checked to make sure the toes of his boots weren't sticking out at the bottom because he was hiding behind them and nearly smiled again at her own foolishness. Though she did glance at the lock on the door to make sure it was turned. It was.

"What do you know about Castillo Jameson?" she asked on a whim.

"Not much, miss. I've seen him a few times in town."

Well, there was no information there. Mary pulled the silk over Caroline's head before laying it over the high back of the chair sitting in front of the vanity. Then she returned to untie the bustle and unlace Caroline's corset. When those were put away in the armoire, Caroline said, "Just bring me my wrapper and take the gown to Willy. I can do the rest." Mary didn't argue and helped her shrug into the cream silk dressing gown.

When the maid left, Caroline locked the door and leaned back against the cool mahogany to wait for her heart to calm down. Now that she was away from the tension of Castillo's presence, she'd decided that maybe she was making too much of this. It was entirely possible there was a reasonable explanation for why Reyes and his friend had been chasing that man on the train. She tried to focus on the information she did know. They'd called the man Bennett, so they'd known his name. They'd also been interested in the location of his father. Perhaps the man's father had wronged them, somehow.

Clearly, she'd stumbled into something larger than a simple theft on a train. She wasn't sure what to do about it. Just stay calm, Caroline. You can figure this out. Bringing her hand to her chest, she took in a deep breath and closed her eyes. She'd do nothing until morning. She'd sleep on it and probably be thinking more clearly in the morning.

Crossing the well-appointed room decorated in tasteful shades of blue and cream, Caroline checked the lock on the door leading out to the veranda, even though she could see that it was turned. She was being silly, but she felt much better when she found the knob wouldn't turn and she went ahead and drew the curtains over the door. She even laughed to herself a bit as she walked to the armoire, her hands pushing the wrap from her shoulders. No one was trying to get her. She'd get into her night rail and go to sleep. Everything would seem better in the morning.

"I'd like a moment before you undress."

Her heart jumped up into her throat and she gasped and turned to see Reyes stepping out of the small washroom attached to her bedroom. He was dressed in his shirtsleeves and suspenders with no coat or waistcoat, as if he'd been about to retire before deciding to pay a call on her. He still wore the dark trousers and boots he'd been wearing downstairs. Tall, with wide shoulders, his chest roped with muscle beneath his shirt, he seemed to take up most of the space in the room and all of the available air. She had to force a breath into her tightened chest. "What are you doing in my bedroom?"

He turned his hands palms out to show he wasn't armed, though he left them at his sides. A quick glance to his hips and waistband found no weapon stowed there. "I want to talk to you, and I'd appreciate it if you didn't scream."

"Why would I want to cooperate with you?" Screaming wasn't a natural response for her. She very much preferred rational thoughts and actions. But she'd closed the drapes, and now the room seemed very small and very intimate. When he stepped forward, he was closer to the door leading to the hall than she was. They were both an equal distance from the veranda door, but one glance at his long legs and she knew he'd be able to stop her before she reached it.

Perhaps screaming was a viable option in this situation.

"Because I have a man in your father's room." He didn't continue the threat, but he didn't have to. If she screamed, her father's life would be in danger.

Her spirits sank to settle like a lump in the pit of her stomach. When they'd passed her father's room there'd been no light coming from beneath the door, so she'd assumed he'd gone to sleep. She'd been too consumed with her own fears to even worry that he was in danger. Guilt clawed its way past her fear, digging its talons into her heart and giving her courage. "If you hurt him, I swear to God that you will pay," she said through clenched teeth.

Reyes didn't move, but something changed in his eyes. It was difficult to tell in the low light of the lamp, but she thought she saw a gleam of respect. Then his lips twitched, one corner of his mouth coming up in a grin that he fought, and she realized that he was only amused. He didn't believe she had any power to bring him to justice, and maybe she didn't. "He won't be harmed, and I swear not to touch you, either. I only want to talk to you."

"You mean that you want me to do your bidding. I won't be harmed as long as I do what you want."

He hesitated and then inclined his head a little in agreement. "I'm certain we can come to an arrangement favorable to both of us."

Caroline wasn't nearly as certain. The only remaining door was the one that led to the sitting room. Only it had been turned into a maid's chamber because of the extra help the Jamesons had hired for the wedding. It was her only hope of getting away from him, so she backed toward it and hoped it wasn't locked from the other side. "We don't have anything to talk about."

She turned and ran, but he was on her before she reached the door. One hand went over her mouth while an arm went around her waist to pull her back against him. It was eerily similar to the way the man had grabbed her on the train and almost sent her into a panic.

"You have no reason to fear me." His deep voice spoke softly against her ear.

As if the fact that he'd appeared in her bedroom wasn't a good reason to fear him. She jerked her face away, but he followed, keeping his hand firmly in place.

"I want to explain about the train and who I am. Please, mi corazón."

The endearment got to her. For that brief moment, he wasn't an intruder in her bedroom, he was the handsome stranger she'd met on the train. His voice moved like warm honey through her veins, and his warm body was firm against her back. His strength was reassuring, as it had been two days ago. He was so broad, so strong, that her heart quickened for an entirely different reason as her body began to awaken.

Sensing her capitulation, he slowly lifted his hand from her mouth, but kept his arm wrapped around her waist. The fingers of that hand gently bit into her hip, but not in a way that was painful. His touch was a quiet exploration as each finger seemed to become aware of her with soft pressure. She took in a deep breath and his cologne filled her senses. It was the same as the one he'd worn on the train, only this time she had the presence of mind to examine it. Hints of citrus mixed with leather and a woodsy scent she was certain he must have brought in with him from outside. Whatever it was, it gave her the strange urge to turn around and bury her face in his neck to get closer to the smell. Strange how a scent she'd only smelled once before could be comforting and remind her of how he'd soothed her.

Once his hand lifted completely from her mouth, he dropped it to her arm, where it moved down in a slow, almost absent-minded stroke that ended much too soon. She closed her eyes as she tried to contain the shiver that traveled down her spine. This was wrong, but despite her best intentions, she was intrigued by him. She had to remind herself that he was an enemy now.

"In the last few minutes, you've threatened my father and restrained me. I'm finding it a little difficult to believe that I have nothing to fear from you."

His grip on her hip loosened, hesitated and then fell away. A moment later he moved back, putting enough space between his chest and her back that she actually missed the heat of his body. Taking a deep breath, she turned and faced him, looking up a bit to meet his gaze. She was taken aback by the green-gold of his eyes. They caught the glow of the lamplight and seemed even more vivid against the shadowed darkness of his skin.

"I'm sorry that was necessary." His eyes filled with regret. "We seem to have a knack for being tossed together."

"That appears to be true, yes." She pressed herself back against the door. She knew running wouldn't get her anywhere, but she felt safer, more in control, knowing that she could leave.

"Please sit." He gestured to the two armchairs set near the windows. "I'll explain to you what I can."

She hesitated, but there wasn't any other option aside from screaming. She'd hear him out and could always scream later, if need be. Nodding, she made her way to one of the chairs and perched on the edge, ready to jump up. He took the other one, his long legs stretched out before him, his shoulders spreading from one wing of the chair to the other.

"I've met you as a man named Reyes and now as Castillo Jameson. Who are you?"

"My given name is Castillo Jameson. Reyes is my mother's family. It's the name I went by after my father left us when I was a boy."

He spoke so matter-of-factly that she was inclined to believe him. Something about the image of him as a little boy, abandoned by his father, tugged at her heart. She found herself saying, "I'm sorry about your father."

The words settled into the space between them. He drew in a breath and his eyes widened almost imperceptibly, but she was so aware of him that she noticed; her nerve endings were alive with his presence. It was wrapped around her with an almost tangible thickness.

Clearing his throat—a deep masculine sound that rumbled through her in a most unnerving way—he said, "It...It's in the past."

She nodded. "Mr. Jameson is your father...the one who abandoned you?"

"Tanner is my father." He nodded.

Well, that explained the two names easily enough. She almost felt silly expecting there to be some darker reason, except he had been chasing a man who'd been afraid enough to threaten her life. There had to be more to this.

She hadn't met Tanner Jameson before this trip west, but Aunt Prudie had always been his champion. However, Aunt Prudie championed anyone who was on Isabelle Hartford Jameson's bad side. She despised Hunter's mother and always had. As far as Caroline knew, the feeling was mutual and stemmed from some childhood slight she was unaware of. She had to wonder how much Aunt Prudie knew of Mr. Jameson's history with his first wife and child.

"Tanner had just been discharged from the army after being shot in the leg. He went home to Texas and met my mother. They were married, but he didn't stay around long."

Caroline hadn't expected more of an explanation, so could only murmur another, "I'm sorry." She was angry at her parents for their ridiculous demand that she marry, but she couldn't imagine not having grown up with them. If her father hadn't taken so much time with her, she probably wouldn't have plans to become a physician.

"It's not important. My grandfather raised me and he was a good man. Honorable. I don't know who I'd have become if he hadn't been around to guide me." His eyes focused on the lamp beside her bed, clearly reliving a memory.

Was Miguel also Mr. Jameson's son? If Mr. Jameson's first

marriage wasn't officially dissolved, did that make Hunter illegitimate? It was hardly her business, but she couldn't quite process the implications. "You said you had a younger brother, Miguel?"

He nodded. "My mother remarried years later. Miguel is my half-brother, just as Hunter is. Miguel's father was a good man, too, but he died only a few years into their marriage."

Caroline sat back in her chair as she watched him. And now she was feeling silly about her earlier outburst and escape attempt. He'd been kind to her on the train, and he was being fairly open with her now. Of course, he could've knocked on her door like a normal person and not threatened her father, so she held onto her anger for those transgressions.

After a few moments of silence, he drew in a deep breath and turned his gaze back to her. "A few years ago, a man my grandfather trusted very much murdered him and ran off with his investment funds. I've been searching for him ever since, without success. He vanished. But that man on the train was his son. He recognized us and ran. Unfortunately, he ran into you."

"I'm very sorry for your grandfather. But you couldn't knock on my door to tell me this? Ask me to sit in the study with you so we could speak?" She crossed her arms over her chest.

He laughed and sat back in his chair, crossing his legs at the ankle. She couldn't help but notice how long and powerful he was. "No, I saw the look on your face at dinner. You weren't going anywhere with me."

"Probably not," she agreed. He watched her, a hint of a smile still curving his lips. She felt herself blushing even though she couldn't figure out why she would, or why her skin felt sensitive wherever his gaze touched. "Still, in the future, I'd appreciate it if you ask for a moment of my time. It's disconcerting to find you in my room."

He didn't reply right away. Instead, he kept watching her with those eyes that were as intense as they were teasing. "I need your promise not to speak to anyone about what happened on the train. Don't mention the name Reyes. If the man I'm looking for is in the area, I'd rather he not know that I'm here and looking for him. It'd be best if the wedding guests don't know about that part of my life."

"But that man, Bennett, mentioned that he'd hurt your friend. Given him that nasty scar on his face. What did he mean by that?"

Castillo stared at her as he shook his head. "That's not my story to tell."

Despite her curiosity, that seemed fair. He'd explained the incident on the train and that was all she was entitled to know. "If that's the entirety of the story, then why do you have someone stationed in my father's room ready to harm him at your signal?"

He surprised her by smiling broadly, and it transformed his already-handsome face into something breathtaking. Gone was the edge of darkness and the tension. He was relaxed and looked like a man lounging in his bedroom before turning in. She imagined him with a snifter of brandy, smiling at her and talking before they retired to their bed for the evening and...dear Lord, she was losing her grip on reality.

"I lied to you about that. I couldn't think of another way to make you listen to me. I'm sorry." He leaned forward then, his forearms on his knees as the smile fell from his lips and his eyes implored her for her cooperation. "I need you to promise me that you won't tell anyone what happened."

She'd never been so relieved to have been lied to. Caroline opened her mouth to assure him that she'd never tell anyone. It wasn't her place to gossip, and besides that, it sounded like it'd be safer for everyone if the man Castillo was hunting wasn't on the loose. The sooner he was found the better. But then she struck on an idea that made even more sense.

She sat in stunned silence as the plan formed in her mind. It was a bit devious, but her parents had pushed this upon her. What choice had they left her with? Marry someone she barely knew, which could very well ruin the rest of her life? No, this would be better.

"Carolina?" That name spoken in a whisper in his deep, raspy voice made butterflies take flight in her belly. The fluttering of their dainty wings sent ripples of awareness out along her nerve endings. He said the name using the Spanish pronunciation. Caroleena. She quite liked it. "Your promise."

Licking her dry lips, she said, "Perhaps we could trade. My

silence for your cooperation." Her pulse beat like the wings of a hummingbird against her wrists.

Castillo sat up straight, and his jaw tightened as his hands moved to rest on his thighs. He was clearly unhappy that she'd make any sort of demand on him. Caroline actually did feel a little twinge of guilt, but she managed to squash it down when she remembered the alternative was marriage.

"What sort of cooperation?" he asked.

"Would you allow me to explain a bit about myself before I tell you?" At his curt nod, she continued, "My father is a physician. He has a small practice in Boston and runs a clinic that serves some of the poorer areas of the city. He's also on the board of a hospital. Ever since I was a little girl, I've been fascinated by his work. I thought his ability to heal was otherworldly, until I grew up enough to understand there was a whole area of study behind it."

She smiled at the memory of herself as a child, amazed when he'd taken the wrappings off the arm of one of the servants' children. The little boy had broken it in a fall from a tree, and Caroline had been sure it'd come out of the wrappings bent and misshapen. But the forearm had been perfectly straight, and she'd been convinced her father was a sorcerer.

"I've spent countless hours with him, years observing him work with patients. I worked as his assistant for a few years and have seen patients with minor ailments on my own. I've known my entire life that I want to be a physician, too. Thankfully,

I have that chance. I've been admitted to Boston University's medical school, and I'm scheduled to start in September."

He'd been watching her solemnly as she spoke, but now he sat back, relaxing again, though his brow was furrowed. No doubt he was wondering what any of this had to do with him. He rubbed his fingers over his mouth, his fingertips settling on his chin where she could see the beginnings of a bit of stubble. "Congratulations."

He didn't say anything else, but Caroline let out a breath, only just realizing that she'd been waiting for him to laugh at her, or worse. Most people looked at her with mild amusement when she told them of her plan to become a physician, as if she were a child they were humoring. Sometimes they went on to lecture her on a woman's duty being in the home.

"Thank you. Unfortunately, my plan has hit a snag." She took a deep breath and swallowed against the unexpected well of emotion in her throat. The pain of betrayal was so new and raw that she still found it difficult to talk about.

"The problem is that my parents have decided that they want me to marry first. I'm their only child. I think they'd probably given up hope of ever having a child, so when I came along they indulged me. Or so I've been told."

Her friends had been slowly getting engaged, one by one, over the past few years. Most of her extended family fell into the group that believed she should be engaged, too, now that she was approaching twenty-two.

"My father has had some health issues recently, and my mother has never been in good health. I think they're worried that if I go off to medical school without being married, then they won't be around to see me properly wed and taken care of." She blinked against the tears that welled in her eyes. Aunt Prudie had tried to convince her that that was the reason, that her parents only had her best interests at heart, but it hadn't sunk in until now.

He took in a breath through his nose, shifting again to rest his elbows on his knees as he leaned forward, his intense gaze holding hers. "Don't you want to get married, have a family?"

She bristled. It wasn't the first time that someone had questioned her, and no matter how she tried, she couldn't seem to accept the question as anything other than an attack on her. As if she couldn't somehow follow her dream of helping people and become a wife and mother. "Of course, but not now. Not yet." She did want that. She wanted a husband who danced with her and held her hand as they read the newspaper. She wanted babies with chubby little hands and soft skin.

But if she was honest, the question prodded a deeper bruise. Most of the men she met seemed to be put off by her ambition. What if no man wanted to marry her after medical school? What if that was the reason her parents wanted her married off now?

She swallowed past that ache in her throat and looked away from him. She'd seen the beginning of interest in Castillo's eyes when he'd looked at her on the train, and then again tonight. He found her attractive. She didn't want to see that interest change now that he knew the truth about her.

The seconds passed, ticked off by the clock on the mantel above the fireplace, and he didn't say anything. With every bit of will she possessed, she forced herself to meet his gaze. It didn't matter what he thought of her. It wasn't as if that little flirtation on the train meant anything.

His expression was unchanged, though, and unreadable. Finally, he said, "You admit that you do want to be married, so why not marry before medical school?"

"It's not that easy. For one, it would require me to find a husband who is supportive of my choice. You can't imagine how difficult that is. For two, I don't know of a man I'd want to marry or who'd be interested in marrying me. Not in the next few months."

He smiled then, and his gaze flicked over her features and down to her bosom and even lower to touch on her hips. She blushed at his scrutiny. Her face burned hotter when his gaze moved back up to hers and she could see that he appreciated what he saw. His eyes were a deeper green, somehow, and his smile...she couldn't describe it. It wasn't lecherous, like the men she sometimes passed in the street in the shabbier parts of town. It was admiring, appreciative, the way one might look upon a much-revered—friend? No, not a friend. It was too intimate for that. A lover?

Her body came alive at the thought, just as it had begun to

come to life when he'd had his arms around her. Her heartbeat fluttered, and something pulsed dangerously low in her belly. Somehow, she became even more aware of his presence across from her. His powerful frame radiated heat.

"I won't believe that you don't have suitors." Something about the way he said that, with that hint of an accent and with such certainty, had her squirming in her chair.

"Well, I haven't." She stared at her recently buffed fingernails because she couldn't hold his gaze anymore. "That's why I need your help."

"Oh?" He seemed only mildly interested now, and she couldn't fathom what he must be thinking.

Taking a deep breath to steel her nerves, she said, "I'll keep quiet about who you are, about what I saw on the train, but I need you to compromise me."

Chapter Four

Castillo took in a deep breath and let it out slowly. It didn't help though, because even across the distance he could smell the lavender on her skin. The scent was still on him from when he'd held her against him. His gaze went to her lush mouth, and he imagined how soft her pink lips would feel as they opened beneath his. He closed his eyes before he could imagine anything more, but he only saw her disheveled. All of that golden hair down around her waist, her creamy skin flushed with need.

He'd been attracted to her on the train because she was pretty and kept her wits about her when she'd faced death. He'd admired her then. But this woman...this woman was all of that and more. She stood up for herself, she challenged him and she did it all while making him imagine how great it would feel to have all of that energy focused on him. She was so different from what he'd thought he wanted in a woman, but all he could imagine was how explosive they could be in bed. His eyes shot open and he had to look away from her, but he couldn't banish the thoughts.

"I'm not in the habit of compromising innocents, Miss Hartford." She was an innocent, and she wouldn't welcome what he had in mind.

She was silent, and he finally looked back at her, curious as to her thoughts. She stared at him pensively, her head tilted to the side. He couldn't tell if she knew the direction of his thoughts, but he couldn't stop his gaze from drifting down to her soft lips.

"No, I suppose you aren't, Mr. Rey—Mr. Jameson." She didn't look away, even though she blushed, and he knew she felt the attraction between them. Her heated gaze held his for far longer than was appropriate. But, hell, he was in her bedroom, alone, late at night. They'd passed appropriate a long time ago.

"I'm sorry." She blinked, looking down at her hands clasped in her lap. "I don't mean to stare, it's just that...I know this sounds silly, but I feel that I can trust you. I know that I met you on a train while you chased a man with a gun, and now you're asking me not to reveal your alternate identity or why you're looking for that man, but—" she laughed "—I do. I look into your eyes and I trust that you are a man of honor."

He clenched his teeth and swallowed the bitter taste on the

back of his tongue. He'd been a man of honor once, but that was long ago. There was too much blood on his hands to ever claim to be honorable again. He hadn't even been completely truthful with her. Yes, his name was Reyes and he was searching for the man who'd murdered his grandfather. However, he'd conveniently left out the list of crimes he'd committed in that search and the fact that he and his men had somehow become a band of notorious outlaws.

The Reyes Brothers. The papers called them a gang. Castillo had never thought of them in that way. There'd even been a drawing in one of the papers once. Castillo, Hunter and Zane had been drawn with kerchiefs over the lower halves of their faces as they faced down a sheriff. The shootout had never happened, though the artist had captured Zane's scar perfectly. But that was back in Texas, and far away from Montana Territory, where his identity was still secret. Castillo hoped like hell he could keep it that way. Her silence could help ensure that.

He didn't know why he felt the need to warn her away from him, but he found himself saying, "You should take care in placing your trust. You don't know me."

"I don't," she agreed. "But I know people, Mr. Jameson. And I know you find me pleasing." Even in the dim lamplight he could see the blush that rose to her cheeks again. "I know that...that you've thought about compromising me, and yet you don't. Why?"

He shifted again, finding her candor unsettling. "You don't

mince your words, do you?"

She chewed her bottom lip and her eyes shifted across the room toward the cold fireplace. "I'm told it's a flaw."

Something twisted deep in his gut. "You're not flawed from what I can see."

She smiled, but it seemed sad and hollow, and it slipped away before he was ready for it to go. She met his eyes again with her startlingly direct gaze. "Thank you. Now, if you don't mind, I'd like to get to sleep. As you can imagine, I have a few things to think over." She started to rise, but he leaned forward, holding out a hand, though he stopped just short of touching her.

"Wait. I'm afraid I can't leave until I have your promise to keep silent."

"And I'm afraid I can't give it to you. I need to go to medical school, and it appears I can't do that until I'm either wed or so ruined that no man will want to marry me."

"You can't mean that. Even if I were to do as you ask, you've said yourself that you want to be married one day. Don't you think the scandal will follow you for years? Don't you think that it could ruin your ability to marry in the future?"

She smiled at him then, like he was a simpleton who clearly didn't understand her argument. "No, I'm not worried in the least. You see, the man I'll eventually marry won't care. I don't plan to marry one of those gentlemen who trots out to our fundraisers, gives a pretty speech, pledges a donation and then returns to his parties and the theater. I plan to marry a physician or perhaps a professor. Someone scholarly who won't care for gossip and who'll listen to me when I explain the circumstances of my being compromised."

Castillo leaned back in his chair and raked a hand through his hair. Not that he'd ever put himself in the running as a contender for her hand, but had he, she had just shot down all hope. He wasn't the least bit scholarly. She deserved someone exactly like the man she described. Someone who would listen to her and honor her. "I hope you find such a man, but I imagine that he would prefer it had you chosen not to compromise yourself."

She shrugged. "Is that your position? Would you prefer your future wife—I'm assuming you're not married?" At his nod, she continued, "Would you prefer your future wife chaste and pure and all of that?"

"I haven't thought much on marriage." But that was another lie to add to the growing list he'd already told her. He thought of marriage more than he wanted to admit.

In his youth, growing up on his grandfather's hacienda, there'd been a small village nearby. At the ranch's peak they'd employed so many of the villagers to help with the cattle that they'd built quarters to house them all. His grandfather had even built a chapel, and a priest had lived there year round.

Castillo couldn't say that he was very religious now. He still prayed sometimes, but he hadn't attended Mass in years and couldn't recall when he'd made his last confession. He'd seen his mother married in that chapel to her second husband—with some not-so-subtle persuasion from his grandfather, since her first husband hadn't been dead—and Castillo had taken it for granted that he'd be married there, as well.

In that life that seemed so far removed from who he was now, he'd been taught that women should be obedient and keep themselves chaste for their future husbands. But he'd also been taught that to take a life was a sin. He couldn't very well expect a wife who was virtuous when he only had a tarnished soul to offer in return. "I suppose you're right. It wouldn't matter so much. I'd assume she had her reasons."

She adjusted the prim little spectacles perched on her nose before crossing her arms over her chest and narrowing her gaze at him. "And yet you still won't compromise me, even though you know it's for my own good? That it's what I want?"

He shook his head, as much from the need to deny her as the need to deny himself. Something about her—he couldn't quite put his finger on why he was so drawn to her—made him want to say yes. "I wouldn't steal from your husband."

That infuriated her. Anger burned from her eyes as she sat up straighter, gripping the arms of the chair. He had to fight not to smile at how it transformed her beauty from prim and elegant to fiery and almost wild. He wanted to see her wild, to see her lose control of that fire she kept carefully subdued. And he wanted her beneath him when it happened. She was beautiful. She was strength. She was all the things he wanted and admired.

"My virtue doesn't belong to my husband. It belongs to me. I can do with it what I like."

He inclined his head in a minor concession. "As you wish. My answer is still the same."

"Have you considered that it's possible to compromise me without actually taking my virtue? We could simply arrange to have someone see us in an embrace. It needn't be very dramatic."

He hadn't thought of that at all. Probably because he'd been too busy imagining the act of compromising her. "No, but I wouldn't insult your honor in any way."

She wanted to scream at him. He could tell from the way she jerked her head to the side, her jaw clenched tight, and he was tempted to push her until she lost her grip on her restraint. What would she look like raging at him? And, just as quickly, he was back to imagining his tongue on her body, his hands wrapped in that gorgeous hair as she bucked beneath him.

Mierda, he needed to stop. His blood was already starting to rush south, tightening his trousers.

"Fine, then we have nothing more to discuss. Get out."

Castillo felt the first stirring of panic and his shoulders tensed. He'd been too soft with her, letting her think this was her choice instead of his demand. He kept his voice calm, and didn't move at all. He'd played enough poker to know not to show his hand. "I could play the role of suitor. Would that help?" He had no right offering to associate his name with hers in any way, but he felt compelled to offer some compromise. It wasn't right that she wouldn't be able to continue her education.

Her widened gaze jerked back to his. She was clearly as surprised by the offer as he was. She began to shake her head, but then stopped and a smile spread across her face. It nearly stole his breath away. "Yes! Yes, that's perfect. I don't know why I didn't think of that before. It's even better than compromise."

She rose to her feet to pace the length of her room as if she was working out all the details in her head. She practically glowed with excitement, and Castillo shifted in his chair, uneasy with the direction of her thoughts. He'd meant to only discourage other suitors with his attention while she was at the wedding. It had been a paltry compromise, but the only one he could think up. He was actually worried about what wild scheme she'd come up with.

Finally she turned to face him, her eyes bright with enthusiasm. "I have the most wonderful idea. This is what we'll do." The smile on her face was so enchanting that he didn't bother to interrupt her. "You become my suitor for the week. We'll convince my father that we've fallen madly in love. He may disapprove at first, because you're not from Boston, but I know he'll come around. Then, after Hunter and Emmy's wedding, you'll propose."

Castillo shook his head emphatically at that, but she kept on talking.

"I'll accept and we'll put on the charade of a gloriously

happy couple. You'll voice your support that I be allowed to go to school. We won't be able to wed until the autumn in Boston—it'll take weeks and weeks to plan such an affair. By that point, my parents will have to let me attend classes or I'll risk losing my place. Then, once the semester is under way, we break off the engagement. We'll have to come up with a compelling reason for that. Something that doesn't reflect too unfavorably on either of us."

She adjusted her glasses and resumed her pacing. "I'm sure by that time I can convince them that I must continue my studies. I may have to concede to searching for a suitable husband while I attend, but that's preferable to not going at all."

She'd walked all the way to the corner of the room, but she turned then, beaming at him. "Thank you so much for suggesting this, Mr. Jameson. It's absolutely the perfect solution."

She looked so hopeful that he hated to disappoint her, but there was no way he was agreeing to this farce. "That is not what I suggested. I'd be willing to agree for the week, up until the wedding, but after that I'm afraid I have to go."

Depending on the leads Zane found in Helena, Castillo might even need to leave before the wedding to follow up on Derringer's location. He'd make sure to be back for the wedding, but the possibility that the man was nearby was something that couldn't be ignored. He didn't have time for what she wanted.

She walked back toward him, her hands steepled under her

chin in thought. "That's the perfect reason to put off the wedding until autumn. You have to leave...business we can say?"

He laughed. Hunting down his grandfather's killer was a business, of sorts. "Yes, business."

"There. So you see. It's all coming together."

He rose to his feet and noted that her eyes widened a bit. She took a step back. At least she didn't trust him completely. "Except it's not. I'm willing to bet Derringer's put in a lot of time, effort and money into making sure I don't find him. If your name is connected to mine—and it will be if an engagement is announced—then I can't be certain he won't come after you. He doesn't want to be found, and I don't think he'd hesitate to use you in some way." Just a few short weeks ago Hunter had almost lost Emmy to a shootout in the barn outside with a band of outlaws. Castillo wouldn't be responsible for something similar happening to Caroline, especially not over a sham of an engagement.

"That seems a bit dramatic," Caroline said, crossing her arms. "I've seen the men outside, riding in the distance. They're all armed. They're sentries, aren't they? They're keeping an eye out and making sure we're safe?"

He inclined his head in acknowledgement. "You're observant, Miss Hartford. I'll give you that."

"Then I'll be safe here on Jameson Ranch. After the wedding, you'll go off on your search, and I'll return home to Boston. I don't think what I'm asking is all that risky. Besides, it's a small risk I'm willing to take."

Castillo sighed and raked his hands through his hair. If she only knew the real risk. If she knew about all the things he'd done on his search for Derringer and the fact that Reyes was a wanted man, she wouldn't be so cavalier. It wasn't information he could share, however, so he just stared her down. "The answer is still no. I'm sorry. But you'll still have to keep my secret. I've never threatened a woman—" He paused, because that wasn't precisely true. "I'll remove you as a threat if it comes to it, Miss Hartford. You don't know me or what I'm capable of."

Her eyes widened, but she looked more angry than afraid. He'd half expected her to go pale or tremble, like the men on whom he'd used that tone. But not her. He wasn't certain if it was because she didn't believe him or because she was too angry to care. Her eyes blazed and an ember of attraction flickered through him. She was magnificent when she said, "Then I'll scream now." And she opened her mouth to do just that.

Castillo lunged at her and covered her mouth, jerking her against him to keep her from struggling. "Fine, damn you, but we'll keep it quiet. Nothing will be published in the paper. This is strictly between us and your parents." But that wouldn't stop people from talking and word getting out to Derringer. This could be a mess.

She stilled against him, and he cautiously removed his hand from her mouth, doing his best to ignore how soft and warm she felt in his arms and how her lavender scent enveloped him like an embrace. When she turned to face him, she smiled and he had the sinking feeling that she'd manipulated him into accepting her plan.

He felt compelled to offer one last argument. "Has it occurred to you that your parents may not be happy with your choice?"

Her expression blanked and he realized that not only had that not occurred to her, but that she had no idea what he was talking about. "I'm not from Boston Society," he explained with a wry grin.

She touched his hand, which was resting on her arm, and her gaze did one quick sweep of his face in a way that made him think she liked what she saw. "You're not flawed from what I can see," she whispered.

Chapter Five

Castillo slipped quietly from her room. He was still trying to figure out what the hell had happened in there. One minute he'd been in charge, and the next she had him agreeing to be her fiancé. His response to having her repeat his own words to him was so visceral that it had taken his breath away. Instead of replying, he'd had to leave.

Walking a few steps away, he turned, half intending to go back in there and tell her the plan wasn't going to work. He had more important things to do than pretend to court her. But he paused because he didn't have a suitable alternative. He couldn't keep her tied up in her room the entire week.

An image of what that'd look like swam through his mind. Damn, keeping her tied to her bed all week did hold a certain kind of appeal. He remembered the way she'd looked at him back on the train when she'd thought about kissing him. He doubted she'd admit it now, but he'd seen the way her eyes had gone soft and lit on his mouth. She'd imagined he'd kiss her right there on the train. If he kept her tied up then he'd have plenty of time to make her look at him like that again. Then she'd be all his.

He shifted, his body already responding to that image in his mind. Damn. Her presence here was ruining his concentration and his plans.

"Cas?" Hunter called his name.

Castillo gave one last quick, befuddled glance toward Caroline's door and made his way to Hunter.

"What's going on with Caroline?" Hunter asked when he was close enough to not be overheard.

"She was on the train when Bennett saw us. She heard him call me Reyes."

Hunter cursed under his breath.

"I talked to her," Castillo said and put a hand on his brother's shoulder. "I explained about my grandfather and she's offered her cooperation. She's not a problem."

Hunter raked his fingers through his hair. "That seems a little too convenient."

"She doesn't know everything. Just that Derringer went missing with the funds he stole and that Bennett is his son. She has no reason to say anything." Castillo believed that as long

70

as the dust settled and Bennett or Derringer didn't make an appearance, she'd stay quiet about the train incident. Or maybe that was just him hoping for luck to land on his side for once.

But Hunter nodded and started walking back toward the stairs. Castillo walked along with him. "That's good. I don't want anything to ruin the wedding for Emmy."

"It won't, Hunter. Zane and I will make sure of that." Once again a pang of jealousy threatened to rear its head. God knew he didn't begrudge his brother his happiness, but that didn't mean Castillo wasn't mourning his own lack of a family.

"We'll make sure of that," Hunter said, pausing at the landing and meeting his eyes. "I'm still in the brotherhood."

"You are, but this week is about you and Emmy."

Hunter smiled, his eyes going warm as they usually did when he talked about his bride. "Come on, the old man wants to talk to you downstairs."

Castillo sighed. He'd known this confrontation was coming. Better to get it over with now so that he could sleep in peace tonight, but he was so bone weary he didn't think sleep would be a problem. He and Zane had spent the past two days looking for Bennett and finding dead ends.

"There'll be whiskey." Hunter smiled as if that would sweeten the deal.

Castillo conceded that it did make the talk more palatable. He barely grumbled as they made their way down the curving staircase to the study in the back of the house. The women were either still outside on the porch or had already gone up to bed, because he didn't see them anywhere as Hunter led him through the semi darkened house. Wall sconces lit the way, their light gleaming off the polished wood floor where it wasn't covered in Persian rugs.

The study door was open, and Tanner was seated in one of the tall, wingback chairs before the fireplace. A low fire was burning to chase away the little bit of coolness in the air. He stood when Castillo and Hunter walked in. "Castillo. Thank you for joining us." His hand came up to offer a tumbler of dark, amber-red whiskey.

Castillo nodded as he accepted it, aware of the door closing behind him and how it made the room feel stuffy. He tried to ignore the way the skin at the back of his neck suddenly felt two sizes too small. Instead, he focused on the man before him.

Tanner had aged well and still had a headful of hair the same tawny color as Hunter's with just a few strands of silver at the temples. His forehead was grooved and lines spread out from his eyes and bracketed his mouth. But they made him look distinguished instead of merely aged. He must be around fifty—Castillo didn't actually know how old his father was—but he was the image of vitality.

As a child, Castillo had listened to his mother talk about Tanner Jameson often. Usually when she was putting him to bed at night. She'd smile in that way she'd had that brightened her entire face and tell Castillo how he'd gone to seek his fortune, that he'd come back for them one day. Castillo had never been sure if the blurry images of the man he'd carried in his mind had been memories of his father or pictures she'd painted with her words.

That was, until his mother died and he'd knocked on the front door of Jameson Ranch five years ago and come face-to-face with the man. His face had matched the image in Castillo's mind, except the grooves had grown deeper. Castillo had been surprised that he'd remembered the man so clearly. He'd also been surprised to not feel anything at seeing his father—not happiness, not sadness. Nothing except a swell of anger that this man had made his mother cry.

Tanner indicated Castillo should take the seat opposite him, and he sank down into the matching chair and brought the whiskey to his lips. The familiar warmth of the liquor going down soothed him. Hunter poured his own drink and sat on the sofa. When Tanner settled down, the leg he'd injured in the war jutted out a bit because the knee didn't bend properly. Firelight gleamed off the black lacquer of the cane propped next to him.

Tanner cleared his throat, breaking the awkward silence that had settled in the room. "Thank you for coming to the wedding. I'm glad you could make the trip."

"No need to thank me. I didn't come for your benefit." Castillo grimaced at how harsh the words sounded. He didn't particularly like the man for what he'd done to his mother, but he wasn't bitter.

Instead of taking the bait, Tanner gave a little shrug of his wide shoulders and inclined his head. "Nevertheless, I'm glad you came. I hope everything went well with Miguel. He settled in fine?"

Castillo nodded. "Well enough. He didn't want to go, but I think he realizes an education is best for his future." It was a damn sight better than being chased like a criminal until someone eventually gunned him down. That situation with Campbell's gang had been too close.

"Hunter didn't want to go, either." Tanner chuckled and shared an amused glance and some unknown memory with Hunter before looking back at Castillo. "I had to take him myself, much like you had to take your brother. I'd like to meet Miguel someday."

Castillo stayed silent. In recent years, Tanner had made attempts to get to know more about him and his family—mainly with requests sent through Hunter—but that didn't even come close to making up for the years his father had been absent or how the man had hurt his mother. Maybe Castillo was a little bitter.

When it became apparent Castillo wouldn't reply, Tanner asked, "When did you meet Emmy? Back in the dining room...well, it seemed that you knew each other."

Castillo took another sip of whiskey and glanced to Hunter. Together they'd all three concocted a story about how Hunter and Emmy had met. Due to his venture breeding horses,

Hunter had met Emmy's stepfather through business. When the man had needed to take an extended overseas business trip, he'd implored Hunter to take in Emmy and her younger sisters because they had no other relatives to see them through such a lengthy absence. Naturally, it had been love at first sight for the young couple and here they were getting married just weeks later.

They couldn't very well go around telling everyone the truth. That her stepfather was Ship Campbell, leader of a ruthless gang of bank robbers who'd kidnapped Miguel in an act of retaliation. Or that Hunter, Castillo and Zane had kidnapped Emmy, and then she'd escaped to a brothel and Hunter had bid on her virginity. Not even Tanner knew about their legally questionable activities. Castillo was still unclear about how he was supposed to fit into that story, so he smiled as Hunter took the lead in answering.

"Castillo and Miguel came up from Texas not long after Emmy arrived. They spent a little time here before taking the train to Boston."

"I'm sorry to have missed the visit," Tanner said. "With any luck, the vote for statehood will go through soon and I won't have to spend so much time in Washington."

"Is it luck or money that's involved?" Castillo wasn't involved in politics, but he knew enough to understand how it all worked. Whoever had the most money could generally get what they wanted.

"A bit of both, I suppose," Tanner said with an easy grin. "There's no question it takes money. Lots of it. But it also takes a lot of convincing the right people that we're not just a bunch of lawless, immoral heathens. I expect we'll see some changes coming to Helena soon. Saloons, brothels and gambling dens will have to be brought down to a manageable number. We'll have to do our part to fit in with Eastern expectations."

"I've known many heathens with greater moral character than most of the men in Washington."

Tanner paused, perhaps wondering if he'd been included in that group, before inclining his head in agreement.

"Won't closing those places anger a lot of people?" Castillo asked. "Those places cater to the people who work the mines."

"They do, but the times are changing. We're not just a mining town anymore. There are families here, businesses, schools and churches. It's time to move forward." Tanner took a deep breath, as if he had something else he wanted to say but didn't know how to start. Finally he let the breath out and met Castillo's gaze. "We can talk about Montana statehood all night if you want, but that's not why I asked you to come in here."

Castillo clenched his jaw, already preparing for what he knew was coming.

"I want you to accept the income from your silver mine and acknowledge your interest in the Jameson Mining Company."

On Castillo's first and only other visit with his father, Tanner had mentioned the silver mines he'd bought in both of his sons' names years ago. Apparently they both produced a healthy income. Castillo had refused his in no uncertain terms. But when he'd returned home to Texas, and his grandfather had made him aware of the financial state of the hacienda, Castillo had been tempted to soften his stance. His outrage at his father couldn't withstand his sorrow at seeing his grandfather's dream crumble around him.

When he would've weakened, his grandfather had urged him to stay strong, saying that he'd never allow Tanner's dirty money to sully the hacienda's good name. Hunter had taken over the management of both mines, and Castillo still wanted no part of his.

At some point since his first visit, Tanner had redrawn his will so that Hunter and Castillo shared in the estate equally. He'd also made them partners in the Jameson Mining Company. Hunter had urged him many times to accept his share, but Castillo had refused. If standing strong against Tanner was the only way to honor his grandfather, the man who'd raised him, then that's what he'd do. Making the hacienda a success wouldn't mean anything if it was accomplished with Jameson money.

"I have no interest in your money, Tanner. You know that." Castillo clenched his hand around the tumbler, while the other balled into a fist at his side, as unreasonable anger coursed through his body. He shouldn't feel this angry. Logically, he knew that it wasn't productive. He'd spent too many years rationally weighing his options and outsmarting those who were a threat to the brotherhood to allow anger to rule him now. But, just for a moment, he indulged it, allowing it free rein. "I don't want anything from you."

"It's your inheritance, Castillo." Hunter's voice was soft but firm when he spoke, his expression earnest.

"No, it's your inheritance, and you're entitled to it. Take it with my compliments." Castillo looked back to Tanner's wary eyes. "It's not my inheritance. You abandoned her." He'd never spoken so plainly to the man. On that first visit, he'd barely said more than to introduce himself and hand him the letter his mother had written. Tanner had spoken, but Castillo hadn't. He'd been too angry, and too surprised and overwhelmed by that anger and his grief over his mother's death, to say much.

"Castillo, you must know...I didn't simply abandon Marisol. I asked her to come with me."

Castillo's breath caught in his chest. He'd never heard Tanner say his mother's name before. Something about hearing it now made their relationship seem more real, which was foolish because of course it had been real. Castillo was living proof. The green eyes with a tint of gold he saw every time he looked into a mirror were staring back at him now. The strong jaw and wide shoulders had both come from the man sitting across from him.

He'd never known that Tanner had tried to take his mother with him when he left. She'd never told him that, but it didn't matter. "If she said no it was with the understanding that you'd come back for her, and she never saw you again. You abandoned her."

"There's more to it than that, Castillo. It's more complicated." Tanner was agitated. He set his whiskey on the table beside him and dragged a hand over his chin.

"I'm certain there's more to it, but it's not all that complicated. You were more interested in building a fortune, in this—" Castillo raised a hand to encompass the opulence of the room "—than you were in honoring your commitment to her. After all, what better way to solidify your ambition than to marry into a political family like the Hartfords? Something tells me a Reyes for a wife wouldn't have held as much political weight." Castillo jerked his gaze toward the fire. He hadn't meant to drag those old demons out. He'd told himself when he found out Tanner would be here that he'd stick to benign topics and avoid the man as much as possible.

The room went silent, with only the crackling of the wood as it burned filling up the air. Finally, Tanner said, "I'm sorry for what happened with your mother. Sorrier than you'll ever know. I can't change the past, but I'd like a fresh start with you."

A fresh start. As if Castillo could just wipe away how it felt to grow up without his father. As if he could forget how helpless he'd felt every time he found his mother crying. As if he could forget the way people looked at him when it had become known that Tanner had married someone else. Castillo wasn't a bastard, but having it known that your father had thrown you away to start another family was pretty damn close to the same thing. "Why do you deserve that, Tanner?"

"I probably don't. I deserve as much of your anger as you want to throw at me. But that's not going to bring either of us any happiness. Also, I'd like for you to call me Father, at least this week while people are here."

Castillo shook his head and rose to his feet, setting his tumbler down on the mantel. "Thank you for your recommendation. Miguel wouldn't have been accepted to the university without it and whatever favors you requested. I do appreciate that." Castillo had also paid the tuition from the silver mine's account. It was the least he could do after Miguel had almost been killed, but that'd be the only money he'd take. "But that's the extent of this. I'm here because of Hunter, because he's asked me to stand up next to him when he marries Emmy. Alejandro Reyes raised me as his own. He's my father."

"You're just like him, Castillo. Too proud and stubborn. He wouldn't accept any of the money I offered him over the years. If he had, maybe things would've gone better for him."

Maybe he'd still be alive and the hacienda wouldn't be a failure. Tanner didn't say that, but that's what he meant. Castillo hadn't known about Tanner offering his grandfather money over the years, but it didn't change anything. Turning, he walked from the room.

There was some rustling behind him, and he assumed Tanner or maybe both of the men got to their feet. Then he heard

Hunter say, "Let him go, Pop."

Whatever else Hunter said faded into the darkness as Castillo made his way to the stairs. He took them two at a time and found his bedroom. He'd take his things and move into the bunkhouse for the week. They'd need as many bedrooms as they could get for the guests that would arrive, anyway. He wouldn't sleep under this roof, not while Tanner was here to see it as some sort of capitulation. Yet as soon as he walked into his bedroom, he realized that he couldn't leave.

Caroline was down the hall and he needed to stay close to her. He cursed and kicked over the ottoman just before plopping down into the overstuffed chair before the cold fireplace. That woman was going to be trouble. He'd have to watch her day and night to make sure she kept her end of their ill-advised bargain.

An unwelcome vision of her as she'd been on the train swam through his mind. She'd been soft and sweet in his arms, an almost direct contradiction to the woman he'd met earlier tonight. That woman had been all challenge and confidence. He wanted to figure out how both personalities melded together.

He sucked in a breath and leaned forward to hold his head in his hands. Spending time with her was going to be challenging. There was no denying that she intrigued him. He'd never met a woman so certain of herself and what she wanted. It didn't help that he was attracted to her.

This was going to be a tough week.

Chapter Six

Caroline awoke the next morning more excited than she'd ever been in her life. Well, perhaps more excited was extreme. She'd been excited when she'd been accepted to the medical program. This feeling was simply a different kind of excitement, a new excitement. It was similar to when she was ten and she'd been given a pony for her birthday. She'd unwrapped the papers for her new treasure and had had to wait until Sunday when her father could drive her out of town to the stables to see it. The whole way there she'd felt like she might burst out of her skin because she was too wound up for it to contain her.

This excitement was like that. Only better. Because it wasn't a mere pony who waited for her. It was Castillo. One of the most intriguing men she'd ever met in her life. Hunter Jameson was very handsome. A few of the men at the charity balls in Boston had been every bit as handsome. This man was handsome in a different way. He was dark sensuality mixed with rugged intensity, an enigmatic combination she'd never encountered before. And when she looked into his eyes, she saw that he knew things that she'd never know on her own. Things that she wanted him to teach her.

Castillo. Even his name was exotic and mysterious. She said it to herself as she sat in front of the mirror at her dressing table. He'd called her Carolina. Not Caroline. Nothing so boring and normal as that. She'd lain awake in bed for hours last night just remembering the way his smooth voice had practically caressed the sounds as they came out of his mouth. If she wasn't so befuddled by her reaction to him, she'd take the time to chastise herself for it. But that'd have to wait until after she saw him again. Right now she was too busy getting ready.

She tugged on one of the perfect sausage curls that fell across her shoulder and wondered if she shouldn't have had Mary spend the time with the hot iron. Caroline had perfected a series of simple twists and pins years ago to deal with her heavy hair. It's how she wore it every day at her father's office. Father and Aunt Prudie were bound to know something was amiss if she was putting extra effort into her hair now, when it wasn't even evening. Then she smiled at her own foolishness. If she was pretending to fall in love with Castillo, then they'd expect her take the extra time with her appearance.

She kept forgetting that. This was all pretend, only the flutters in her belly didn't know that.

Standing, she ran her hands down the skirt of her morning dress. It was a sunny yellow with white tulle around the bodice to keep it modest and with just enough of a bustle to keep it fashionable. The fact that it went well with her coloring had only figured a little into her reasons for choosing it for this particular morning. The blush staining her cheeks in the mirror called her a liar. The truth was that she'd never felt this way about a man before. She'd found some handsome, but this level of attraction was beyond her experience.

She shook her head at herself as she made her way to the door to collect her father and go down to breakfast. There she hoped to see Castillo again. She practiced saying his name, trying to get the Spanish double L to sound the way it had when Hunter had said it.

"Castillo." The sound of a man's voice saying his name left her dumbfounded.

Castillo was leaning with one shoulder against the wall just outside her door with his arms crossed over his chest. He smiled and repeated his name, this time enunciating each syllable, taunting her. "Go ahead, try it again."

Her cheeks flamed in embarrassment. "I thought...if we're to pretend...I thought I should know how to say it correctly."

Castillo inclined his head in acknowledgement. "Of course, Carolina."

A shiver of pure pleasure snaked through her body at the sound of his voice saying her name again. It raised gooseflesh on her arms and made her skin tingle. Even her breasts seemed to tighten somehow, though Caroline had no firsthand experience with what that meant or even why it happened. She cleared her throat and pulled her shoulders back to disguise her reaction. Surely he couldn't tell what he did to her.

He smiled as if he did know. His eyelids lowered slightly, heavy, and one corner of his mouth quirked upward, bringing her attention to his fuller bottom lip. He was dressed like a gentleman this morning in a plain yet perfectly tailored suit of dove gray. The coat was stretched across the broad width of his shoulders, emphasizing their strength. The men at the charity functions in Boston definitely did not have shoulders like that. His dark hair was parted at the side and pushed back from his forehead. It fell in rich waves just past his collar, too long to be fashionable but it looked appealing on him. He was a strange mixture of gentleman mixed with rugged handsomeness that she found very appealing.

"Why are you here?" she asked.

"To watch you."

He didn't mean that with any sort of intimacy, quite the opposite actually, but the words plucked a chord of longing deep inside her. Across the hall, just a couple of yards back toward the staircase, her father's door was cracked open. She lowered her voice a bit so her father wouldn't hear. "And what if someone catches you here?"

"I'll say that I'm enamored of you and can't stay away." His lips twitched as he tried to contain his smile. "You do look lovely." His glance went from her hair to her morning gown before lighting on her face again.

Her heart pounded in her chest. Never had such a casual, possibly disingenuous compliment had such an effect on her. Instead of addressing that, she said, "The charade was my idea. I'd hardly change my mind about it."

"Trust must be earned, Miss Hartford. I can't very well give you my trust after one conversation. For all I know, now that it's morning, you might've reconsidered."

She sighed, but she couldn't dispute that. If she were in his shoes, she'd be equally suspicious. "Well, I can assure you, Mr. Jameson, that I'm not some faint-hearted dolt. I made a commitment and I'll see it through."

Something like respect shone in his eyes. He straightened a bit and gave her a once-over, as if sizing her up in a different light. "Then let's go down to breakfast." He held out his arm as if he intended to escort her like a proper gentleman.

This man was so contradictory that she was quickly becoming fascinated with him. Here, in this hallway on this grand estate, he had the aura of a gentleman, but that dangerous man she'd seen on the train lurked just beneath the surface. "I need to collect my father first."

He nodded once and led the way to the bedroom, though

he stayed in the hallway while she pushed the door open and went inside. Her father was sitting outside on his balcony with a medical text in hand. She recognized it as the one she'd read on the train. "Good morning. Are you feeling rested?"

Her father set his book down on his lap and took off his reading glasses. A gentle wind blew wisps of his gray hair out of place. "I'm feeling much better. Thank you, dear. I apologize for my disappearance last night."

"I assumed you'd decided to go to bed early when you didn't come down for supper." She crossed his room and took in the healthy color in his cheeks and the clear whites of his eyes. The sallowness was gone. The rest had done him good. His tired spells were happening more often lately, but they never seemed to last long. "You look much better." She leaned over and gave him a hug and a kiss on the cheek.

"As do you. I don't think I've ever seen you curl your hair when your mother didn't demand it for a function." He grinned and rose to his feet, going into his room and placing his book on the bedside table. "I'll let her know as soon as she arrives."

Caroline smiled. He was right about that. Her mother was constantly after her to pay more attention to her dress and hair, all in the name of catching a husband, of course. "We're on an adventure. I thought the change was called for."

A twinge of guilt at the fib tugged at her chest. She wanted to tell him about the plan she'd concocted with Castillo. She'd never kept anything from her father before. While a part of her thought that he might understand and actually go along with it, another part knew of his deep loyalty to her mother. He sent her daily letters whenever he traveled. There was no way he could keep quiet about this, and then Caroline would be right back in the position of facing marriage to a virtual stranger in order to continue her education. Or worse. That stranger might actually demand she not go through with medical training. As much as she despised the deception, it was necessary.

He smiled back at her as he offered her his arm. "You look beautiful. You may find yourself a husband yet." He winked at her and she took his arm and laughed at the jest, but she thought of Castillo. Somehow she knew that there would be no one else to draw her attention the way he had. In just two brief meetings he'd fascinated her in a way no one else ever had. Her reaction to him was almost frightening, because it was completely unprecedented in her experience. She'd been attracted by a handsome face before, but this was more. This was deeper. She reacted to him on a visceral level she didn't quite understand.

Castillo was standing at attention when she and her father stepped into the hallway. "Good morning, Mr. Hartford. I'm Castillo Jameson, Hunter's brother. I've come to escort you and your lovely daughter to breakfast." He offered his hand and her father shook it.

"Ah, Castillo Jameson. It's a pleasure to meet you. Your father and brother speak highly of you. You must have arrived last night. My apologies I wasn't downstairs to greet you. I was a bit under the weather."

"I did arrive last night, but I must confess, with your sister and daughter for company at supper, I hardly noticed anyone else."

Her father laughed at this and Castillo winked at her. She smiled back, impressed with his commitment to their ruse. If she didn't know better, she'd think he was an overeager suitor looking to make a good first impression on her father. Of course, she did know better, but her father didn't. Another twinge of guilt twisted in her chest when he looked back at her and raised a knowing eyebrow, as if to say she'd found her first prospective admirer.

"They are quite a duo when you get them together," her father agreed. "I'd love to hear all about your trip to Boston. I'm sorry our paths didn't cross while you were in town."

As a group they turned toward the stairs. When Castillo stood back to allow her and her father to precede him down, her father gently shrugged off her hand from his arm. "You two go ahead." Castillo offered his arm, and just like that, he was escorting her down with her father behind them.

Castillo's arm was strong beneath her hand. Even through the layers of his clothing she could feel the dense muscles flexing in his forearm. She wanted the time to touch him at her leisure, to explore the sinew and tendons wrapped across his body.

A part of her curiosity was intellectual. She'd studied the

illustrations in books on human anatomy her father had given her and taken notes as she read them from cover to cover. But since her father limited her to female patients and children, she'd never actually had the chance to study the male form for herself.

Castillo was such a spectacular specimen that the physician in her wanted to see and feel those muscles up close, to learn how they moved and worked together. The woman in her wanted to see and feel those muscles for an entirely different reason.

"You're very clever," she said, mainly to distract herself from how solid his presence was beside her.

He smiled. "Committed to your cooperation, I believe, is the appropriate description."

She laughed. "That, too."

***

Castillo walked into the dining room with Caroline on his arm and received a roomful of surprised looks...again. Tanner was at the head of the table in deep discussion with her aunt about something—probably politics—but he paused with a hand in midgesture. Emmy and Hunter had equally baffled expressions. A grin spread across Prudence's face from one ear to the other when she saw Caroline on Castillo's arm. This plan was going to be easier to execute than he'd thought. It seemed as if they already had one person willing to believe the ruse.

Castillo had debated avoiding walking her downstairs that morning because, well, because he'd wanted to see her. Obviously, after their discussion the previous night, he needed to keep her in his sight at all times. But he couldn't deny that he wanted to keep her in his sight for more than logical reasons. He wanted her, and that wasn't a feeling he could indulge. This arrangement between them needed to be kept cold, a simple exchange of words and gestures to fool her family. He couldn't slip up and let himself think that it was anything more, because it could never be more. Not with the price on his head. Not with her plans to return to Boston.

A spread of delicious-smelling food had been set out on the buffet for them to prepare their own plates, so Castillo led her in that direction.

"Good morning, dear," Prudence said.

"Good morning," Caroline said to the room, and received a chorus of greetings in response.

Hunter had lowered his paper just enough to glance over the top and pinned Castillo with a look that clearly demanded to know what the hell was going on. It was tinged with disapproval. Castillo hadn't had a chance to go over the finer details of their arrangement last night. He'd have to see to that soon.

As her father greeted the group, Caroline let go of Castillo's arm and grabbed a plate. She filled it with a poached egg, sausage and some of the strawberries left over from last night. He waited for her father to go ahead before filling his own plate and following them to the table. Everyone seemed to be watching him, waiting to see where he chose to sit. He inwardly grimaced and followed Prudence's not so subtle glance indicated that he sit at the empty space next to Caroline. Caroline smiled at him as he sat. It was genuine and free of artifice. He couldn't help but wonder how it might feel to be the recipient of those smiles every day.

"Did you sleep well?" Prudence asked no one in particular. After getting a handful of remarks, she said, "You're looking well, Samuel. Have you recovered your health?"

Caroline's father murmured a reply in the affirmative, and Prudence nodded before turning her attention to Caroline. "You look radiant. I love what you've done with your hair. I don't think I've seen you wear it that way since the night of the Higginbotham's musical."

Caroline blushed at the compliment, pink staining the apples of her cheeks. Had she fixed her hair for him? "Thank you. I wear it like this from time to time. Mary offered to do it, so I accepted." She glanced at him before taking another bite of her breakfast and he thought that maybe she had. An unexpected warmth swelled in his chest. What if he'd never met her on the train and this ruse hadn't been necessary? How would this morning be different? Would they have flirted? Would they have realized they liked each other? Would she have wanted him to court her?

Prudence didn't miss much, and her narrowed gaze took in her niece and then Castillo. "Good morning, Castillo."

"Good morning, Mrs. Williams." Castillo gave her one of his most charming smiles. "You're looking lovely this morning."

She smiled at his compliment, but her calculating gaze landed on Caroline. "Not nearly so lovely as Caroline."

He paused and turned the full force of his attention on the woman sitting next to him. She blushed even more. He allowed his gaze to make a slow sweep across her face and her hair, and down to her bosom, which was tastefully covered for the morning hour. But he remembered how she'd looked last night. She'd been covered but her wrapper had been thin and shown far more to him than she probably realized.

Her lips parted as she drew in a ragged breath, drawing his gaze back to them, and he nearly smiled at how he affected her. Maybe it could be fun pretending with her. "She is very lovely," he agreed. For a moment there was heat in Caroline's gaze. Then he turned his attention back to her aunt. "And I told her as much upstairs."

"Oh?" Prudence perked up and looked to Caroline for an explanation.

Caroline shifted as if she was uncomfortable, and then her foot kicked him under the table. It wasn't hard, but it was enough to get his attention. He smiled and brought his coffee cup up for a sip. Apparently when she'd proposed that he court her, she'd meant for him to do it at her direction.

"We met in the hallway on our way downstairs," she explained.

"Oh." The look of disappointment on her aunt's face was so comical, Castillo couldn't help but snicker. It seemed as if the woman was in favor of her niece's plan, whether she knew it was a plan or not. He wondered what Prudence knew of her brother's intentions to have Caroline married off and if she supported it.

The thought sobered him. It had started to bother him that Caroline didn't have anyone in her corner advocating for her. She was clearly intelligent, and her family had the funds to pay her tuition and had apparently helped to foster her ambition by allowing her to train with her father. It seemed unfair that they'd try to curb her ambition now.

After a moment the conversation continued around them. Castillo offered a random comment here and there, and nodded politely where appropriate, but when he glanced at Caroline he could tell her eyes were troubled. He wondered if she was second-guessing this plan of theirs.

"Tell us more about this hacienda of yours. Jameson here says it's the best cattle ranch in Texas," her father said, drawing his attention to the older man.

The last thing he wanted to do was talk about his family with these people. He wanted to keep that part of himself separate from Tanner and from this ruse. Except he had no choice but to open up a little. "My grandfather came from Spain as a young man to build it. It was his dream to own the greatest cattle ranch in middle Texas. For a while, it was one of the best," he acknowledged.

"Cattle's a hard business, I'm told." Samuel wiped his mouth on his napkin and folded the square of linen back over his lap. He did it meticulously and with concentration, just as he seemed to do everything.

Castillo nodded. "Indeed. Fortunes have been lost to disease and rustlers." That's what had happened to his grandfather's fortune. Bitterness and anger welled within him, but he forced it down. Derringer was close, and Castillo would find him and settle the wrong. He gripped his cup to take another sip, but Willy swept in with fresh coffee in a silver pot. She gave him an affectionate smile as she stopped to refill his cup, and he nodded his thanks.

"It's true. I've heard stories of men losing everything. Didn't Hamish follow the cattle markets, Prudie?" Then he turned to Castillo and added, "Prudie and her husband lived in Chicago for some time early in their marriage."

"Oh, Samuel, you know I dislike discussing business at the breakfast table. It's quite rude," Prudie chastised him, but her tone was playful.

Samuel shrugged as if he was clueless when it came to social graces, and he went back to talking to Hunter about his stallions. "Tell me, Hunter, how often do you breed a female with a stallion for a season?"

Caroline nearly choked on her coffee. Animal husbandry definitely wasn't appropriate breakfast conversation.

"For heaven's sake," Prudence said. "I'm going to need whiskey with my coffee for this conversation." Everyone laughed while Caroline's father shook his head in resignation.

"Maybe we should save the specifics until we're in the stable. We have three foals already this year," Hunter said, leading the conversation into safer territory.

"Forgive my father." Caroline surprised Castillo by leaning over slightly to talk to him in a low voice, treating him to the scent of her lavender perfume. Her arm brushed his, making his nerve endings come alive. She smiled as she gave her father a fond glance. "As a physician he's fairly liberal in his discussion of reproduction. He never seems to understand why others aren't. Once, when I was a child, he sent my mother fleeing from the room because he'd taken the time to answer my question about how babies are made."

Despite his best effort, an image of her splayed out naked in his bed as he took her flashed through his mind. His entire body immediately tightened in response. Clearing his throat, he couldn't stop himself from teasing her. "I could clarify if he left anything out of his explanation."

She drew back, the smile dropping from her face as she seemed to realize what she'd just said to him.

From some distance away, a bell rang. "Ah," Hunter folded his newspaper and stood. "I believe our first guests have arrived."

Chapter Seven

M r. and Mrs. Bonham arrived with their three teenaged
daughters as breakfast was coming to an end. They
were friends of Tanner Jameson's from another part of the
territory. They'd spent the night in Helena before getting up
early to make the ride to the ranch. Caroline was torn between
welcoming the distraction and mourning the fact that more
people meant she'd have less time to spend getting to know
Castillo.

The activity for the day was a ride to the river where they'd
have a picnic. It took over an hour to get everyone ready to go
and then a little bit longer to get them mounted on horses. A
wagon was brought around for the children. Emmy's sisters,
Ginny, who had proudly proclaimed herself almost thirteen

when Caroline met her, and Rose, who was a few years younger, climbed into the back of the wagon, which had been filled with hay. The three Bonham children climbed in behind them. Hunter held the reins up front with Emmy beside him and, once everyone was settled, set off at a sedate pace across the field. Mr. Jameson rode on his horse beside them.

"Thank you," Caroline said to the stable hand who brought out a beautiful chestnut-colored mare for her to ride.

"I'll take her, Jim." Castillo came up beside him and took the reins.

The boy, who couldn't have been more than fifteen, nodded his thanks and ran back into the stable. On the tour Hunter had given them when they'd arrived, Caroline had seen a few men working the stables and the corral beyond, but today they were all gone, leaving the boy to do all the work of getting their mounts. Hunter had even helped him hitch the wagon. It made her wonder if their absence had something to do with Derringer's possible presence.

Castillo led the gentle horse to the mounting block where he held her steady. "Her name's Cinnamon."

Caroline smiled her thanks and took his outstretched hand as she mounted. Even through the leather of their gloves, the electricity found a way to spark between them. Instead of lingering, she focused on getting herself settled in the saddle and withdrew her hand.

"She's a beauty," she said, running a hand over Cinnamon's

neck. The horse gave her a look before nudging Castillo for a treat. He laughed and obliged by taking a sugar cube from his pocket and holding it out on his palm. Then he ran his hand affectionately down her nose while murmuring something in Spanish. His touch was gentle and confident, as if he knew exactly how to touch her. An irrational pang of jealousy tore through Caroline. "Cinnamon likes you," she added, to cover up her envy. She refused to be jealous of an animal.

He smiled up at her. It was a smile that momentarily lightened the heaviness in his eyes, giving her a glance at the man he might have been without this horrible tragedy hanging over his head. "She's a good horse. Stroke her the right way, give her a little sugar and she'll follow you anywhere."

Caroline had to look away, afraid that her face had turned red. She was sadly aware that it wouldn't take much more than that to make her forget her scruples and follow him anywhere he asked her to go, and she barely knew the man.

"Are you coming, Caroline?" Mrs. Bonham laughed as her horse, eager for exercise, trotted after the wagon. She was an astute horsewoman, though, because she easily controlled her enthusiastic mount, and her husband caught up with her.

"Yes, coming," Caroline replied. "Aren't you joining us for the picnic?" Caroline called to Aunt Prudie who stood perched on the porch steps.

"No, I'm staying behind. Your father has challenged me to a game of chess and I cannot let him go on thinking the last time he beat me proves anything."

Her father laughed from his rocking chair on the porch. "The only thing you have to prove, dear sister, is that you can maintain your grace in losing. Have a good time, Caroline."

Caroline smiled. "I will," she called back and started off behind the Bonhams. Though she'd barely cleared the stable yard before she was looking back to check on Castillo. Just as she did, he came riding out of the stable on a beautiful chestnut. He hurried to catch up to her but slowed his mount to ride beside her.

They rode in amicable silence for a little while. Caroline took in the big mountains in the distance, rising up to meet the even bigger sky. She'd never seen anything so beautiful. She loved Boston, the people, the variety, the culture. But this was different. It was what she imagined heaven might be like. Everything was so green and fresh, like it was created brand new every morning.

"It's so beautiful. I can understand why Hunter prefers it here over Boston." She swung her gaze over to Castillo to see that he was staring at the mountains before them, his shoulders a little tense. Alert.

"It's one of the most beautiful places on Earth," he agreed, his eyes roving over the hills in the distance. A little bit of the tension seemed to leave his shoulders.

Their horses waded through the knee-high grass that swayed in the cool breeze blowing in over the hills. Butterflies fluttered happily from one bluebonnet to another. The girls' excited voices could be heard from the wagon far ahead, but it was tranquil where they were. Quiet enough to allow her to ponder the man beside her.

Caroline hadn't considered his life outside of the train incident and the Jameson Ranch. He'd told her last night about his mother and his grandfather, but she hadn't considered that he had an entire ranch back in Texas. For some reason, the conversation at breakfast had made her heart drop into her stomach.

"Is Texas as beautiful?"

"It's different. Flatter. With blue sky as far as the eye can see." He gave her a little smile before looking ahead again. "It's home."

Something passed over his face. It was difficult to tell from his profile, but the corner of his mouth tipped downward and she thought it might be sadness. Was he thinking of his grandfather and all he'd left behind in Texas? Did he have a woman waiting for him? He'd said that he wasn't married, but maybe he was involved with someone. Maybe she was waiting for him to complete his vow to find this criminal and then return home and marry her. A twinge of guilt for forcing him to play this charade twisted in Caroline's chest.

What sort of man would devote years of his life to chasing the man responsible for the death of someone he loved? She found the quality admirable and decided she'd try to learn more about him in their brief time together at the ranch. When he caught her looking at him, his gaze dropped to her lips, making them tingle almost as if he'd touched them. She licked them and looked away. Best to keep her interest purely on the side of intellectual curiosity. Anything more would be too dangerous. "Will you tell me about your grandfather?"

He looked away, and she wasn't certain he'd answer. She certainly had no right to ask him anything so personal, but she wanted to know what would push him so far for justice. He'd apparently been hunting this killer for years, when most men would've given up.

"My grandfather was a good man," he finally said. "Devout in his faith, tireless in his work, uncompromising in his character and demanding when it came to instilling those same values in me."

"He sounds...formidable." He sounded harsh.

Castillo laughed at her word choice.

"That means difficult?" he asked.

"Yes, and tough, intimidating."

He nodded with a smile. "He was all of those things, yes. I'm certain he never met anyone who wasn't a little afraid of him."

"Then he taught you well. That describes you, too." She noted the rifle in a saddle holster and that his coat bulged like he might have a gun holstered there. Between all the men being gone from the stables, Castillo's tense demeanor and his weapons, she was beginning to wonder if something might be wrong. If he'd had word that Derringer was, indeed, targeting the ranch.

He followed her gaze to the rifle before looking back at her. "You're not afraid of me." The sunlight caught the gold in his green eyes and made it shine.

She was afraid of him, but not for the reason he might think. She'd experienced his gentleness with her on the train, and even in her room last night when he could've been harsher than he had been. She was afraid because she felt so many things that she couldn't even name with him. She should call off this ruse and be done with him, but she couldn't. Not yet. Swallowing to moisten her suddenly dry mouth and throat, she said, "I am."

He shook his head, one side of his mouth tilting up in a smile that was everything sensual. "No, you're not." Then his gaze dropped to her mouth. She could feel it tracing the contours of her lips.

"I am," she repeated, licking her lips, unable to stay still under his scrutiny. "But I can't seem to stay away from you." That last came out on a breath.

He dragged his gaze back to hers and something nearly tangible leaped between them. It was so potent that she had to look away before she said something else that she probably shouldn't. Something like how much she wanted to kiss him.

"Would you mind sharing what happened to your grandfather?"

He shifted, looking off toward the mountains, and it was a few minutes before he spoke, keeping his gaze on the horizon.

"Derringer was an investor. He claimed to be from California, but I doubt he'd ever set foot there. He came recommended by someone my grandfather respected, a neighboring rancher who'd done business with the man. He visited us for a couple of weeks. Was knowledgeable about cattle. Ours weren't hardy and had been dying from disease. The cows had stopped having calves. Even the first-year heifers weren't producing the next year."

He ran the back of a gloved hand over his forehead. She wondered if he was remembering the despair and frustration that situation must have caused him and his family. "Derringer talked of a new breed of cattle from California. This new breed was resistant to all disease. I didn't know it at the time, but my grandfather gave him money to buy a new herd."

Caroline didn't know anything about cattle, but she knew a little about disease. It was unlikely an animal would be born impervious to disease. There was inoculation, but that wasn't the same thing as what he was describing, and she didn't even know if such a thing was being done to cattle. Her stomach churned with the fear that they'd been betrayed. "The herd never came?"

"He took the money. My grandfather went to the authorities and about a week later I woke up one night to our house on fire." He took a deep breath. She could hear it over the plodding of the horses' hooves, and closed her eyes because she didn't want to know what she knew he would say next. "He died in the fire.

At times I still smell the smoke."

"Oh, dear God, Castillo, I'm sorry." She raised her hand to her mouth, while in her mind's eye she imagined that horrible night.

He nodded to acknowledge her words, but he kept his gaze on some point in the distance. "Derringer was there that night. He was angry that we'd gone to the authorities. He'd figured no one would pay attention to an immigrant, but my grandfather was respected in the area. Derringer wanted to silence him." Castillo sighed. "We nearly caught Derringer that night, but in the madness he got away while my home burned to the ground."

She didn't know what to say to that. Her life in Boston seemed so...so protected and privileged after hearing his story. "I'm sorry," she whispered. "I can't imagine what it'd be like to lose someone close to you and your home in the same night."

He looked toward the hills on his left, away from her. The river was coming into view, a silver ribbon reflecting the sun as it wove out through the green field before disappearing into the mountains again.

"Of course you can't. No one should have to imagine that," he said after a moment. His gaze turned to the river.

"I hope you find Derringer." And she meant it. She hoped with all her heart that he'd find the justice he sought.

Castillo gave her a long look, filled with intensity but completely unreadable. She opened her mouth to tell him that she understood. That she wanted to help him, but was interrupted by one of Emmy's sisters running toward them.

"Cas! There's a snake. Come look!" The girl looked entirely too pleased with herself for someone who'd just seen a snake before she ran back toward the river.

Castillo smiled and dug his heels in to make the horse go faster, following the happy girl.

Caroline continued at her sedate pace, stunned in the knowledge that she'd been just moments away from releasing him from their deal. If he didn't have to spend so much time pretending to court her, he'd have more time to look for Derringer. Right?

But then where would she be when she returned home to Boston? She'd be facing a future where she was at the mercy of a husband who almost certainly wouldn't allow her to pursue her profession. She'd already met the entire crop of suitors her mother had in store for her, and not one of them had interested her. They'd all seemed very foppish and vain.

If she married one of them, it could be disastrous. Aunt Prudie had warned her many times about the importance of marrying the right man. Caroline didn't know very much about Aunt Prudie's marriage, but it had never seemed to be a particularly happy one. She and her husband appeared to be little more than distant strangers who occasionally shared the same social engagements, which was the primary reason Caroline didn't want to marry a stranger herself.

Aunt Prudie had once said that she should make sure to find

an honorable man with a gentle temperament. It was a funny twist of fate that she had found that man, and he seemed to be the one most ill-suited for her.

Chapter Eight

Caroline Hartford had enchanted him. There was no denying it anymore.

After dinner that night everyone retired to the gold salon where the tall French doors had been opened to allow in the cool breeze blowing over the mountains. The sun had just set, leaving the horizon with a burnished glow directly at odds with the bright stars struggling to shine in the velvet eastern sky. As beautiful as that sunset was, Castillo was having trouble pulling his gaze away from Caroline to properly enjoy it.

He'd been captivated by her on the train. And then annoyed with her when he found her here and she'd offered that proposal. But then—though he couldn't say when it had happened—he'd started to become captivated by her again. She sat across the room on the settee next to Tanner, discussing her plans for the future. He'd tried not to listen, but her voice kept drawing him in. It wasn't the sound of her voice, though that was pleasant...soft, with enough of a husky timbre that it spoke directly to his baser instincts. It was her words and the conviction with which she said them.

She knew what she wanted to do with her life, and it wasn't at all what anyone else in her position would want. She didn't value marriage, not the way his mother had. His mother had been crushed when she'd been abandoned by Tanner. Some of that had been heartbreak, but Castillo had come to realize that much of it was because the life she'd imagined for herself had been taken away.

Marisol Reyes had been raised by very conservative parents, and that meant her only calling in life was to be a wife and mother, to be obedient to the needs of her family. A caretaker of her family who ran an efficient household. She'd never had a chance to develop interests beyond anything domestic, and truth be known, as he thought back, Castillo wasn't certain she'd have wanted anything more. She'd been the perfect mother.

Caroline was different. Her family was affluent. She could've been just like all the other women in her life, content to allow her future to be planned for her. Content to follow her given role in society. He'd seen those women in Boston and had met a few during his visits to Helena once he'd been recognized as

Tanner Jameson's son. Not one of them had intrigued him like Caroline did. She wanted more. She wanted control of her destiny. There was something about that independence he found appealing.

No one understood it better than Castillo. His destiny had been planned out for him from the start and he'd been trying to take back control ever since. The Reyes hacienda was his destiny. But with his grandfather gone, he was struggling to make it his.

"Yes, I've been influenced greatly by Dr. Mary McLean. I was fortunate to attend a lecture she gave last year. She's a fascinating person," Caroline was saying, raising her glass of champagne.

Amelia, the eldest Bonham girl, played a soft tune on the piano in the corner, offering a pleasant, melodious backdrop for the evening. Castillo looked outside and caught a flicker of light in the distant hills. It disappeared too quickly to be a fire. Was it a flicker of the dying sunset against a piece of metal—or a signal?

"You certainly sound as if you're set on this plan," Tanner remarked.

"Oh, I'm quite set on this. I hope to run my own practice someday. I think there are strides to be made yet in the area of women's health."

"As long as you stick to females and young children, and avoid taking on male patients, you'll do fine. I'm certain of it." This was said by Mr. Bonham, who'd just walked back into the room after smoking his after-dinner cigar on the veranda.

Castillo whipped around to gauge Caroline's reaction. She

was as elegant as usual, her spine straight, shoulders back. She'd changed from the dress she'd worn on the picnic into a pale-green evening gown. The hair piled on top of her head shimmered like liquid gold in the candlelight. She made her expression deliberately bland, but something burned in her eyes.

"Why do you say that, Mr. Bonham?"

"Because it's less challenging. Caring for women and children is a fair extension of the woman's role at home with her domestic duties. Continuing that role outside of the home will be challenging enough to keep you occupied without overly taxing the intellect." The bastard actually grinned as if he was explaining a well-known fact to a child or someone of lesser intelligence.

"Now, Bonham," Tanner said before she could answer. "While there are a few notable differences between the genders, human anatomy is much the same between them. Disease doesn't discriminate."

Bonham shook his head and sank down into the chair next to the settee facing the piano. "But it does. The same disease works much differently in the male anatomy. We've a much stronger constitution." Looking back at Caroline with that indifferent smile, he continued, "You'll learn all about that in your studies."

Castillo couldn't hold silent any longer. He'd never read a book about human anatomy or disease, but even he knew Bonham was talking nonsense. He itched to put his fist through the man's smile, but thought Tanner might not appreciate the violence. "Miss Hartford has spent her entire life studying under her father. You're a banker. She knows far more about the subject than you ever will." Castillo turned his attention to Caroline. She had a little smile on her face and the anger had left her eyes. "Come walk with me, mi corazón?"

Her mouth dropped open, much like Bonham's, except hers changed into a smile while Bonham kept opening and closing his mouth as if he couldn't quite figure out what to say. Caroline quickly regathered her wits and rose to her feet, setting her champagne down on the spindly side table. Castillo deliberately ignored the smile on Tanner's face as he held out his arm to her. She slipped her small hand through it and he led her out to the porch.

"What an ass," he muttered, keeping his gait calm and steady as he led her on a walk around the veranda.

"It's fine." There was a smile in her voice.

"No, it's not fine. To imply that you—"

"Castillo." She placed her hand on his forearm, drawing his attention. "It really is fine. I've been dealing with that sort of ignorance for my whole life. It doesn't bother me anymore."

They'd come to a stop around the corner of the house. The soft music from the piano still reached them here and a lantern hung from the rafters, flickering softly. The cadence of Tanner's voice along with the occasional word could be heard coming from inside, but they were nearly alone. She was beautiful, smiling up at him, and she was all that he could see.

His gaze dropped to her mouth and the small white teeth pressed gently against her lush bottom lip. The blush over the soft curve of her cheekbone. The small nose with the delicate, gold-rimmed spectacles perched on the bridge. Everything about her was delicate. Everything except her height. The top of her head caught him at his chin, when he was accustomed to most women being far shorter.

He liked it, though he had no reason to pay attention to anything about her enough to like it. This courtship was a farce. "Anymore? It doesn't bother you anymore?" he asked, because he'd been staring at her for way too long.

"There was a time it bothered me." She nodded. "I've heard it all, from how it's not fair to the patients because I'll almost certainly faint at the first unsightly lesion I see, to how my female brain is too small to comprehend everything I'll need to learn. I couldn't understand why anyone would think that way. I've spent so many hours learning under my father that I know as much as he does in some areas. I know more than the people saying those thoughtless things. Eventually, I realized that it doesn't matter what they think. They hold onto their prejudices because it comforts them in some way. I don't claim to understand it, but I know that I can't dissuade them with words. Only my actions can prove them wrong."

"But, Carolina, he just said your intelligence was inferior."

She shrugged. "I know, and I also know he's wrong. I can't go battling every ignorant comment. Believe me, I've tried and it's exhausting. I do feel sympathy for his daughters, though."

His gaze had settled on her clear blue eyes. They shone with intelligence and warmth. He couldn't believe that she could be so calm when anger still swelled within his chest trying to force its way out. The only way to assuage it would be to go back in that room and confront Bonham, but Castillo wouldn't ruin the rest of the week. There were still days until the wedding.

But then she tightened her grip on his forearm, her fingertips pressing gently into his flesh. Her touch was warm and reassuring through the fabric of his coat and shirt. Immediately, all the blood in his body took a drastic turn south.

"Thank you for standing up for me. You didn't have to, but I appreciate it."

He sucked in a breath to cool the heated blood in his veins. It didn't help. He merely pulled in her lavender scent, which was mixed with something that he couldn't identify. Something feminine and sweet. A scent that was hers alone.

An image of her pale skin glowing in the darkness of his room flashed through his mind. He was licking that scent from her skin, tasting her, shattering her composure. He moved his hand to the railing, dislodging her touch as he stared out across the field and tried to scrub the image from his mind. He replaced it with memories of that time he and Hunter had been holed up in a muddy canyon for two days with no food, in the cold rain, while being shot at relentlessly. It helped, but only a little.

"It's ignorance—like you said. I'm sorry you have to deal with that." And this is why she was so worried about marriage standing in her way. If she married someone with Bonham's attitudes there wasn't any way she would be attending school. Of course, he knew many people felt the same. Except that he'd been too much in his own world the past few years, obsessed with finding Derringer and earning money to resurrect the hacienda, and he'd stopped interacting with society. He tightened his hand on the railing. Perhaps she wasn't that much different from him. She was fighting for something she wanted against a world that seemed intent on making it tougher for her.

He blew out a breath, the dark, looming shadows of the hills in the distance drawing his attention. There was that flicker of light again. Definitely a signal. They'd had men take watch over the east field and west field. Was it one of them? He'd need to check it out before heading upstairs to bed. He was tired and was scheduled to take over the watch well before sunrise. Playing suitor and tracking Derringer was proving to be exhausting work.

"Does that light mean something?"

He whipped his head around. She was looking out toward the same light he'd seen, her brows knitted together.

"No." It was an automatic response. He could simply tell her that it was likely a signal that one of the men on watch had found something. But he still couldn't trust her completely. He'd been keeping things quiet for so long in his quest to find Derringer, he wasn't certain he'd ever be able to trust anyone outside of his small circle of brothers ever again. "Why would it mean something?"

She shrugged. "You tensed when you saw it."

Mierda, she was observant. She hadn't mentioned it, but she'd noted the weapons on their ride today. Her brows had knitted together like now, like she was trying to figure him out. He'd have to be more careful. There was no sense in creating panic when he didn't even know if Derringer had his sights set on the Jameson Ranch. The ass would be stupid to target it. It was common knowledge that it was well protected. "I'm always tense." He tried to smile but failed miserably.

"Maybe, but that's not it. You were tense on the picnic today, too. And while it's true this is my first visit here, I don't think it's normal to travel to a picnic at the river armed with a rifle and at least one revolver, not to mention the guns Hunter carried."

"Never hurts to be cautious." Even he could admit that was a weak argument.

"Cautious?" She turned to face him, leaning her hips back against the railing. It seemed so natural to put his hands on either side of her, to lean in, that he almost did that, catching himself just in time. "Do you think we're in danger?"

He took in a deep breath. He was in danger right now. His gaze darted down to her mouth and she licked her lips, as if getting them moist for him. His brain stuttered over some way to allay her fears without raising her suspicions even further, but her next words ground his thoughts to a complete halt.

"Will you kiss me, Castillo?" she whispered.

His breath stopped in his throat and he stared into eyes that widened as if she'd only just realized she'd voiced the request. His heart punched against his chest, trying to make him move toward her, and before he realized it, he was mere inches from her mouth.

"I can't do that."

"Why?" she whispered.

Why couldn't he do it? She was right here in front of him. Her plump bottom lip shimmered in the light of the oil lantern. Her tongue darted out again nervously and he wanted to chase it, to suck it into his mouth and learn her taste. His hand stroked the silky skin of her bare arm as his palm moved up to rest on her shoulder. He could feel her delicate bones beneath her flesh, smell her lavender scent, feel the heat from her body as he angled himself closer.

"One kiss wouldn't be enough," he said. It wouldn't be. He hadn't really touched her yet, but this longing she created within him wasn't asking for something so casual as a kiss. It wanted more. All of her. Yet even as he warned her off, he tilted his head, already anticipating the touch of her mouth. Her breath brushed across his chin. "Carolina," he whispered.

"Is wanting more so bad?" she whispered back.

Yes. Very bad. His mind yelled the words, but couldn't make his body listen to them. He just kept moving toward her, crowding her back against the porch railing. She reached up and grabbed his biceps, her fingers squeezing into him gently.

His lips touched hers, a soft caress that was more teasing than kiss. It wasn't nearly enough, but he drew back before he gave into the temptation to dip his tongue inside her. His breath came as fast as it did after a fight.

"This is only an agreement." He said it as much to remind himself as to remind her. If it were only an agreement, then why did it feel like more? "We have no future together. You know that." Even as he spoke, he couldn't draw his gaze from her mouth. Her lips were pink and perfect. He knew the bottom one would be lush and soft between his teeth.

"I know, but I don't think a future is required for kissing." The words, or perhaps it was the way he was looking at her, made her blush. It rose from her breasts all the way up her neck to her cheeks.

His whole body tightened. His mind had gone far past kissing—at least, in the way she meant it. He wanted to kiss her mouth, but he also wanted to dip his tongue into that indentation where her neck met her shoulder, to savor the pink of her nipples, to taste the nectar between her thighs. Somehow, his body had gone far past mild flirtation faster than it ever had before.

He shifted his hands to the railing at her back and leaned down, afraid that if he held on to her he'd crush her against him and she'd feel how hard he was. "You're right." He covered her mouth with his and she sighed against his lips as she opened for him. He traced the wet rim of her lips with his tongue and found her hot and so damn sweet he couldn't resist pushing further. His tongue delved deeper, brushing hers and sending fingers of pleasure dragging down his spine.

Shrill laughter rent the night air, dispersing the haze of arousal that held them locked together. Prudence, along with Caroline's father, approached around the corner, their heels echoing on the wood floor of the veranda. He drew back, gasping for air. Despite his vow not to compromise her, he'd been very close to doing just that. Tanner and Bonham's voices could still be heard coming from inside.

He hadn't even waited for privacy to touch her. Pushing off the railing, he walked in the opposite direction of her aunt and father, and jumped down to the ground, heading off into the darkness to get himself under control.

***

Castillo disappeared into the inky darkness of the night as soon as he stepped from the ring of light cast by the lantern. The moon was covered by clouds. Caroline's only clue to his whereabouts was that she could still hear his boots on the packed dirt as he hurried away. Each step matched the nearly frantic beat of her heart. Her lips were warm from his and she still tasted the heady mixture of whiskey and peppermint from his tongue.

"Caroline?" Aunt Prudie's concerned voice came from far too close behind her.

She turned to find her aunt standing just feet away, a puzzled look on her face that told Caroline she'd almost certainly missed something the woman had said. Caroline's father was coming up behind Aunt Prudie, his gaze narrowed in the direction in which Castillo had disappeared. Their presence explained why he'd left so abruptly. Caroline had been too absorbed in the kiss to even hear them approach. How much had they seen?

Caroline couldn't resist one last glance over her shoulder, but Castillo was gone. When she looked back, Aunt Prudie's concerned expression had changed to one of amusement. "Enjoying your evening, dear?"

They hadn't seen the kiss. Caroline couldn't allow herself to believe it, but her aunt's gaze had dropped to her lips. The impulse to touch them was too great for Caroline to ignore, so she'd pressed her fingertips against them before she'd thought better of it. They felt a little tender. Caroline dropped her hand, curling it into a fist at her side. "It's a lovely evening. How about you?"

"Lovely indeed. Samuel and I have been having a pleasant walk. Perhaps you'd like to take a stroll with Mr. Jameson?" Aunt Prudie raised a brow and tilted her head toward the path Castillo had taken.

"I don't...um...I think he had to go talk to someone." Caroline glanced back at her father. He didn't seem angry, but his brow was furrowed in concern as he stared out at the night sky. Perhaps he hadn't seen the kiss and only knew they'd been talking.

Guilt tightened her chest. She didn't like lying to these people she loved more than any others in the entire world. It suddenly felt wrong to give Aunt Prudie hope when Caroline knew that nothing would ever come of her relationship with Castillo. It seemed wrong to continue allowing her father to worry, as he so obviously was worrying right now.

But most of all, it seemed wrong to keep Castillo from the mission that called to him. He could have been out all evening searching for the man responsible for his grandfather's death, but instead he'd been here with her.

"I'm going to go to bed. I haven't been sleeping well." She needed to get away and think about what to do.

"Is everything all right?" her father asked.

"I'm tired." Caroline smiled and kissed his cheek goodnight. After some murmured words of concern from Aunt Prudie, Caroline made her way to her room to think.

Chapter Nine

A saloon on the wrong of side of Helena wasn't how Castillo had wanted to spend this night. He'd spent two days chasing Bennett Derringer only to have to deal with the unexpected presence of Caroline Hartford at the ranch the night before, coupled with the unpleasant conversation with Tanner. A day of playing attentive suitor to Caroline and that damn kiss just a few hours ago had nearly made him forget all the reasons he couldn't have her.

Castillo was in no mood for saloons. He wanted to sleep in his comfortable bed back at the Jameson Ranch for one whole night and forget the mess his life was in right now. But that fire had been a signal. He'd gone out to meet one of the hands who'd told him Zane wanted to meet him in town.

It was early in the week, but the place was busy. A sign written in chalk out front had advertised a faro tournament, so most of the tables were filled with men competing. A woman in a low-cut gown and an abundance of cosmetics played what might have been a pleasant tune on a piano in the center of the room, but Castillo's head pounded with every chord.

A few men at the tables took in his presence inside the door, but most were too busy concentrating on the cards before them. It was just as well. Castillo was in no mood to be friendly. In fact, he might appreciate a fight tonight to ease some of the frustration threatening to boil over inside him. It was a stupid disposition to bring to a saloon, evidence that he shouldn't be here. He wouldn't be here if Zane hadn't sent him a message to meet.

Castillo kept his hat on as he stepped into the room on his way to the bar in the back. He wasn't Castillo Jameson tonight. He wasn't even Castillo Reyes tonight. He hoped that, with his hat pulled down low, he looked just like any other straggler passing through town. Someone these men would notice just enough to avoid.

He caught sight of Zane sitting at a table in the corner and changed course. "Do you have anything?" he asked as he pulled out the chair beside his friend and sat down facing the door.

"Good evening to you, too, brother." Zane flashed a smile that did nothing to make him look friendly and upended a shot glass, filling it with whiskey from the bottle on the table.

Castillo grunted and looked over the men around them. He didn't expect Bennett to be there playing faro, but Castillo had made many enemies over the last few years, so he was always looking for them in places like this. "Have you found out anything?" he asked again.

Zane threw back the whiskey and the smile dropped from his face. "I think there's a spy at Victoria House. Someone went through my room. They didn't take anything, so I can only assume they were looking for information."

"Money?" Castillo asked.

"I keep a hundred or so in the armoire. It was still there."

Castillo let out a breath. "A hundred is a lot, especially for someone working at the brothel."

"It wasn't touched."

Castillo grimaced at the implication. Victoria House was the most exclusive brothel in Helena. Glory Winters, the brothel's madam, had approached Hunter for help a couple of years ago when a group of men had decided that they'd be better at running such a lucrative establishment than she would. Castillo and the gang had provided the necessary muscle to make the men realize they'd have more success in another town. Since then, Castillo and Glory had become associates of sorts, coming to each other with bits of information the other might need. He didn't want to think of her as a traitor, but he couldn't rule out the possibility.

"The spy either didn't need the money or is being paid more

than that." Glory was richer than sin and, as far as he knew, was the only one in that brothel who wouldn't be tempted by that amount of money. She was also the only one who knew about their outlaw activities. It didn't make sense that she'd have anything to do with Derringer, but Castillo had to consider it. "Have you mentioned this to Glory?"

Zane shook his head and his jaw clenched as his gaze passed over the room. Clearly, the possibility that she was somehow in cahoots with Derringer, or whoever had ordered Zane's room searched, had occurred to him. Zane, who knew firsthand the risks involved with loving the wrong woman, harbored a soft spot for the madam. For his sake, Castillo hoped she wasn't a spy.

Castillo tossed back the drink and rose to his feet. "Let's go talk to her."

Zane nodded and followed him out. A light drizzle had begun to fall while they were inside, but Castillo didn't hurry his steps. It was a short walk to Victoria House, and they'd need to keep their eyes open for anyone who could be following them. Castillo had given it a lot of thought and he didn't think Bennett's presence in the area was a coincidence. Derringer had likely figured out who he was and was hoping to take him out before Castillo found him. That was the most logical explanation.

Castillo had stabled his horse across town and left one of the men behind to keep watch. But the streets were dark in this part of town, and now that they were deserted because of the rain, he wondered if it wouldn't be better to have another man with them. The air was thick with the smells of mud and horses. The sounds of music and revelry were partially muted behind closed doors and windows. If there was ever a time to corner them alone...this was it. Zane's hand went to the gun hidden in the holster beneath his coat, and Castillo knew he was worried, too.

Victoria House was a three-story brick building that towered over all the other squat structures in the district, and it would've been at home on the reputable side of town had it not been a brothel. Castillo exchanged a look with Zane and they navigated the two blocks to reach it. Despite the mud, they kept to the street and avoided getting too close to any darkened storefronts. Part of him wanted Derringer to confront them now, just to get it over with. But a confrontation in the dark on Derringer's terms wouldn't be wise.

"Let's go in the back," Zane said and took the turn into the alley. "There's a dinner tonight and likely to be too many people in the foyer."

Castillo agreed and followed Zane, but they both stopped when a shadow separated itself from the dark exterior wall of the general store. As they watched, it darted across the alley to disappear around the corner of the building and down a small alley barely wide enough to walk through without turning sideways. Castillo caught Zane's eye, who nodded and went back the way they'd come to make his way around the building and intercept the shadow at the other end. Drawing his gun, Castillo quietly headed to the corner and drew back the hammer as slowly as he could so it wouldn't make more than a soft, metallic click. He paused when he reached the corner, his back against the brick wall and his pulse pounding in his ears.

The shadow wouldn't be Derringer. If the man was connected to him, he'd be a lackey, but at least Castillo would be one step closer to the man. He strained to listen, but couldn't hear anything except the steady patter of rain on cobblestones. Out of habit, he pressed his palm to the golden cross that hung on a chain around his neck, tucked inside his shirt. His mother had given it to him when he'd been a boy, telling him that it would keep him safe. It had seemed to work so far, though he was certain dodging bullets and chasing outlaws wasn't what she'd had in mind. Nevertheless, he mouthed a prayer, not daring to speak the words aloud. When he'd waited long enough for Zane to make his way around the building to reach the other end of the narrow outlet, he yelled, "We have you trapped. Throw down your gun."

For a full minute there was nothing and then the shadow reappeared, brandishing a scrap piece of wood that had probably been lying in the darkened alcove. Before Castillo could react, the length of wood knocked his gun out of his hand. Castillo dove forward, tackling the shadow to the ground. The man grunted at the impact when he hit the ground with Castillo's weight on top of him, but he wasted no time in striking back, catching Castillo with a fist to his chin that left him reeling. He rolled from the impact but didn't loosen his grip, so his assailant rolled with him.

Castillo recovered before the man could get another punch in and hit him hard with a right hook that knocked him backward. Following him down, Castillo took another hit to his cheekbone before landing enough blows to leave the man on the defensive, his hands raised to cover his face. Footsteps approached from the narrow alley, coming so fast that for a moment Castillo wasn't sure if it was another attacker, but he turned to see Zane running out of the alley.

"There's no one else down there," Zane said.

Castillo turned his attention back to the man on the ground beneath him. "Who the hell are you?"

The man's head lolled. He seemed to be only half conscious.

"Let's get him inside before someone else comes," Zane said. As if to emphasize his point, a wagon drove by on the main road, the driver whistling a tune though rain continued to drizzle.

Castillo nodded. "We'll take him to Glory's." Though the madam wouldn't like it, they needed somewhere to question him. Castillo took the man's gun and rose, and Zane reached down to sling him over his shoulder. Castillo picked up the gun that had been knocked out of his hand, and together they made their way through the dark alley to the gate in the tall, wooden fence that led to the courtyard behind the brothel.

"Good. Still unlocked." Zane kicked it open and led the way inside with his burden over his shoulder. Castillo latched it behind them and rushed up the steps to the back door.

The door led into a servant's hallway. A girl he vaguely recognized screeched when he forced the door open and stumbled inside. She dropped the pile of linens she'd been holding and rushed away from them toward the front of the house, no doubt going to alert her mistress. That meant they'd have only a few precious moments alone with the man before Glory found them.

"This way." Castillo led them to a storeroom off to the left and shut the door behind them. Zane set the man down onto a crate of bottled whiskey. In the light, Castillo could see the man was young, probably around twenty. The flesh around his eye was already beginning to swell, but he was alert as he looked back at them, fear making him tremble.

"Who the hell are you?" Castillo demanded.

"J-Johnson, Rob Johnson." He gave them an insolent glare as he spat a mouthful of blood onto the wooden floor.

Zane shrugged when Castillo looked at him to see if the name meant anything to him. Castillo wasn't able to place it amongst the lowlifes they'd met over the past several years, but then again, it wasn't a very memorable name. "Do you know who I am?" Castillo asked.

"No, didn't ask." Johnson drew forward a little as he gave Castillo a closer look.

"What's that mean?"

When Johnson just glared, Zane reached forward and

grabbed a handful of his shirt, nearly pulling him all the way up to his feet. "Better start explaining yourself real quick, boy."

Johnson's eyes widened as he looked from Zane to Castillo and back again. "I meant that I was told to follow this one." He nodded at Zane, who still held him. "He's been staying at the brothel here, and I was told to watch him and follow him."

"Who told you this?" Zane asked. "Glory?"

The man's eyes widened and he shook his head. "Fella I met over at the Alhambra." The Alhambra was a saloon just a few blocks over, nearer the edge of town. It was said that men went into that hell hole and never reappeared. "Gave me twenty dollars to take the job. Said he'd give me fifty if I could deliver the Spaniard to him." He tilted his chin up toward Castillo. "You're the Spaniard, ain't you? The fella said he wanted you dead or alive, and the big fella here would lead me to you."

"What man?" Castillo asked. There must've been something menacing in his voice, because Johnson began to quake.

Before Johnson could answer, the door swung open and Glory stood framed in the doorway. Her dark-red hair was piled artfully on her head and she was dressed like she'd just stepped from the most elegant salon in Paris in a gown of black silk with an underskirt of pinstripes in gray and white. She looked like an elegant lady, but her eyes were blazing with fury. "What are you doing?" For all its anger, her Southern accent put a cultured slant on her words.

"Do you know who this man is?" Castillo asked.

She narrowed her eyes at Castillo, as if considering if she would deign to answer him, but after a moment looked at the man Zane was still holding. "No. Now get him out of my house. All of you, out."

Zane dropped the man, who landed hard on the wooden crate of whiskey bottles. The bottles wobbled and clinked together inside the crate. "You're saying you didn't hire this man to follow me?" Zane asked.

"What? No, of course not." Glory drew herself up to her full height, which was still short of Zane's chin even though she wore heeled shoes.

"I told you," the man said, drawing everyone's attention back to him. "A man hired me."

"What is going on?" Glory demanded.

"This ass was following us. Trapped him in the alley and he attacked Cas." Zane explained without looking away from the man. "Who hired you?"

The man shrugged. "I didn't catch his name."

"A man hired you to kill me and you didn't ask his name?" Castillo raised his voice.

"Didn't say I didn't ask, just that I didn't know it. He wouldn't tell me. He paid me twenty dollars. Looked like he was good for the rest."

"What did he look like?"

"Dressed like a dandy and had real soft hands. Talked like he was better than me. Figured he was from one of them mining companies. What'd you do to piss him off?" Now that Glory was here and obviously not on their side, Johnson seemed to have rediscovered his courage.

"What color was his hair?" Zane asked.

"Hard to tell. He was wearing a hat, but what I saw was white," Johnson answered.

Derringer. Castillo's blood ran cold at the confirmation. Derringer was probably in his early fifties, but he'd had a headful of the purest white hair that Castillo had ever seen. They'd figured he'd dyed it, since he was trying so hard to hide, but apparently not. It wasn't absolute confirmation, but Castillo knew in his gut the man was Derringer.

"How were you supposed to meet him to collect your money once you had me?" Castillo asked.

"He said to ride south and he'd find me."

Castillo nodded toward the hall and Zane turned. Johnson started to get to his feet, but Zane turned back toward him. "Sit down and stay there. We'll be right outside the door. If you break one bottle, I'll put a bullet through your skull."

Johnson blanched and nodded as he sat back down. Glory backed into the hallway, and Castillo and Zane followed her out, closing the door behind them. "I don't like this brought into my house," Glory said as soon as the door shut. She kept her voice low so it wouldn't travel down the hall or through the walls to the high-society gentlemen eating a late-night dinner in the various dining rooms on the ground level. "I don't allow guns in here or men like that creature." She jabbed a finger at the storeroom.

"Apologies." Castillo inclined his head in mocking deference. "I had nowhere else to take the man who was trying to kill me."

She took in a deep breath, and her voice was calmer when she spoke again. "Who is after you this time?"

Castillo debated how much to tell her. He didn't completely trust her, but he did need her as an ally in this. "His name is Derringer. He's the man who killed my grandfather."

She nodded. "I haven't heard that name before. Now I understand why Mr. Pierce has been my guest the past couple of days."

Zane flashed her a grin. "Your charming company is always reason enough to stay."

She rolled her eyes and pointed toward the storeroom. "You all have to go. I can't risk the law knowing he's here. And I can't have you here if someone is looking for you. I'm sorry, but I have to protect the women who live here."

"Sorry, pretty lady, we can't leave. He stays until we know what's going on." Zane crossed his arms over his chest.

"You cannot stay." She forced the words out through gritted teeth.

"You have a spy," Castillo said. "If Zane stays he'll help you figure out who it is."

"I don't have a spy," she said.

"You do," Zane said. "Someone went through my room."

She sighed and crossed her arms over her chest, mimicking Zane's stance. "That was me. I was in your room. I knew something was going on and you weren't telling me what it was, so I went through your room to try to figure it out," she admitted. "You should know I didn't find anything except a sketch pad full of drawings many would consider obscene."

Zane didn't say anything to that, but he smiled—a real smile—the skin around his eyes crinkling.

"Let Johnson stay, Glory. Just until after the wedding, then we can move him out to the ranch. We can't keep him there with all the guests arriving. Zane will stay here and keep an eye on him."

"I'd be willing to offer any other..." Zane paused and allowed his gaze to travel down her body "...services you might need."

"Keep your breeches on, cowboy." Then she looked at Castillo. "Fine, he can stay until the wedding, but Zane watches him and is responsible for him. You pay for any damage he causes, and you owe me big after this—all of you, and that includes Hunter." She moved her finger between them both. "Take him down to the cellar. I have to get back to my guests."

She turned to go but stopped and turned back. "And I won't have anyone killed here in cold blood. If he's hurt or conveniently disappears, I will contact the sheriff." With that, she swept down the hallway and disappeared through the door that led to the main part of the house.

"It has to be Derringer."

"Bennett was no coincidence," Zane agreed. "Don't worry. I'll keep asking around and see if I can get anything out of Johnson in there."

Castillo nodded. "I can't stay. Remember the girl from the train? She's a Hartford. She was at the ranch when I got there."

Zane cursed under his breath. "She recognized you, I assume?"

"Yes. It's a long story, but now I have to pretend to be a suitor so she won't tell anyone."

At this confession, Zane threw his head back and laughed. Castillo didn't find it particularly funny, but something about the laughter was contagious and he chuckled.

"That's rich, brother." When he finally stopped laughing, Zane said, "Can't wait for the whole story. I hope you know what you're doing."

Castillo wanted to say that he did, but he couldn't. The truth was that Carolina had barely left his thoughts the entire ride into town, and—if he was honest—he was looking forward to seeing her tomorrow. Instead of commenting on that, he said, "I need to get back to the ranch and let the boys know what's happening."

Zane nodded. "Let me know if you need my help."

"Many thanks, as always, brother." Castillo clasped his arm and then made his way through the large house. Since he didn't have a captive with him, he took the hallway to the front door. He'd rather walk the main road and avoid dark alleyways for the rest of the night.

Unfortunately, there was a group of men in the foyer, looking as if they'd just arrived for a bit of late-night entertainment. They were taking off their coats and handing hats dripping rain to a couple of maids. Castillo barely spared them a glance, as he had no time for conversation tonight and he'd not spent enough time in Helena to make social acquaintances.

The butler murmured "Goodnight, Mr. Jameson," as he opened the door for him. At the words, one of the new arrivals swung his head around as if recognizing the name. Castillo caught a glimpse of light brown hair and a thin, pale face. He didn't recognize the man, so he kept walking. He needed to ride home tonight and meet with the men about increasing the numbers on watch.

Chapter Ten

Castillo was a little late for breakfast the next morning. When he walked into the dining room, he noted that Carolina sat with the Bonham girls and Emmy's younger sisters, but their conversation stopped as soon as he walked in. The oldest one, Amelia, gave him a timid smile and leaned over to whisper to Carolina, who blushed and glanced back at him. She wore her hair in a simple braid this morning, which made her seem young and carefree, a juxtaposition with the fiercely intelligent woman he was coming to know. Did she know how beautiful she was? How young and innocent she looked sitting there with those girls? She was all of those things in one.

He smiled at her, but it was just another reminder of why he needed to leave her alone. All night he'd relived that kiss they'd shared, but there couldn't be another one. And he needed to remember to call her Caroline; to call her anything else was too personal...too intimate.

Breakfast was a buffet like the day before. He walked over and grabbed a plate, aware of the eyes on him as he made his choices.

"You fancy him, don't you?" Amelia mock whispered.

Castillo only barely restrained himself from turning around to see Carolina respond. Of course she'd say yes.

"Yes, I fancy him very much," Carolina answered. It was part of the game, but he couldn't stop himself from glancing over, and her expression didn't look like part of their arrangement. She genuinely looked pleased to see him. Her eyes were deep pools of blue, saying far more than her words.

Continuing to uphold his role as suitor, he walked over to her when he'd finished piling his plate with food. "Would you do me the honor of joining me, Miss Hartford?"

"Of course, Mr. Jameson." As she rose, the girls erupted in a chorus of giggles. Carolina rose with her bowl of berries and led the way to the two places at the end of the table recently vacated by Emmy and Hunter, near Tanner, her father and aunt, who smiled at them with interest.

Castillo set his plate down and pulled out her chair for her. After she'd settled herself, Castillo took his own seat and greeted Tanner. Tanner looked back and forth as if just noticing there could be something between Castillo and Carolina. "You seem taken with our fair Caroline."

"I am." As he said it, Castillo realized it was true. He didn't know her. Not really. He knew he liked the way she looked and he liked the way she'd handled herself, both on the train and then again the night when he'd tried to threaten her. She'd held herself together and faced both situations with calm assertiveness. He respected that.

But he didn't know her. He didn't know what she wished for beyond becoming a physician. He didn't know why that goal was so important to her. What had pushed her to break the mold she'd been given and become something else? He didn't even know basic things like what she liked to eat or how she'd spend rainy days back in Boston, so he couldn't quite understand why he kept thinking about her. He only knew that he wanted to know the answers to all of those questions. So, yes, he was taken with her.

Her father gave him a quizzical look. Castillo shifted as he forked a bit of ham into his mouth. He wasn't certain what that look meant. It wasn't quite disapproval—he was familiar with that look and the subtle disgust that accompanied it. This look was confusion. It didn't matter to Castillo if her father liked him—his end of the bargain was upheld either way—but he found himself wanting to make a good impression on the man.

This was madness. The perfect nonsense of the moment struck him. This courtship was fake, but he actually quite liked sitting here with her by his side. Would it be so far-fetched if he actually did court her? Of course it would be. She'd return to Boston and her plans to further her education, and once Derringer was taken care of he'd go back to Texas and what was left of the ranch. He'd need to rebuild his grandfather's dream.

How in hell was he supposed to court her and stay away from her at the same time?

The girls finished their meal and shuffled out of the room, leaving the five adults in solitude. Tanner waited for them to go before saying, "It's a pity Caroline will be going back to Boston for the autumn classes, so she can't stay longer." He smiled, giving Carolina a wink.

"It's not a pity. She'll make a good physician," Castillo said. He couldn't resist a quick glance at her father and Prudence to gauge their thoughts.

Her father nodded his agreement. "That she will. An excellent physician."

Prudence gave Carolina a barely perceptible nod in Castillo's direction, as if she were giving her approval of him. It made him almost feel guilty that this was a ploy.

"Well, now, that all depends." Prudence's words were so unexpected that they all paused and took note of her. She waited until she had everyone's attention before continuing. "No one doubts for a minute that our sweet Caro will be a capable and talented physician, but there is a question about her actually getting the chance to prove herself."

Samuel huffed out a breath and focused his attention on folding and refolding the napkin in his lap. Carolina went still next to Castillo. Prudence just smiled, bringing her cup of tea to her lips, waiting for someone to take the bait.

Tanner had been looking from one person to another as if trying to figure out the missing piece to the puzzle and finally asked, "What do you mean? I thought she was starting her medical training in September?"

Castillo almost smiled in admiration at how the woman had brought the subject to a head. Instead, he took a bite of ham to hold it in.

"That is the plan, yes, but her parents have decided that it's best if she marries before school. She'll attend pending the state of her nuptials." Prudence explained.

Tanner looked from Prudence to Carolina—who hadn't moved a muscle since her aunt had begun talking—to Samuel. "Is this true, Samuel? Will she not be attending if she's not married?"

To his credit, Samuel looked suitably conflicted about the whole thing. "Her mother and I have spoken at length about this issue. We feel that it's best for her to marry sooner rather than later."

Carolina shifted then, a small movement Castillo probably wouldn't have noticed had he not been so attuned to her. She was uncomfortable. Without thinking, he reached over and clasped the hand in her lap with his own. She stiffened in surprise, but after a moment, she squeezed his fingers.

"Can she not attend and look for a husband at the same time?

Or do you have someone in mind already?" Tanner asked.

"We have a couple of options." Samuel shrugged. "You don't understand, Tanner. You have sons, not daughters. We have to make sure she's taken care of. Her mother and I are getting older. What if we have difficulty finding a husband for her after she graduates?"

"Oh, Father." Carolina stood, flinging her napkin down on the table. "You really don't think I can take care of myself, do you?" Before her father could answer, she hurried from the room.

"Samuel, this is hardly appropriate conversation for the dining table," Prudence admonished, rushing after her niece and leaving the men to an awkward silence.

Finally, Tanner broke the quiet. "My apologies if I overstepped, Samuel. After my conversation with her last night, I was...well, I was surprised."

Samuel waved him off, leaning back in his chair with a heavy sigh. "I understand. I feel the same way. Of course I want her to become a physician. Other girls wanted gowns and parties and holidays, but she only ever wanted to work with me. Her mother is convinced that we have to see her settled first, and I can't disagree with that. It makes sense. She'd be married and her future secure. She'd be free to do what she wants."

Castillo had kept quiet all this time because it was none of his business. He didn't want to be involved. It irritated him that her father, the one person who had supported her in her apprenticeship, would allow her future to be decided so impulsively. He found himself questioning him. "Would she be free? What if her husband doesn't approve?"

Tanner shot him a critical glance, but Samuel nodded. "It is my belief that we can find someone who would approve and support her."

Castillo doubted that. Mr. Bonham's commentary last night had been a look into the attitudes of the men of Carolina's social circle. He didn't say anything further. This wasn't something he could involve himself with, no matter how much he'd enjoyed kissing her. He had to find Derringer and end this quest for vengeance, once and for all. She'd only be a distraction. Maybe the more he kept telling himself that, the more he'd believe it.

***

After Caroline had left breakfast, Aunt Prudie had talked to her and calmed her down, reaffirming her belief that they'd figure out a solution to the marriage problem. Caroline believed they'd try, but there was no guarantee her mother wasn't set on whichever suitor she'd alluded to in her letter.

What made it worse was the guilt Caroline felt the entire time they'd talked. She'd been so tempted to share her secret with her aunt, but she'd held back, mainly because she wasn't even certain she could go through with it. She didn't want marriage forced on her, but she couldn't in good conscience hold Castillo to their deal. After their talk yesterday, she now fully understood what was at stake for him. She'd feel horrible if her predicament was the only thing standing in the way of his justice.

Last night she'd stayed up late, conflicted about their plan. She'd been on the balcony outside her room when she'd seen him ride out. She might've even questioned that it was him, except she'd acquainted herself with the sight of his broad shoulders. He'd gone out to search of Derringer. She was certain of it. And this morning he'd come into the dining room with an abrasion on his cheekbone, just below his eye. No one had mentioned it, but Caroline was almost certain he'd obtained it last night doing whatever it was he'd been doing. It only made her feel guiltier for keeping him from his mission.

She couldn't stop thinking of what awful thing had happened to him last night to put that abrasion there. How much danger had he truly faced? Had he come close to dying? She shouldn't care more than she'd care about anyone else who was in danger. But this was Castillo, and instead of simple, understandable concern, she felt a deep and lingering fear. It was absurd to feel frightened for him, because she barely knew him. It was absurd to allow this affection for him to become anything more than it already had, but she couldn't seem to stop it.

After her talk with Aunt Prudie, Caroline had tried to rejoin the activities planned for the day, but she'd been too worried to enjoy herself. She needed to talk to Castillo privately and end this ridiculous charade. Then this whole thing would be behind her, and the weight of this awful guilt would leave her. She'd be able to avoid him for the rest of the week and pretend that he didn't make her feel anything. Retiring to bed soon after dinner, she allowed Mary to help her change into her night rail and wrapper. But instead of going to bed she waited for Castillo to go to his room.

After an hour had passed, she walked out to the balcony and thought she saw a light flicker from the room she'd deduced was his. There was no light coming through his window when she got to it, but the door was open to allow in the cool night air. The pale curtains fluttered in the gentle breeze.

For some inexplicable reason, her heart was pounding. Maybe it was from fear of getting caught in his room. The more likely answer was that her body remembered that kiss from last night. He hadn't mentioned it all day and had been a little reserved, which led her to think he regretted it. She didn't plan on mentioning it, but that didn't mean it hadn't replayed itself over and over in her mind while she waited for him.

"Castillo?" She kept her voice low as she pushed the door open a little farther. A thin beam of moonlight spilled across his empty bed. The sheets were rumpled, and the blanket was folded back to the foot of the bed, as if someone had just been lying in it.

"Carolina?"

The sound of his voice was so close that she gasped when she turned and saw him standing behind the door. His gun was in one hand and the sheet from his bed was in the other, pressed against his male parts, but that was the only bit of him that was covered. His chest, stomach and most of his legs were nude. "Castillo?" It was the only thing she could think to say as her verbal skills had deserted her.

Neither of them moved.

Stop looking! Stop looking! Stop looking!

Her stubborn gaze refused to obey her brain's command and wouldn't leave the sight of his hand fisting the sheet to shield his nakedness. The part of the sheet that wasn't wadded against his...his manhood, trailed down to fall limply in a puddle between his feet. His muscular thighs were quite naked on either side of it. Her gaze caught the narrow trail of dark hair visible above the sheet and followed it upward over his ridged abdomen to the broad expanse of his lightly furred chest. His entire body was wrapped in lean muscle.

Castillo found the will to move first. Setting his gun on a low table beside a chair, he rushed forward and pushed the balcony door closed behind her. She watched this happening as if she had no ability to move, except to turn and follow him with her gaze, only to get a good look at his naked buttocks. They were pleasantly rounded and the muscles shifted and flexed as he walked. The sight was enough to shock her system back into some semblance of functional, because she turned away from him and pressed her cool fingers to her hot face. "I'm sorry. I didn't think you'd be nude."

There was some shuffling that sounded as though he was

arranging the sheet around him. "What are you doing here?" He kept his voice low, but the way he bit out the words told her he was upset.

She peeked back at him to see that he'd wrapped the sheet around his waist and held it closed at his hip. His strong calves were still visible as were his bare feet. He cleared his throat, regaining her attention, but her gaze lingered on his powerfully built chest. His pectoral muscles were clearly defined even in the dim light, and there were small indentation lines where his deltoids met them.

He was a magnificent specimen of a man. She wanted to believe scientific curiosity was the only reason she stared, but it wasn't. Her breasts became taut and her breaths became shorter, while her lower body tightened in a way that was new to her. But she recognized it as arousal and tried to mentally shake herself out of it.

"I'm sorry," she said again when she met his gaze, because clearly she needed to apologize for herself. She'd invaded his privacy and here she was leering at him like some depraved lecher. After this trip out West, with all of the lying and gawking she'd done, she planned to reevaluate herself.

His gaze narrowed at her words and his jaw clenched, making his eyes go intense and angry. She should've been frightened of that anger, but the fluttering in her belly wasn't fear. Neither was it fear that caused her blood to feel heavy and warm, the same way it did after drinking a glass of wine. Something about his anger excited her almost as much as that kiss had. "Really, very sorry."

"Have you come here to get yourself compromised?"

She was so shocked that she couldn't speak. When he started walking toward her, she moved backward with his every step. "What are you talking about?"

"You're here to break your word and make sure someone finds us," he clarified.

His words flipped some switch inside her that turned her growing excitement into anger. "That's preposterous. Why would I do such a thing?"

"You tell me. Why else would you be in my bedroom in the middle of the night?" His eyes widened as if coming to some realization. "This explains that kiss from last night."

She came up against the wall and realized she'd been retreating like a coward. "Do I have to remind you that you kissed me?"

"You asked me to, and then your father came around the corner. Did you set that up, too?" He moved in closer but didn't touch her. This confrontation was a little more like that first night in her bedroom. She missed the gentle man she'd come to know, but couldn't deny that she was excited by this version of him in a completely different way.

"Of course not, you ass. I just wanted to kiss you, but for the life of me I can't figure out why." She brushed past him on her way to the balcony door, but voices could be heard from outside followed by the sounds of muffled laughter. It sounded like Mrs.

Bonham's laughter.

Castillo's hand covered Caroline's mouth as he grabbed her and pulled her back, retreating further into the bedroom, away from the balcony doors. Instinctively, she struggled to get away and managed to put some distance between them, before he dropped down to the bed, holding her down with his hard body on top of hers. She pushed at his shoulders, but he stretched out over her and somehow wrangled her so that her arms were flattened above her head with his forearm holding them down. His other hand kept covering her mouth though she was doing her best to give him an earful even through the barrier.

"Shh." His breath brushed past her cheek as he lowered his head. "I won't have them find you in here."

She wanted to buck him off and tell him to go to hell, but she thought of the reason she'd originally come to his bedroom. Then she thought of how disappointed Aunt Prudie and her father would be if they did find her here. They'd be heartbroken if she was compromised. It was for them that she kept herself still and quiet, certainly not for the large man on top of her.

Her heart pounded in her ears as the pair came to a stop just outside the door, possibly at the railing to take in the view of the stars. Their voices were so low and muffled it was impossible to hear what they were saying, but Mr. Bonham chuckled, leading her to believe that they were simply out for a late-night stroll.

As the time ticked by, Caroline became acutely aware of the weight on top of her, and not in any way that was unpleasant.

Since she'd stopped struggling, he'd positioned his lower body off to the side so he wasn't too heavy, but his torso pressed against hers from shoulder to hip. His scent settled over her, that subtle blend of citrus and leather mixed with clean male sweat. It wasn't the scent of one of the expensive colognes the men wore in Boston, but it was his own smell and infinitely more appealing because of it.

Slowly and irrevocably her body became aware of his where it touched her. The hard yet satiny feel of his muscled chest above her. The heat from his body as it seeped into her pores. The gentle scratch of his jaw against her temple. She became aware of him as a man. The same man who'd kissed her. The same man who'd treated her so gently back on the train. She turned her head slightly toward him, taking in his shadowed form. Self-preservation demanded that she harden herself against him and forget this dangerous fascination, but she could not make her body or her heart understand.

She knew the exact moment he became aware that something had changed. His body tensed and, though he didn't remove his hand from her mouth, he eased back just enough to look down at her. Only a faint light came in through the pale curtains, but she could see his eyes and they weren't angry anymore, and his breaths came faster than before. The change was so subtle she probably wouldn't have noticed had they not been so close to each other. His chest moved with each breath and it brushed past her temple on the way out. Her blood went heavy in her veins, moving slowly like warm honey to settle deep in her core.

The Bonhams moved on. Their voices receded as they continued their walk around the veranda. Cautiously, he removed his hand from her mouth, but he stayed on top of her.

He took a deep breath, the movement pressing her down into his bed. "Why are you here?" he whispered.

She knew she should shout at him, or at the very least tell him exactly what he could do with his questions, but she tried and failed to conjure her previous anger. "I came to release you from our deal." She kept her voice low, just in case someone happened by in the hallway or balcony.

He didn't move, and she knew she must have shocked him. He really had thought she'd come to get herself compromised. The knowledge hurt because, while she wouldn't have gone so far as to call them friends, she really did think they respected each other. He'd defended her with Mr. Bonham, held her hand when she'd confronted her father, and then there was that kiss.

"Why would you do that?" He still hadn't released her arms, so she gave them a tug. He relented, and she pulled them down, but he didn't move to get off her.

"When I made that deal with you, I didn't realize what was at stake for you. I didn't really understand what had happened with your grandfather and why it was so important for you to find the man responsible for his death. It occurred to me today that instead of being here, pretending to court me, you could've been out there looking for Derringer. I was selfish. I'm sorry."

She took a breath and tried to read his expression. She could see his eyes but not clearly enough in the dim light to know what he was thinking.

It was only when he let out his breath that she realized he'd been holding it. The arm that had been pressing her arms above her head curled down so that the pad of his thumb brushed gently across her forehead. It was such a gentle stroke that she barely felt it, but it sent a shiver through her. "You'll do this for me? You'll keep quiet about what you saw on the train without asking for anything in return?"

She nodded. "I want you to be able to find Derringer. What he did to you isn't right and I know I can't help you, but I want to do what I can to make things easier for you. You deserve to have an end to your pain."

He cursed under his breath—or she thought he cursed but couldn't be certain because he'd said it in Spanish—and hung his head. Before she realized what she meant to do, she took his head between her hands and tilted it back up. His hair was thick and soft against her fingertips, but she tried not to pay attention to how good it felt. "Castillo...."

"I'm sorry, mi corazón. I accused you of a bad thing," he whispered.

Her heart clenched at his obvious regret. "I understand why you would think that. I haven't done much to redeem myself, I'm afraid."

He was shaking his head before she'd even finished. "You

didn't deserve that. I was angry at myself for the way I kissed you."

"Why were you angry about that? I...I thought we both wanted it?"

"That's why I'm angry. I did want it, but I don't have time for that, for you. Even if I did...I'd only end up hurting you." He shifted and moved off her to sit on the bed. He tucked the sheet more firmly around his hips and leaned over toward the bedside table, where he struck a match and lit a candle. The air smelled like sulfur and burning wood.

Caroline was genuinely disappointed that he'd moved away from her, but tried to cover the misplaced emotion by adjusting her night rail and wrapper. The small candle only lit the area where they sat, but it was enough to give color to the gray night. He sat in silence, his fists gripping the edge of the bed as he stared down at the floor.

She couldn't resist taking in the view of his wide chest and shoulders in this new perspective. She wanted to trace his muscles with her hands to learn all of the hollows and planes of his body. A pulse beat between her legs at the thought, so she clenched her thighs together and looked down, silently reminding herself that she should leave him alone. He couldn't be hers. His bare right foot was next to her left one. She'd never seen a bare male foot before, she realized with some surprise. His were wider and longer than hers. His skin was a few shades darker, too.

She didn't know what he meant by the remark that he'd end up hurting her. She sensed it was because of the things she didn't know about him. That sense that he was dangerous. She wanted to ask him, but her self-preservation was hanging by a thread. To know more about him, anything about him, could break it.

"I was wrong. Please accept my apology for my behavior." He was looking at her now, and she nearly caught her breath from the intensity. The look in his eyes was certainly one that shouldn't exist outside a bedroom.

She nodded, but all she could muster was a weak, "Of course."

When he didn't look away, she licked her lips, aware that the strange pulse between her thighs hadn't lessened. She became aware that she was completely naked beneath her nightclothes, and this encounter was inappropriate in every way possible, but she couldn't muster the energy to stop it. She didn't want to stop it.

"What will you do about school?" he asked, his expression earnest.

Caroline licked her lips again. Her mind churned on his question, but she couldn't think right now. What was wrong with her? She was about to jump out of her skin and he sat there, clearly upset, but calm. He was trying to figure out a solution to their problems, while she was ogling him as if she didn't have a brain in her head. Surely he wouldn't be so calm if he was half as affected as she was. She pulled her wrapper tight around her, hoping to hide the way her nipples had tightened. "I'm not sure. I'll have to think of something." To break the tension, she smiled and said, "I'm guessing compromising me is definitely out of the question now?"

He smiled, a beautiful smile that lightened his face and crinkled his eyes, and his shoulders shook in silent laughter. The flickering candlelight caught the gold cross hanging on a chain around his neck. He relaxed his posture and shifted toward her a little, bringing his knee up to rest on the edge of the bed. The movement drew her gaze and she saw the only true evidence that he was as affected as she was. His male part bulged beneath the sheet that was stretched tight across his lap, definitely erect. The knowledge flooded her limbs with a leaden weight and liquid heat pooled between her thighs. She bit her lip and glanced up at him to see if he'd noticed her looking. He had.

His humor had fled, to be replaced by that look of intensity she now recognized as arousal. "Carolina," he whispered, and that name in his passion-roughened voice made her catch her breath.

She wanted to be Carolina. She wanted to be his. Her mind raced in a hundred different directions as he moved in closer. The weight of his gaze touched her mouth, followed by the whisper of his breath just before his mouth claimed hers. One strong hand went to her hip, while the other wrapped itself in her braid and he took control of her.

She opened for him, eager to taste him again. Of their own

accord, her hands found his shoulders and she finally—finally—was able to explore his smooth skin the way she wanted. Her palms roved over his shoulders and down his back, but couldn't decide on a place to settle because he felt so good. His skin was warm and satiny, but the muscles underneath were firm and she wanted to feel them all. Before she realized what was happening, he'd lowered her down on the bed and risen over her, so they were in a similar position as before. Only this time he didn't hesitate to kiss her again. His tongue dipped into her mouth to brush against hers, creating a delicious friction she felt all the way down to her toes and making her moan in the back of her throat.

He echoed that sound with his own deep-throated groan and his lips moved down her neck in a trail of hot, open-mouthed kisses. His hand moved to the tie on her wrapper and tugged it until it fell open, leaving her with just the thin, soft cotton night rail. His palm roamed up over her belly to settle over her breast, and she nearly jumped out of her skin when he touched her sensitive nipple through the fabric.

As his hand shifted to cup her breast, his thumb stroked over her nipple. She bit her lip to keep another moan from escaping, but couldn't stop herself from pushing her hips up into him. His leg slipped between her thighs, and the coarse hair on his bare calf abraded her skin where her gown had ridden up, sending shivers through her body. His erection strained against her thigh, so impossibly hard she could barely believe it. She'd had no idea that a man would be so hard.

"Carolina," he whispered against her overheated skin, the tip of his tongue tasting her. When she realized he was bound for her breast, she gasped aloud. It had never occurred to her that a man would want suckle her, but that's just what he did. His hot mouth closed over her and he sucked her through the thin fabric. His teeth scraped across her puckered nipple, and there was no stopping the cry that fell from her lips as her entire body tightened.

A wave of need rolled through her, sending a dart of pleasure straight to her core. The pulse between her legs became a full-on ache for some sort of gratification. "Castillo," she whispered as she shifted against him. Her fingers delved into his hair, holding him against her.

She hadn't even realized he'd moved until the cool night air touched her leg. He shoved his hand under her gown, pushing the thin cotton fabric up to her hip. His knee pressed against the inside of her thigh, urging her to open for him, so she did, tilting her leg out to give him access. He groaned against her breast when his fingers found her swollen and wet for his touch.

"Oh, God," she whispered, arching up toward his touch. She'd never imagined in all her life that a man's touch could feel so good. Dipping briefly into her wetness, his two middle fingers moved up to circle her swollen clitoris. She bit her lip again to keep from making a sound and found herself circling her hips to counter the friction and the ache he was building.

Very soon, quicker than she'd realized it would happen, that motion wasn't enough. She dug her fingertips into his shoulders and shifted restlessly as the ache within her expanded and she felt an indescribable pressure building inside her. "Please," she whispered.

"Dammit, Carolina." He held himself over her as if he'd realized what he was doing, but didn't stop touching her between her thighs. "I shouldn't be doing this to you."

Her arms tightened around him at the mere hint that he might stop. One leg curled around his thigh. She felt as if she couldn't touch him enough, couldn't get enough contact with him. "Castillo, I need…" What did she need? His fingertips slanted over her clitoris, giving her just enough pressure to take the edge off the relentless ache.

"What do you need?" His voice was a hoarse rasp against her lips as he kissed her and his hips pushed against her in a faint thrust.

"More…you…more." His shaft was so hard against her that she realized exactly what she needed. She needed him to fill her. It'd be so easy to push the sheet down from his hips and free him. He'd already be there, ready to thrust himself inside her.

Taking pity on her, his fingers moved down to her opening. She nearly came out of her skin when he circled her and eased a fingertip inside, stretching her to accommodate him. It was a slow in and out movement that had her desperate for more, until finally he pressed his broad finger deep and she saw stars behind her eyelids.

"Are you a virgin, Carolina?" He kept up a gentle rhythm, but he didn't try to fit another finger inside her.

"Yes." It came out more as a breath than a formed word.

He mumbled something. It had to be cursing with the way he growled it, though he spoke Spanish and she couldn't say for sure. Before she could respond, his mouth covered hers once more, and his finger found her clitoris again. He alternated between touching her there and stroking deep. When her body began to tremble from the pleasure, he spoke to her, his words soft and encouraging. The fact that they were in Spanish only somehow increased her pleasure. She didn't need to understand them. It was enough that his smooth, deep voice was saying them to her.

Finally, everything within her narrowed to his touch on her body until she exploded. Waves of pleasure rushed over her, and he kissed her to keep her silent. When she finally stopped trembling, he took his hand away and pulled down her night rail. She was breathing hard and her limbs were leaden, but she wasn't finished. She wanted to touch him. When he moved to her side, she reached for the sheet, but he stopped her with his hand on hers. She wasn't willing to give him up just yet, though, so she ran her palms over his chest, savoring her ability to touch him. He closed his eyes and shivered as he leaned into her touch. Her fingers delved into the hair on the back of his head to pull him back to her. He kissed her hard, his hand going back to cover her breast. She sighed against his lips.

"We can't go further, Carolina." His voice was low and rough, raking across her senses. "That was already too far."

"But I want to touch you."

"No." He said it with such authority, it brought her up short and she pulled her hand from his chest. "If you touch me, I'll go too far."

Her heart raced at the implications of that. They should stop. Somewhere in her mind, she knew that. He was saying that if she touched him, he'd take her. Her body woke up to a brand new state of desire just from the thought of that, but he was right.

He sat up on the side of the bed and took her hand to help her sit beside him. Uncertain of what to do or say, she tensed to rise, but he reached over and touched her face. His palm was warm and her skin prickled beneath his fingertips, longing for more of his touch. "Thank you. For what you gave me just now and for releasing me from our agreement."

She nodded. "I'm sorry things can't be different between us. I like you, Castillo. I...I like you very much." It was true. She admired his dedication to his grandfather and his drive for justice. She appreciated that he seemed to understand her own ambition, when almost everyone else didn't. She relished the way he'd stood up to Mr. Bonham on her behalf. Suddenly it dawned on her. He was everything she'd ever thought she wanted in a husband. Strong but kind, intelligent and compassionate, honorable yet passionate.

Oh, God. If given half the chance, she could love him. But that couldn't be. Her future was in Boston. His was in Texas or maybe even here. She actually had no idea what he planned to do after he found Derringer, which only proved it wouldn't work out. None of that even included the fact that he was a dangerous man. Loving him was sure to bring her heartache. The very idea of it terrified her, but the logic didn't do anything to stop her heart from opening up and letting him in.

Since she couldn't rely on her perfectly logical brain to protect her, she decided that distance was the only thing that could. Pulling her wrapper around her body, she murmured a hasty, "Goodnight," and fled the room before he could stop her.

Chapter Eleven

C aroline spent the next morning in a daze. Part of it was that she couldn't stop reliving the night with Castillo. She'd never imagined that such pleasure could be had with a man. Between all the whispers and giggles of the women of her acquaintance, she'd assumed that it could be pleasant, but Castillo's touch had been so much more than that. And the connection between them went far deeper than pleasure. He touched her and it felt like she was rediscovering a part of herself she'd lost, or maybe never even known about. He looked into her eyes and saw who she was, not who he wanted her to be.

Nothing had changed overnight. She was still going back to Boston and he was still searching for Derringer, so her brooding was quite pointless, but she couldn't seem to snap herself out of it. Castillo and Hunter had already left when she came down for breakfast that morning. Mr. Jameson had said they had some business in town to attend to, and she could only assume that meant Derringer. In addition to brooding, that meant she was worrying about him, too. That worry was a perfect reminder of why they'd never work out together. She'd end up hurt in the end.

"Caro?" Aunt Prudie stood in the doorway of the parlor, a frown on her face. "Are you all right?"

Caroline had been staring off into the cold fireplace, a book forgotten on her lap. "Yes, of course. Why do you ask?"

"You didn't hear the bell? Your mother is arriving."

The housekeeper had taken to ringing a bell located near the front door whenever new guests had been spotted coming down the long driveway. Since the parlor was located just off the front hallway, Caroline should've heard it. She would've heard it had she not been lost in thoughts of Castillo. "Oh, I suppose I wasn't paying attention."

"Is this about Castillo Jameson? When you said this morning that you'd both decided it best not to continue your flirtation, I wasn't happy but agreed. He doesn't live in Boston, so I'm not certain how that would've turned out." Aunt Prudie walked over and put her hand on Caroline's shoulder. "But you seem sad, dear. Did he mean more to you than you let on?"

Lying to her aunt had been one of the hardest things she'd ever done. When she answered she tried to stay as close to the truth as possible. "He does mean something to me. It's strange because I've only known him for such a short time, and yet I feel as if I do know him. But I also know we don't have a future." She was coming to realize that what she felt for him was on the cusp of being so much deeper than she let on. She feared that if she blinked she might fall right into those feelings...especially after last night.

Aunt Prudie clucked her tongue and cupped Caroline's cheek. "I'm sorry, dear. I like him, too. I think sometimes we just have to have faith that everything works out as it's meant to be."

Caroline nodded, though she wasn't entirely sure how she was supposed to find comfort in the fact that she and Castillo weren't meant to be. The front door opened and people could be heard coming inside. It was probably for the best. She'd have spent the day moping and pretending to read if left to her own devices. Placing her book on the table beside the chair, she plastered on a smile and followed Aunt Prudie into the foyer.

"Caroline!" Her mother squealed and rushed over to pull her into an embrace. A familiar rose scent met her nose as Caroline hugged her. When her mother pulled back, her smile was so radiant and full of love and happiness that Caroline immediately felt awful for the uncharitable thoughts she'd been having about her mother. Perhaps after a chat they'd be able to come to an agreement about school. Perhaps if she simply agreed to marry within the next year. But even that compromise made her stomach churn.

"Hello, Mother, how was your trip?"

"Wonderful, darling. I can't wait to tell you all the things we did in New York. The shopping was marvelous. I bought you some things and I'll show you as soon as our bags are brought in." Then she turned to Aunt Prudie. "Prudence, it's lovely to see you."

As her aunt and mother spoke, Mr. Jameson made his way into the foyer. Emmy was upstairs undergoing a final dress fitting, so probably wouldn't be down for a while.

Isabelle, Hunter's mother and Mr. Jameson's estranged wife, swept in behind Caroline's mother. Her blond hair was streaked with strands of silver, swept up elegantly onto the crown of her head and topped with a black velvet hat that matched her traveling dress. Caroline walked forward and greeted her. The woman responded with a very cold and bland, "Good afternoon, Caroline. Lovely to see you." Her gaze lit on Aunt Prudie before moving back to her estranged husband. "Wilhelmina!"

Willy stepped out of the shadow of the stairs where she'd stood unobtrusively observing the gathering. "Good afternoon, Mrs. Jameson. It's good to have you back."

"Have our bags unloaded and I'd like a bath immediately. The dust out here is insufferable." Walking toward the stairs, she paused at her husband. "Where is my son?"

"Good to see you, Isabelle." He smiled at her, glossing over her rudeness. "Hunter's in town. An urgent business matter, but he should be home for supper."

"I see you've yet to teach him any manners. I'll be in my room until supper. Tell him I look forward to meeting his bride." She didn't wait for a reply as she swept up the stairs, saying a brisk word to Caroline's father as she marched past him.

Mr. Jameson appeared to be unmoved by his wife's demeanor. He kept a slight smile on his face as he called to her back, "I certainly will."

Caroline sighed as she shared a knowing glance with Aunt Prudie. She genuinely regretted that Emmy would have to endure such a woman for a mother-in-law, and thanked her stars that she'd only have to spend a few days in the woman's presence. She couldn't understand how her mother could be friends with such a cold woman, but Kathleen Hartford was a social butterfly and had never had trouble making friends with anyone.

"Samuel!" Her mother held her arms out as she hurried to the foot of the stairs to greet her husband.

Caroline's father smiled broadly and picked up his pace down the stairs until he pulled her into his arms. "Kathleen. I missed you." The sight was so joyfully intimate that Caroline had to look away. She'd always hoped to have that in a marriage, but now she realized how naive she'd been.

"Hello, Miss Hartford." The masculine voice came from the open front door. Caroline turned to see a tall man step into the foyer. He was lean, handsome in a cultured sort of way, with light brown hair and eyes, and he was vaguely familiar. She searched her mind for some memory of him. Perhaps they'd met at a function of some sort. He smiled at her, and it was a very knowing smile. His gaze was direct and shrewd.

"Caroline." Her mother's voice drew her attention. The woman beamed at her as she crossed the foyer to stand next to her, Caroline's father behind her.

He was smiling, obviously thrilled to have his wife in his arms, but when he saw the man standing in the doorway, the smile fell from his face. "Kathleen, we shouldn't—"

Her mother turned and patted his cheek. "Nonsense, Samuel, now is perfect." Then she turned back to the young man. "Caroline, this is Grant Miller. Don't you remember meeting him last year at the Christmas gala?" Without even giving Caroline time to respond, she hurried on. "I invited him to come out with us, and he said he'd never been to Helena and thought it sounded like a wonderful idea."

Caroline vaguely remembered the man from some event. If she recalled correctly, his father had donated a generous amount to the hospital. She didn't know what that had to do with anything or why he'd want to come all the way to Helena for the wedding of someone he didn't even know. None of that made any sense. When she realized that no one was saying anything, Caroline cleared her throat and offered her hand. "It's nice to see you again, Mr. Miller." He took her hand and gave a very courtly little bow over it as he returned her greeting.

"Oh, Kathleen." Aunt Prudie's voice was so low, Caroline might've thought she'd imagined the words had her mother not acknowledged them with a wave of her hand and a shake of her head. It caused the first crack in the mental barrier Caroline had somehow managed to keep in place this whole time, while her stomach churned on the knowledge that something was happening. Even then, even with the proof of her mother's deception standing there and staring her down, Caroline couldn't quite bring herself to believe what was happening.

"I had a long talk with Grant's parents back in Boston, and we've agreed that you both would make such a lovely couple."

"Mother...." Caroline couldn't quite get her mind around what she wanted to say. Her entire body went cold and prickly, and then she felt numb.

"Well, Mrs. Hartford." The man smiled and dipped his head in the perfect semblance of modesty, but his eyes weren't timid at all as they settled back on Caroline. "I think Caroline and I should get to know one another before we settle on calling us a lovely couple."

Caroline clasped her hands before her so hard she was sure her fingers were turning red. Her own mother had invited this man all the way across the country to court her. It was the most outlandish thing she'd ever heard. "I'm not clear on what's going on here," she began, though she was pretty certain that she knew. "Mr. Miller is here to court me?"

Her mother laughed and linked her arm with one of Caroline's. "It's a little more than that. Why don't we have some tea while we discuss it? Prudie? Could you arrange some tea and refreshments for us in—" They came to a stop in the front parlor where Caroline had so recently been daydreaming about Castillo. "This should do nicely. Have it brought in here, Prudie dear."

Aunt Prudie squeezed her arm just before she hurried off to see to the tea. Before Caroline knew it, she was sliding down to sit on the settee while her father took the chair she'd vacated. Grant Miller was, mercifully, absent. Whether he'd stayed in the foyer or had been ushered off to some other part of the house, she didn't know nor did she care. "I don't understand what's happening."

"Caroline—" her father began, but her mother cut him off.

"Caroline, we feel—"

"Kathleen." Her father's sharp tone drew them both up short. He rarely spoke in any way that wasn't calm and measured. When it was clear her mother would cede him the floor, he began again. "Caroline, as I explained to you, and as your mother's letter explained, we feel that you need to be married soon before the opportunity seems less...attractive to some suitors. I, personally, feel that any man who would eschew your hand after your education, doesn't deserve it, but we live in the world in which we live." He shrugged as if he couldn't comprehend that world. "Your girlhood friends are all married now, or at least engaged."

"But, father, you specifically told me that you supported me going—"

"Yes, yes. I do support you going to medical school. I've made it my mission to find you a husband who also approves. Grant and I spoke before I left Boston, and he approves of your going. He actually spoke very highly of you and your pursuits."

"As do I," her mother put in. "I'm very proud of you for being accepted, Caroline. Very proud. But we have to be realistic. This is your future."

"What are you saying? I am being realistic. I can be a physician. That is my future."

"Of course you can," her mother was quick to reassure her. "But eventually you'll want a family. You won't want to continue being a physician then, will you?"

Caroline had never thought about how having children would impact her profession. She assumed there'd be challenges, but she'd never thought about giving up being a physician. "Well, yes, yes, I think I will want to continue." This wasn't some passing fancy that she'd abandon to move on to something else.

Her mother frowned, but didn't interrupt as her father took over. "As I said, I've spoken with Grant and he's an upstanding young man. His father owns a foundry and invests in several downtown buildings. They're an old family."

"Are you...were you holding meetings with suitors to find one who'd take me?" A wave of nausea churned through her belly.

"No, of course not." Her father frowned and darted a glance at her mother. "I did speak with a couple of gentlemen who'd expressed interest in the past in coming to call. Though I have to agree with your mother and say that I received fewer inquiries once your plans became known. And that's no reflection on you. I fully support your decision. However, it did bring to my attention the particular challenges you might face in the future when it came time to marry. I confess that I hadn't bothered to concern myself with the prospect of your marriage until your mother brought the question to my attention."

Her mother nodded in agreement. "You know how your father tends to leave the day-to-day thinking to us sensible folk while he goes off into one of his books." Then she leaned forward and took Caroline's hand. "Please understand that we do not take this decision lightly. We only have your best interest at heart. We've spoken to Grant at length, and we do very much feel that he'll be the best option as a husband for you."

The very idea that they'd think she'd entertain the notion of marrying this stranger was perplexing. Her heart pounded so hard she could barely hear anything over the roar in her ears. "And if I don't like him?"

Her father sat back in his chair, but her mother only smiled. "Please don't be unreasonable, darling. Give him a chance. I'm certain you'll find that you quite like him."

"What if I don't?"

Finally, her mother's smile cracked a little. "Let's hope it doesn't come to that. We've made a good match for you."

Caroline could hardly believe her ears. They were behaving as if this was normal. "I won't commit to this engagement. I have not chosen him. I don't even know him. We're not in the Middle Ages. People don't just marry off their children." Yet, even as she said it, she knew that it happened all the time. Maybe not quite as straightforwardly as this, but she knew many women who'd had their suitors selected for them.

Her parents merely looked at each other.

Taking a deep breath, she asked, "Am I not to attend medical school unless I marry him?" The words echoed in her mind as the room stayed silent. Neither of them wanted to admit that they'd backed her into a corner. Had they thought she'd just allow them to do this to her?

"Miss Hartford? Caroline?" Grant Miller walked into the room as if unsure of his welcome. "If I could have a word with you, I think I could clear up a little of the confusion. You see, I approached your father months ago. After I met you, I was quite enamored with you and I knew that you had barely noticed me. You were too busy chatting with donors and making speeches to notice your admirers."

He gave a small smile that softened his features and made him appear very young, almost likable if she'd been inclined to view him as anything other than a threat. "I heard every word of your speech that night and I highly admire your passion for the hospital and your chosen profession. If it sets your mind at ease, I support your ambition and would proudly call you my wife, as well as my physician."

He smiled and it did seem genuine. "I apologize for the ambush. Your mother thought it would be fun to surprise you, and I can see now that we were wrong. I'd hoped that my coming here would be a symbol of my dedication. If I've overstepped my bounds, then I humbly apologize."

Caroline stood, rubbing her wet palms down the skirt of her gown. If what he said was true, then he was caught in the middle of this awful scheme her parents had arranged just as she was. She couldn't fault him for that. Knowing her mother, she'd probably played up Caroline's enthusiasm to him a bit too much. "Thank you for your apology. I believe my parents are a little overzealous in their ambitions. I hope you don't think I'm being rude, but they caught me off guard."

"I completely understand. I'll go and leave you to talk with your parents." He turned to go, looking rather dejected, making her feel terrible.

"You don't have to go, Mr. Miller."

He smiled back at her. "I don't want to be a bother. I have a room in town, a very nice room, actually. I'd never have believed Helena had anything to rival Boston, but the Baroness is one of the nicest hotels I've seen."

"Please stay. At least for refreshments. I'll go see what's keeping Aunt Prudie." Caroline forced the same smile she used at the fundraisers and left to go find her aunt. Inside she was seething and very aware that her parents had backed her into a corner. She refused to marry a man they had arranged for her, but she was already starting to wonder how she could get out of it. They very literally held the purse strings to her future. If they refused to allow her to attend medical school—and refused to pay her tuition—then she really had no choice.

As she moved into the hallway and left the parlor behind, thoughts of Castillo began to intrude. The very idea of touching some man who wasn't him was repulsive. What would he say when he came back tonight to find this had happened? What if he didn't care? She closed her eyes and came to a stop in the privacy of the little alcove beneath the stairs.

He wouldn't care...would he? Despite what had happened between them last night, her being forced to marry someone else wasn't his problem. And why should it be? He could do absolutely nothing about it.

Her heart pounded in her chest so hard she thought that it might try to leap out. Closing her eyes, she was afraid that she'd just fallen over the edge into the deeper feelings for Castillo that she'd been so afraid of.

Chapter Twelve

A trail of dust kicked up behind Johnson's horse on the deserted road. Castillo clenched his fingers around the field glasses as he shifted them to evaluate the hills beyond the road. He didn't see any movement, no sign of Derringer or one of his men watching for Johnson.

Castillo, Zane and Hunter had made the decision that it was time to act when there'd been suspicious tracks early that morning on the ranch's southern border. They couldn't wait around and allow Derringer to get desperate and do something stupid, like attack the ranch. They'd need to lure him out with the only bait they had. Rob Johnson.

Castillo had ridden to Victoria House that morning with a couple of the men from the ranch and Hunter, who'd insisted on coming despite Castillo's protest. They'd concocted the plan to have Johnson ride out as if he'd been successful on his mission to capture Castillo. The gang would hide and ambush Derringer once Johnson brought him out of hiding.

It hadn't taken much to convince Johnson to agree to the plan. They'd offered him more money, and it wasn't hard to buy the temporary loyalty of a man like him. There was no question the plan was risky. Johnson could get jumpy. Derringer might smell a trap. A hundred things could go wrong, but it was the only plan they had right now. There'd been no other signs of Derringer and no clear way to find him.

After getting a visual on Zane hidden in the hills across the road, Castillo stowed the binoculars back in the case hanging from his saddle horn. They were only a few miles from town. They'd likely have another few miles before Derringer showed himself. Tightening his grasp on the reins, Castillo led his horse through the trees, careful to keep up with Johnson, but not get so close he couldn't stay out of sight. In the intervening silence and the growing tension of possibly facing Derringer after all these years, misplaced thoughts of Carolina began to intrude. Truth be known, he'd barely stopped thinking about her since she'd left his room the night before.

Carolina. What a surprise she'd turned out to be.

Last night he'd nearly gone against everything he believed in and taken her. She'd come undone in his arms, her body slick with her need for him. It would've been so easy to move the sheet aside and slide between her thighs, claiming her as his. He swallowed hard and gritted his teeth against the half erection just the memory of her caused. Why did she intrigue him as she did?

He'd had his share of beautiful women, and not one of them had been as innocent as he knew Carolina to be. But none of them had gotten under his skin like this. They'd been fun and distracting while he'd had them, but he'd been able to move on with just the memories. He hadn't even slept with Carolina and already she was on his mind more than she should be. Maybe that's why he couldn't forget her. He hadn't had her yet.

No. Even as the thought flickered through his mind, he knew it was false. He liked her, and in some strange way he couldn't quite understand, he understood her need to do something different with her life, to buck the restraints put on her. As much as he loved the hacienda in Texas and planned to rebuild as soon as this journey with Derringer was over, he couldn't help but wonder what his life might be like if he didn't have the yoke of that responsibility hanging over his head. What if he had Hunter's freedom to live how he wanted?

He thought of Carolina as she'd spoken of her chosen profession. She'd been confident and alluring, even as Bonham—that bastard—had tried to demean her. She'd kept her composure and had looked like a queen patiently addressing her wayward subject. Castillo had been proud of her. No, he'd felt more than that. He'd felt proud to walk with her on his arm. Proud that she'd smiled at him when he intervened. His chest had swelled with something he didn't recognize when she'd looked up at him in the light of that lantern with something like admiration in her eyes. It was why he hadn't been able to resist kissing her that night, even though he knew he wasn't good for her. He'd wanted to capture just an ounce of her goodness.

Then that image was replaced with one of how she'd looked last night in the candlelight of his bedroom when he'd kissed her. The dark pink of her nipple under the pale, wet cotton of her nightgown, her luminous eyes as she'd stared up at him, the pink glow in her cheeks. He could almost smell the lavender from her body. His palms tingled at the memory of her soft skin beneath them. It would've been so easy to peel off her gown and run his hands all over her silky body. He'd wanted to dip his tongue between her legs and taste her desire for him. Then he would've taken her.

If he had the luxury of freedom, he would claim her as his.

Castillo took in a deep breath, letting it expand his chest, filling him up with hope and possibilities, before he let it out and the weight of his life settled over him again, indifferent to his musings. She had a life in Boston, and his life was nowhere near Boston. Even without the hacienda, he belonged out here in the wide open spaces, not in the city. She needed to be far away from him where he couldn't hurt her.

He shook his head to clear it, but he couldn't help wondering what she was up to today and how she felt about what had happened between them. He'd grabbed a quick breakfast before the sun came up, but he missed taking breakfast with her.

Johnson quickened his pace, catching Castillo's attention. Retrieving the field glasses, Castillo held them up and saw some movement about a mile ahead at the tree line. It wasn't a very dense copse of trees, so after a moment he was able to make out a man on horseback. He raised the lenses to the hill behind the trees and caught the tail end of a horse skirting around behind it. That's probably where Derringer was camped, out of view of the road but close enough to keep watch. The only problem was that Castillo had no idea how many men Derringer had with him.

Castillo quickened his own pace to catch up with Hunter. But before he could, Johnson yelled out a warning to Derringer. "Son of a bitch," Castillo muttered and put the binoculars away so he could draw his gun.

The first gunshot came out of nowhere and slammed into Johnson's chest, unseating him so that he landed spread-eagled on his back in the dirt. He lay there unmoving. A figure crested the rise just ahead, and Castillo knew that Derringer's man had pulled the trigger. Another one came over the hill to the east and fired in Zane's direction. Castillo wasn't close enough to see if he'd found his mark, but figured he hadn't when the man narrowly missed getting hit by the return fire. Castillo turned his attention to the man who'd shot Johnson and pulled the trigger. The man lurched backward, pulling up on the reins of his horse. He wasn't dead, but he turned around and moved out of sight.

And then it was chaos. Hunter darted from the trees to cross the road and get to a closer and better position, but he drew gunfire, revealing the positions of two other unknown attackers. Castillo was able to take out one, but the other had set himself up behind a rocky embankment. His heart pumping, Castillo followed Hunter and disappeared into the trees where the others were waiting for him. None of them had been hit, but the gunfire kept coming, breaking off bits of the cottonwood trees around them. This wasn't somewhere they could ride out the fight indefinitely.

"We have to get around the hill to that camp," Castillo said. "I saw a man heading over in that direction." He pointed east around the hill, where he'd seen the horse going.

Zane nodded.

Another bullet ripped into a branch, filling the air with the sharp smell of green wood and gun smoke. "We've gotta get out of here," Hunter said, aiming and firing in the general direction of the gunfire.

More shots echoed from the valley behind the hill and Castillo prayed that it was the two men from the ranch they'd brought with them. His prayer was confirmed when one of them let out a whoop of victory. From the pitiful cover of the cottonwood trees, Zane, Hunter and Castillo fired on the attackers still out there. One of them went down, but there was still the man behind the embankment of rock.

"I'm going around that embankment. Keep shooting until I get there," Castillo called. As long as Hunter and Zane were shooting, the man likely wouldn't chance a return fire. It was a risk, but one that Castillo was willing to take to end this. Even in the midst of this madness, he thought of Carolina and was glad he'd stopped when he did last night.

The two men from the ranch were just riding out behind a trail of dust that headed east, probably Derringer attempting escape. Castillo longed to follow them, but had to take out the man behind the embankment first so that Hunter and Zane wouldn't be vulnerable. He circled around, using the top of the hill as cover, until he'd managed to work himself so that he could see the man's shoulder. Dismounting, he edged around until he could see a dark beard.

It wasn't Derringer, but it could be Bennett. Very much wanting to keep him alive for questioning, Castillo raised his gun and aimed for Bennett's shoulder. Something must've tipped him off; at the last moment he turned just enough that the bullet missed him and fired back. Pain exploded in Castillo's shoulder, as if someone had lanced him with a hot poker. He didn't have time to acknowledge it as he ran forward and fired again, but this time his bullet skimmed off the rock. He was close enough to duck down beside the embankment for cover and could hear Bennett's heavy breathing on the other side.

"Give up, Bennett. We've already taken out the others. It's

only a matter of time for you."

"You think this is getting you any closer to my father?"

"It's taking down a few barriers. As I said on the train, I don't want or need you dead. I just want Derringer. Give up and I'll let you walk."

Bennett laughed. "You think I'll give up my father and walk away?"

Castillo had hoped but had known all along the likelihood that he'd have to kill Bennett. "That's your choice, Bennett. If you want to keep up the fight, then that's on you, but he'll pay for what he did."

Bennett laughed again, and Castillo couldn't help but wonder what the hell the man had to be so jolly about. Something was missing in this scenario, but Castillo couldn't figure out what it was.

Since he was keeping Bennett occupied, Hunter and Zane were slowly making their way to the back side of the embankment. It'd only be a matter of minutes before they had Bennett surrounded. Castillo figured he'd get him to talk as much as he could while they waited.

"You still don't know who my father is, do you?" Bennett taunted.

Something about that made Castillo's blood run cold. It had occurred to him that Buck Derringer wasn't the man's real name, and after killing Castillo's grandfather, he'd simply gone back to assuming his old identity. Was he missing something?

"What do you mean?"

"Just you wait, Reyes. Soon enough everyone here will know who you really are. How do you think Papa Jameson will feel when he realizes his firstborn is a notorious outlaw?"

Castillo didn't particularly care how Tanner felt about anything, but he didn't want things to get difficult for Hunter and Emmy. If it was revealed that Hunter had been involved with the gang, he could go to jail for a long, long time...or even worse. Gritting his teeth, Castillo tightened his grip on his gun, and said, "No one would believe you."

"Not me, hombre. You're right, no one would believe me."

"What in hell are you talking about, Bennett?" Then it hit him, and he realized why the man was talking crazy and laughing like he wasn't in the middle of a shootout. "You've been shot."

Bennett laughed again, and this time it was followed by a moan. Castillo darted around the rock and trained his gun on the man. Bennett fired, but the shot wasn't even aimed and went wide. Bennett's left forearm was bloody where it pressed against his belly. It looked like he'd been shot in the arm, but when Bennett shifted, blood poured from a wound in his gut. It flowed so fast that he only had a few minutes before he'd bleed out.

"Where's Derringer hiding?"

Bennett smiled and it looked gruesome. His teeth were red with blood and some trickled out the corner of his mouth. "You won't find him until he's ready."

There was movement behind Castillo on his left side. Bennett raised his gun in a weak grip, but could barely get it off the ground to fire. Hunter didn't even flinch as he came up beside Castillo. A moment later, Zane came up on his other side, drawing Bennett's attention.

"How do the whores like the scar I gave you, savage?"

"Hasn't had much effect," Zane deadpanned.

Hatred flashed in Bennett's eyes. "I should've killed you for what you did to her." Whatever else he might have said was cut off by a series of deep coughs as he struggled not to suffocate in the blood.

Zane tensed. One look at his face and Castillo knew he was cursing the fact that Bennett's death was depriving him of the retribution he'd planned. All those nights they'd spent out under the stars, eating their dinner around a fire and planning revenge, and this was how it ended for Zane. The man who'd cut his face, the man who'd taunted him and said that he'd rather see his own sister dead than married to a "half-breed savage" was now dying.

"Christine came to me, Bennett. She loved me," Zane said, a muscle ticking in his jaw.

Blood flowed from Bennett's mouth now, far more than the earlier trickle, but still he managed to spew his hatred as he slumped over, too weak to stay upright. "She's married now—" his words were interrupted with a watery cough "—to a decent man." His eyes fluttered and he coughed again. "Doesn't change the fact that she's a whore."

Zane clenched his jaw so tight, Castillo could hear his teeth grinding. Bennett had found Zane and his sister together one night. They'd nearly come to blows, but Bennett hadn't stood a chance against Zane's bigger size. When Derringer had come back to burn down the hacienda, Bennett had come with him, intending to kill Zane. He'd only been able to disfigure him.

Castillo looked over at his friend, but a flash of movement from the corner of his eye caught his attention. Bennett had raised his gun in a surprisingly steady and strong grip and was pointing it at Zane. Before Castillo could adjust his aim and pull the trigger, a shot rang out.

The shot came from so close, it filled the air with the acrid burn of the ignition. Bennett's eyes went blank and he slumped onto the ground. Zane didn't say a word as he holstered his gun. Castillo rested his hand on Zane's shoulder. "Let's go get Derringer. Then it'll be over." Zane nodded and they made their way to their horses, ready to follow the trail of dust, hoping it was Derringer. Bennett's words weighed heavily on Castillo's mind.

Chapter Thirteen

It was nearing midnight by the time Castillo and Hunter made their way to the salon where piano music was being played by the deft hands of Mrs. Bonham. They'd only just returned, and Castillo was in no mood for socializing, but it couldn't be helped. They were late, their plans to return by supper waylaid by the shootout. Hunter had said his mother and Carolina's mother were due to arrive today along with another family, so it would be suspicious if he was absent. Emmy could put them off with the lie of an unexpected business meeting in Helena for only so long.

Castillo had been awake for almost twenty-four hours, and nearly all of those had been spent in the saddle. He couldn't remember if he'd eaten anything aside from that hasty breakfast before taking watch before dawn, but his hunger had long since turned into an empty ache that had moved up to settle in his chest. Four more men, including Bennett, were dead today because of his quest for vengeance. In the past he'd consoled himself with the knowledge that the dead were bad men and his vengeance had saved them from wreaking havoc on the world.

Somehow that reasoning wasn't working tonight.

Tonight he simply felt angry, frustrated and uncertain, when he'd been so damn sure for so long that the path he walked was the righteous one. Even thinking of the hacienda, eventually re-built in all its splendor, didn't help alleviate the doubt creeping up on him. Would it be worth the cost? The cost to his soul? His pulse galloped when he thought of Carolina, but he forced himself to stay calm. She was a hope that was out of reach. That life wasn't for him.

Despite their giving chase, the lone rider had disappeared, or so it seemed. Castillo and Hunter had come back to the ranch to figure out what Bennett's cryptic words meant.

Hunter pushed the double doors to the salon open, and Castillo instinctively reached out to push the left one, but gri-maced when the movement tugged at his bullet wound. He'd taken a look at it during his hasty bath, but hadn't been able to dress it. And he was pretty certain he'd opened it up when he'd shrugged into his coat, but hadn't had time to see to it with Hunter knocking on his door. It didn't matter. He'd stay downstairs for half an hour, long enough to meet everyone, and then he'd head upstairs to bed. Warm, wet blood trickled down his arm beneath his coat and he modified the timeline. Perhaps a quarter hour would be enough time to say hello.

The music kept playing, but Tanner saw them as soon as they entered and called out to them. Emmy rose from the chair at his side, "Hunter! Castillo!" She hurried over to greet them, her face a beacon of relief and happiness as she tried to hug Hunter as if he'd just come back from a business meeting and not a brush with death. Her fingers tightened around him, though, in a white-knuckled grip. Castillo murmured a greeting, but his gaze sought one person. He found her perched on a settee near the piano holding a glass of wine and talking with one of the newcomers.

Carolina. She was perfect in a dark blue gown with her golden hair done up in soft curls. She belonged here in a room just like this, with soft music and fine things. Not back at his hacienda surrounded by decay and failure. Their eyes met. She didn't smile or offer a greeting, but her direct gaze nearly leveled him. Her brow furrowed as she looked him over, as if she knew the hell that had been his day. It seemed as if she could see so much more than everyone else. A part of him wanted to go to her and confess everything that had happened, to bring her into his world. But he couldn't put her in danger.

Tanner drew his attention and introduced him to his wife, Isabelle. She gave him a cold, blue stare, barely managing to utter a greeting or give a tilt of her head. Castillo could only imagine how awkward the encounter was for her, but the way she looked at him reminded him that he didn't belong here. Not really. He wasn't one of them. No matter how he dressed, his life would set him apart.

Kathleen Hartford was next, Carolina's mother. The woman was shorter than her daughter, with a pleasantly plump face, and she smiled at him warmly. Castillo looked carefully, but he didn't see anything of Carolina in her features. He couldn't help but remember the breakfast conversation from the day before, and only barely managed to restrain himself from asking her why she was being so unreasonable when it came to Carolina's profession.

Next were a Mr. and Mrs. Cunningham, some distant relatives on the Hartford side, and their two adult sons, one of whom had brought a wife—the woman Carolina was talking to. He said hello to them all, and social custom dictated that he greet Carolina as well. "Good to see you again, Miss Hartford. How are you this evening?"

He wanted to drag her out to the porch and ask her, while he smoothed out the worried furrow between her brows with his lips, How are you? Did I take too much last night? Can I hold you and pretend that things are different?

"Good to see you again, Mr. Jameson." She offered him a small smile, a social smile that didn't reach her eyes. "I'm doing well. How are you?" Her gaze flicked down to the still noticeable cut under his eye from where Johnson had punched him.

Thankfully, it hadn't bruised too much. Then she took in the rest of his body in a glance that was so fast no one seemed to notice. But she didn't look reassured when she met his gaze again.

Castillo wouldn't lie to her, not anymore, but he couldn't tell her everything that had happened. "Well enough," he said, instead.

Come with me, Carolina. Come and let me hold you.

Did she regret her decision to call off their plan? Had she missed him today? Damn. He was tired if he was wondering if she'd missed him. It didn't matter. She was too sensible to become besotted with him, while he, apparently, wasn't sensible enough. He wondered if she'd mentioned anything to Prudence, and his gaze shifted to the older woman who sat in the chair adjacent to the settee. She didn't bother to smile at him and just raised a disapproving brow. Apparently, her niece had explained that he wouldn't be a suitor to her anymore. He'd probably hear an earful once Prudence could get him into a corner alone.

With a final nod, he moved to the table next to the open double doors that led out to the porch and poured himself a whiskey. Now that exhaustion was setting in, his shoulder was starting to throb. It had pained him the entire ride, but the movement had kept him distracted. The liquid warmed his belly as it went down, so he went ahead and poured himself another, hoping the next one would dull the edges of the pain.

"Are you hurt?"

He whirled at the sound of Carolina's soft voice coming from so close behind him. She stood with her back to the room, her eyes wide with concern. A quick glance behind her confirmed that no one was paying them any attention as Hunter and Emmy spoke about the wedding. "I'm fine," he said, meeting her gaze.

She frowned, clearly unconvinced. "Did you find out anything?"

"What do you mean?" He hated this deception, when all he really wanted to do was talk to her.

"Castillo—" She bit her lip and looked around to make sure no one had heard her. Then she continued in a softer voice, "I know you weren't in town on business. You don't have to tell me what happened, I just want to know if you found what you were looking for."

For some inexplicable reason, an ache welled in his throat. He had to swallow several times to make it ease, and glanced down to the amber liquid in the tumbler he held so that he wouldn't focus on her eyes. Those eyes saw too much. "I don't know what you mean."

"That abrasion on your cheek under your eye. What happened?"

He didn't want to lie to her, he'd already done that enough in their brief time together, but he couldn't tell her the truth. "One of the horses got too anxious. Ran me into a post in the stall."

"That's a new one." She gave him a rueful smile and looked back toward the people in the room, trying to appear as if they were having a normal conversation. "I've heard it caused by walking into a door, falling against a table, but never once has it been caused by a horse."

"What are you talking about?"

"An abrasion left by a fist, Castillo. I see many women at my father's practice, and a few have husbands with unfortunate tempers. I know what it looks like when a fist hits flesh."

"I don't have a husband with an unfortunate temper. And any man who hits a woman is a coward who doesn't deserve his balls."

There was silence for a moment, and then she laughed. She tried to hold it in and it made her shoulders shake. It was one of those laughs that came from deep inside, and it was apparently contagious because he started laughing, too. A badly needed moment of levity for such a tense topic of conversation. He had to turn his back to the room so no one would notice. She did the same, holding onto the edge of the table as she tried to get herself under control. She pulled off her spectacles, wiping daintily at a tear that had escaped her eye. He watched her fingers move over the creamy skin of her cheeks and felt that rush of arousal come back. He had the strangest urge to brush her fingers aside and feel her silky skin for himself. To delve his fingers into her hair and pull her close so that he could cover her mouth with his. To possess her fiery strength and beauty.

Putting her spectacles back on, she looked up at him and her smile had faded. His thoughts must have been clearly written on his face, because her gaze darted down to his mouth. He was watching her pink tongue so intently that he felt the phantom tingle of it against his own lips.

"You're worried. I noticed that the men on watch moved in closer to the house today."

He must've had a question on his face, because she nodded out toward the night. There was a tiny dot of an orange glow from a lit cigar just past the stables, halfway to the hills. Castillo had had them move in closer since he was taking some men out chasing Derringer today, and those tracks from the morning had gone unexplained. She was too observant. "Yes."

She nodded, letting out a breath as if she'd been holding it, then took the last sip of her wine. Forgetting his wound, he reached out and took the empty glass from her to set it on the table, an excuse to touch her, but he grimaced when his shoulder throbbed from the movement. Reading his face, she looked down for some sign of his injury. "You're bleeding!" She kept her voice low but her face registered shock at the little bit of blood that had stained his shirt cuff.

He sat her glass on the table and covertly pulled his coat open. The white sleeve of his shirt was streaked red with blood, and it was making its way across the front of his shirt.

"Mierda..." he muttered and closed his coat before anyone

else could see it.

"No wonder you look pale. What happened?"

"Doesn't matter." He clenched his teeth as he looked from the open double doors leading to the porch to the doors opening into the house, trying to determine which route was best for his escape.

"How long ago did it happen? Have you bandaged it?"

He shook his head, refusing to discuss it here. "I have to go."

She nodded and seemed to realize this wasn't the place for this conversation. "Of course. Go upstairs and I'll follow to bandage it."

"No. I can take care of it." The last thing he needed was to be alone with her in his room again. Wounded or not, he didn't think he had it in him to stop things again if they got out of hand.

"If that were true, you would've already taken care of it," she muttered through a smile she flashed Emmy as the people in the room started to break up into smaller groups for conversation.

"I didn't have time." Castillo didn't know why he was defending himself to her, because he had to admit her concern was nice.

"Go, and I'll follow you," she whispered.

"I can do it," he said, but he turned and slipped out onto the porch, hopeful that she'd ignore him.

***

Caroline had to wait nearly twenty minutes before she could

make her escape. The evening had been winding down until Castillo and Hunter walked in, and then it seemed as though everyone got a second wind. As soon as he disappeared, she'd been pulled into a discussion that she couldn't even remember now as she hurried up the stairs to her room.

Thankfully Grant Miller had realized he should keep his hotel room in Helena for the length of his stay and had left before supper, so he wasn't a complication she had to deal with tonight. Part of her wanted to tell Castillo, but his wound was more important right now. She'd tell him tomorrow. As if the maid had been waiting for her, Mary poked her head out of the sitting room that had been turned into her bedroom, ready to help with Caroline's gown.

Caroline wanted to wave her off, but acknowledged that she couldn't get out of the gown on her own, and it'd look suspicious if she said no. Instead, she plastered on a smile and allowed Mary a few minutes to help her out of her gown, but as soon as she'd put on her night rail and wrapper she said goodnight and locked the door behind the maid. Rushing to the armoire, she grabbed the bag containing her medical supplies and ran to the balcony door. When she pulled it open, Castillo was right there, staring down at her. She would've yelped in surprise had she not remembered Mary just next door and caught herself. His expression was unreadable.

"What are you doing here?" she whispered.

"Waiting for you." He glanced down to her bag. "I knew

you wouldn't leave it alone. I came so you wouldn't risk getting caught in my room. Let me in."

She moved back, and when he'd stepped inside she locked the door and pulled the drapes closed. "Do you really think it matters if I'm in your room or you're in my room? If we're caught, then we're caught." She didn't know why she was arguing the point with him. Her hands shook a little as she fully comprehended the fact that he was in her room and they were alone and there was nothing at all stopping them from kissing as they had last night. A pleasant rush of heat moved over her skin as she remembered it.

Castillo had already taken his coat off and changed his shirt in his room, though this fresh one already had a blood stain growing over his upper arm. Oh. Right. Nothing was stopping them from kissing again but for the fact that he had a potentially serious injury and was bleeding. She berated herself for forgetting even for a moment that he was in her room for a very good reason. "Come sit down by the lamp." She rushed over to set her bag down on the bed and hurried into the washroom to wash her hands and fill up a pitcher with water. Grabbing a towel, she rushed back to his side.

He fumbled with the buttons on his shirt as he eased down to sit on the edge of the bed and shrug it off his shoulders. When he grimaced, she helped him pull it off, draping it over the footboard.

"What happened?" she asked and started to gently wash the

wound. Some of the blood had dried so it was difficult to see the extent of the damage.

"I was shot."

"Shot?" She couldn't keep the surprise from her voice, and what could only be described as absolute terror squeezed her chest. Someone had tried to kill him. Biting her lip, she forced herself not to think about it and concentrate on the wound. There was only flesh and blood in front of her right now. Not Castillo.

She'd never had to treat a gunshot wound before, had never even seen one, and searched her memory for some mention of that type of a wound from her father. Should she go get him?

"It's not bad. It was only a graze," he said, staring at the lamp.

Now that some of the blood was coming away she could see that he was right, there was no bullet lodged in his arm. It looked as if the bullet had grazed his upper arm, tearing out a chunk of flesh with it, but overall it was a clean wound. She tried to keep herself from imagining what sort of activity could've resulted in such a bullet wound and how close he'd come to being killed. There'd be time for those thoughts later. "You're very lucky. A few more inches and it would've splintered bone, which would've required surgery."

He nodded. "It's not the first time."

She had to swallow to keep her voice steady. "You've been shot before?" She kept her gaze on his wound as she cleaned it. The wound wasn't horrific. There were no bits of cloth to dig out and the flow of blood had likely kept any infection from festering.

"I've been shot at before," he clarified.

"Derringer?" she asked, moving the bowl of blood-tinged water to the table and patting his arm dry with the towel.

He took a deep breath and hesitated before he answered. "This," he indicated his shoulder, "is the closest I've come to Derringer in years."

Was he involved in something far worse than simply trying to find his grandfather's murderer? "Then, who shot at you before?" She tried not to sound too interested as she opened her bag and rifled through it for the bottle of iodine and the package of surgical gauze, but she suspected that she failed miserably at keeping the interest from her voice.

"You don't want to know, Carolina. It's better if you don't know." His voice was tired, and his eyes were troubled and wary.

"But I want to know." Lord help her, she did. Instinct was telling her there was more to him than met the eye, but her heart was telling her that whatever was going on, she wanted to help.

"I don't want you involved."

She hesitated, knowing that she should heed his warning. "You might feel a little discomfort from this." She applied the iodine and covered the wound with the fresh gauze. He sucked in a breath but it was the only indication of pain that she saw. "Will you hold this so I can get your bandage?"

He held it in place with his other hand and she moved to pull out a small skein of linen. Pulling out a length, she cut it free and wrapped it around his arm, tying it tight enough to keep the gauze in place but loose enough it wouldn't restrict circulation. "You need to keep it clean for the next few days." She repacked her supplies and pulled out a small bottle of laudanum. "Drink a little of this. It'll help with the pain."

He wrinkled his nose as he looked at the brown glass bottle she held. "I don't need anything."

Rolling her eyes, she said, "You were shot chasing an outlaw. You don't have to prove anything to me. Believe me, I'm aware of your status as a man." Immediately the air between them became charged as visions of last night came to mind. She'd felt him hard against her thigh. Another reason she was aware that he was a man.

He grinned at her and managed to look a little arrogant.

"Open." She held the bottle to his lips. He obeyed and she poured in the approximate amount he'd require, before closing the bottle and returning it to the bag, which she stowed in the armoire. When she turned back to him, he was watching her. "I can make you a sling to keep pressure off," she offered. "You don't want to reopen the wound."

"I think a sling would cause too many questions."

He was probably right, but she couldn't resist teasing him. "You could say you were kicked by a horse."

She could tell he was fighting it, but his lips tipped up in a smile at the reminder of how he'd lied about the abrasion on his cheekbone. "Castillo." She sat down beside him on the bed, unsure of what she wanted to say, but knowing that she wanted to reach him. After last night, things had changed between them. Something special was happening.

"Don't, Carolina." He reached out and covered her hand with his right one. A flicker of awareness came to life in her belly at exactly the same time her mind was telling her to leave him alone, that he was a dangerous man. There was naked longing on his face, despite his words.

"But—"

"You're good at what you do." He indicated the wound on his shoulder. "You've got a nice touch. I can understand why you'd want to be a physician."

She noted the fact that he was trying to change the subject, but allowed it to happen. "My mother thinks I should take up nursing. Actually, she thinks I should have nothing to do with patients and marry a physician if I absolutely must support the profession." She gave him a self-deprecating smile. "But at least in nursing she can imagine me as a sort of Florence Nightingale bringing hope to the sick."

"And you can't do that as a physician?"

She shrugged. "Yes. I admit to not understanding her reasoning, either."

He smiled again, and his gaze flicked to where their hands met. She didn't know if he realized that he was absently rubbing his thumb over hers. Taking a breath, she decided to just confront him. "Castillo, last night—"

"I killed someone today." He blurted out the words before she could finish. "Today four men are dead because of me. Two by my own gun."

"Oh." She sucked in a breath because it felt like the air in the room had become too heavy to breathe. "But they were connected with Derringer. Right?" She only realized that she'd been holding her breath when he nodded and she let it out slowly.

"There was a shootout," he explained, but he didn't elaborate. She realized how tired he looked. There were shadows under his eyes and his skin was pale.

"You had to defend yourself, Castillo."

"Did I?" He let go of her and raked his hand through his hair, keeping his left arm immobile across his stomach. "That's what I thought at one time. But look what's happened. My brother Miguel was almost killed. Kidnapped by enemies I've made in my quest for vengeance. That's why I insisted he go back East to school. I wanted him away from all of this."

"That's understandable. You're looking out for him."

"You're missing my point, Carolina." He took her hand again and shifted so that he faced her. "Last night I let things go too far, because the truth is that I really like you, too. But I'm not good for you. I put everyone I love in danger. Whatever is between us can't go further."

Her heart pounded and she couldn't help but turn her hand

over in his so that they were palm to palm. She nodded because she understood that, even while something inside her fought against it. "I'm going to school in September. Won't you return home to your hacienda in Texas...once everything is over with Derringer?"

"I'll need to rebuild. Somehow." He nodded and squeezed her hand. "You understand? This can't last."

She did understand. She saw it so clearly that it made her heart ache. "I know."

He groaned and pulled her closer, catching her under the chin to lift her mouth to his. It was as if accepting the inevitability of their parting had finally given them permission for this small indulgence. His mouth covered hers and before she knew it her hands were in his hair, holding him closer. They kissed until they ran out of air and then he buried his face in her neck. "Carolina," he whispered, his day's growth of beard tickling her sensitive skin. "I'll never get enough of your smell." His mouth sucked at her flesh. "Can I stay for a little while?"

"Yes, please stay." She should make him go, but she couldn't. If this was all the time they had, she wanted so much more than she knew he'd be willing to give her.

He drew back to look at her face while she tried to memorize the exact shade of gold and green of his eyes. Leaning forward, as if giving her time to pull away, he kissed her again, his good arm going around her to draw her even closer, and then he pushed her back on the bed. He rose up on his right arm over her and gently pulled off her spectacles, setting them on the bedside table. She couldn't help but touch his beloved face, her fingers tracing the strong contours of his cheekbones and jaw before running over his full bottom lip. She didn't want to think that she could love him already, but the ache in her chest certainly felt like something close to it.

He kissed her fingertips, before moving to lay beside her and drawing her against his chest. Caroline curled into him, more comforted by his strength and warmth than she'd anticipated. He kissed the top of her head as she settled her cheek against his chest, and his right arm curled around her. As his hand stroked up and down her back, she listened to the sound of his heartbeat beneath her ear. After a while, the laudanum took effect and his breathing shifted to long, deep breaths as he drifted off to sleep. She tried to savor the moment for as long as she could and then she followed him into sleep.

Chapter Fourteen

"Carolina."

The whisper called her from a dreamless sleep. It was Castillo's voice, deep and raspy, and so close she would've sworn she felt it vibrate through her. It wasn't him, though. It was the dream Castillo, the one who had come to her once or twice before and promised to make her feel good. She always woke up before they ever got to the good part. This time, she was determined to see the dream through.

He said her name again. It was so close that his warm breath seemed to brush past her ear. Her skin prickled with goose flesh. Teeth nibbled the lobe of her ear followed by a gentle bite to her neck, which he soothed with the hot, wet lap of his tongue. That sensation was so real that she couldn't help but open her eyes.

She was in her bedroom, but it wasn't completely dark. The oil lamp still burned low on the bedside table. Castillo's strong body was pressed against her from behind and he gently sucked at her neck. She closed her eyes against the tremor of pleasure that moved through her.

"You're awake." His right hand, which was curled beneath her, pressed against her belly to pull her back against him. He was hard. That male part of him was like iron against her bottom. She opened her eyes wide at the realization, and her body responded instinctively. Her breasts tightened, and a pulse beat between her thighs. She knew she was wet there, too. It was exactly how she'd felt last night. Her blood seemed heavy, while at the same time her heart pounded out an excited rhythm.

"Castillo." Instinctively she pressed her hips back against him, relishing his hard length against her buttocks and the way it intensified the ache building inside her.

"Carolina," he whispered, dragging his mouth along her neck to the narrow strip of flesh bare above her collarbone before it disappeared into her night rail. Then he pressed forward, thrusting his hips into the softness of her body.

She gasped at the answering surge of need that moved through her. Her body was throbbing, clenching, wanting to feel him inside her.

"I want you." His voice was ragged. "If this is the only time we have, then I want to bring you pleasure. I want to make you come apart."

"Yes. Yes, I want that." She tried to turn in his arms, but he held her too tight, his forearm like a vise around her. Needing to touch him, she reached up and buried her fingers in his hair, pulling his mouth to hers for a searing kiss that left her breathless. He loosened his hold on her waist, just enough to move his hand to her breast. His fingers found her nipple through the cotton of her gown and pinched it just hard enough to make her lose her breath.

"Will you open your gown for me, mi corazón? Let me see you."

He'd barely finished saying the words before her hands were at the row of buttons that held the gown closed between her breasts. Somewhere in the back of her mind she was aware of a tiny voice reminding her of her modesty, but she didn't care to hear it. This was Castillo, and she wanted to share these things with him. There was no other man she could ever imagine wanting like this. Only Castillo.

He allowed her to roll onto her back, and he rose above her, propped on his elbow. The look in his eyes was intense and heated. She'd seen a hint of that look the night before, but this was even more piercing, its weight almost tangible. She tugged the corners of her bodice, but stopped just short of revealing her nipples. It seemed she had some modesty, after all. No one had seen this part of her. The corner of his mouth ticked upward, and he moved his left arm, the injured one, as if to assist her.

"No," she whispered. "You'll hurt yourself."

"Then open it for me." The tip of his tongue ran over his bottom lip, his eyes flicking to hers briefly before settling on the exposed mounds of her breasts.

She took a breath as she pulled the edges of the bodice down far enough to show her nipples, and then even further until the entire globes of her breasts were revealed to him.

"So beautiful, mi corazón."

It was strange how she felt beautiful, as though she could see herself through his eyes. "Will you kiss me...like you did last night?" Only this time there would be nothing between her flesh and his mouth. She trembled just thinking of it, and a pulse beat deep within her.

He held her gaze as he bent down to her, and anticipation fluttered in her belly, but he paused inches above her. If she arched she could put herself just at his lips, but she forced herself to wait. And it was worth it. His tongue darted out to tease her, and she nearly came undone at the hot, wet friction. But it didn't prepare her for the surge of longing that flooded her body when he closed his lips around her and sucked. She gasped, and bit her lip to keep herself from being too loud. Mary slept right next door. Finally, he pulled back, but when she would've protested, he gave the other nipple equal attention.

Letting her go with a slight pop, he smiled down at her with a self-satisfied look on his face, and she didn't even care. He deserved to look so satisfied. She wanted him to look even more satisfied. Careful of his arm, she ran her palms over the strong muscles of his shoulders and down his bare chest. She could hardly believe that she was able to touch him at will, and snaked a hand around his neck to pull him down to her for a kiss, just to prove to herself that he was real. That he was here and solid and really touching her. He slipped into the cradle of her hips as he took control of the kiss, ravaging her mouth.

Pulling back to catch a breath, he pressed his forehead to hers and whispered, "I should leave you alone, but I can't."

"I don't want you to leave me alone, Castillo." She gripped his back and pulled him closer, arching up into him. The hard length of his erection pressed against her where she throbbed for his possession.

"I can't take you. I won't." He placed soft kisses on her face to soften his words.

"Please," she whispered, knowing without a shadow of a doubt that she'd never want any other man as much as she wanted him in this moment.

Though he flexed into her, wringing a groan from both of them, he shook his head. "I won't take your virginity. I should go and leave you alone, but God forgive me, I can't." His mouth covered hers after that and his tongue stroked hers. "I want to taste you." He was already moving back to sit on his knees between her thighs.

She took in the sight of his bare chest, her gaze tracing the curves and contours of his muscles. At some point her gown had ridden up her legs to just above her knees. He took the hem in his hand and pushed it up, baring her thighs. Her breath caught as she watched him, slowly coming to realize exactly what he meant to do, though the thought had never crossed her mind before. Just before he revealed her, he stopped and met her gaze, but his hand moved up underneath her gown to find her center. His fingertips dipped into her slick heat, and she fought to keep herself from moving against his hand. Instinctively, she bent her knees to open herself up to him further, and he pushed the hem of her gown above her hips. She thought she'd die of embarrassment when he stared at her sex and clenched her eyes closed.

"Look at me."

She opened her eyes to see him staring down at her. His fingertips grazed over her swollen flesh, making a tremor work its way through her body, but it wasn't enough to make the wave of pleasure crest. Then he let her go, his fingers leaving her desperate and aching to be filled. She opened her mouth to beg him to help her, but he moved down to lie on his belly between her thighs. Pushing up on her elbows, she stared at him, certain that he couldn't mean to do what she thought.

When his face was level with her sex, she said, "Castillo—"

His mouth opened over her—there!—and he kissed her just as he'd kissed her mouth. Though he kept his left arm immobile, he pushed against her thigh a little with his shoulder while his right hand pressed her left thigh, opening her further to him.

His tongue dipped inside her, and he groaned a little. "You taste good, Carolina." His voice was nearly a growl and that, combined with his tongue, sent tremors of pleasure coursing through her. The only sound in the room was the soft, damp sound of his mouth against her.

The flat of his tongue pressed against her clitoris, making the nub throb and ache for more of his attention, and he obeyed her wordless cries. He teased her with a few swirls of his tongue before sucking her into his mouth. She nearly came undone when he did that, falling back against the pillows and not even caring that she was shamelessly splayed out beneath him. Then he moved downward, dipping his tongue inside her and starting the rhythm all over again. She moved her hips desperately to ease some of the ache building inside her.

"Please, more, I need more."

She didn't realize she was talking out loud until he whispered, "Shh..." against her tender flesh.

His tongue flicked over her again, nearly drawing her out of her skin. Her body clenched and unclenched, desperate for something to ease the ache he'd caused. And he did heed her whispered cries. As he went back to laving her, one broad finger slipped deep inside her. It was just enough and not nearly enough all at the same time. She arched toward his touch and he withdrew only to drive back into her and suck all at the same time, creating an amazing friction that promised release. Her entire world narrowed to him and his touch on her body.

Then he curled his fingers upward, the rough pads of his fingers working against a particularly sensitive place inside her. The pleasure was so intense, she bit her lip to keep from crying out.

He groaned, a soft vibration of sound that reverberated through her. He was enjoying this. The frenzy of her pleasure that had her twisting against him made him happy. Her heels pushed against the mattress and his teeth grazed her throbbing flesh. A spark to ignite her into flames. A tiny wave of pleasure crested, followed quickly by another larger one. His tongue stroked her, building her up higher, until her whole body trembled and waves of ecstasy crashed over her, breaking her open.

He rode them out with her until the intensity eased. Soft waves were still crashing over her when he climbed up her body to lay fully on top of her, catching her mouth in a deep kiss. She could taste her release on him and found it oddly appealing that they'd shared something so intimate. It only made her want to share so many other things with him. Wrapping her arms around him, she relished the silk of the warm skin of his back before moving down to cup his buttocks through his trousers. He groaned and flexed his hips into her. She gasped at how good it felt when his hardness pressed against her sensitive sex. He'd only just brought her more pleasure than she'd imagined was possible and she already craved more.

"Carolina," he whispered her name over and over as he kissed from her mouth to her ear.

Without waiting for permission, she moved her hand between them, stroking him through his trousers. He gasped against her ear. "I want to touch you," she said, already working the fastenings so he couldn't let some misplaced sense of duty to her honor make him tell her to stop.

"You should not," he said against her neck, but he made no attempt to stop her. In fact, he raised his hips a little so she could slip her hand inside and grip him.

"Oh, Castillo." He was bigger than she'd thought. She'd felt him through his clothes, but having him in her hand offered her an entirely new perspective. "You're bigger than I expected." His response was to bite her neck, an action that was about a hundred times more pleasant than it was painful.

Testing the size and shape of his erection, she stroked the length of him with her palm. "Is it okay if I squeeze?" A strangled groan was his only response, so she gently squeezed her hand around him, testing his hardness. When she slackened her hold, his hips pressed forward in what felt like an involuntary thrust into her palm. "You're so much harder than I thought you would be."

He groaned out her name, thrusting again, and she flexed around him. She wasn't certain if that meant she'd gripped him too hard or not, but he rose to look down at her. "We should stop before I come." He didn't seem inclined to remove himself from her hand, though, and the slight distance was enough that she could look down and see his hard length in her hand.

"I want you to." She couldn't see him as clearly as she wanted.

She longed to have the time to explore him, but it had to be almost morning by now and they'd already stolen too much time. "Please, Castillo? Please let me help you?"

He shook his head. "It's not right."

"How is it different than what you did for me? I could put my mouth on you—"

He groaned, almost like he was in pain, and covered her mouth with his before she could finish. Then he drew back just enough to whisper against her lips. "It's not the same. I'm not an innocent. I shouldn't have done that. I shouldn't take that innocence from you."

"You're not taking anything. My innocence is mine to give to whomever I want. I want you, Castillo. I choose you."

He mumbled something in Spanish and rolled over onto his back, taking her with him. "Only your hand," he warned, and then covered her hand with his and showed her exactly how to stroke him.

It was fascinating watching the muscles of his body tense and flex as she pleasured him. His hips pumped up from the bed as he thrust into her rhythm. Unexpectedly, his palm found her bare breast and closed over it. She leaned into his touch, her body still alive with need, but this was about him. It was only a moment before his body started to tighten, and he gritted his teeth against the coming wave of pleasure. He groaned her name, his eyes squeezed shut, and then his release warmed her palm. She hardly had a chance to savor the moment of satisfaction, because he tumbled her onto her back, one hand in her hair as he kissed her breathless.

Chapter Fifteen

Castillo got up early the next morning and stayed out all day riding the property from one end to the other. The wedding was coming up and Castillo was worried Derringer was planning something for that day. Though the man must've taken a hit the day before by losing so many men along with his son.

Castillo tried to feel a sense of victory over that, but all he felt was hollow. The lives lost were senseless. Derringer was the only man Castillo wanted to bring to justice for what he'd done.

The sun was low on the horizon, slowly making its way down past the mountains. Beautiful rays of pink and orange painted the land and sky. Normally Castillo would take a moment to appreciate the beauty, but he was too busy appreciating the beauty of the woman on the balcony. She stood next to the railing, her head resting against a post as she gazed out into the distance, looking east, away from the sunset. He wondered if she was looking for him. His heart thumped harder.

Last night was vivid in his mind. He could still smell her on his skin. Every time he'd closed his eyes that day, he'd seen her splayed out before him. Her skin pink against the white sheets as she whispered his name and dug her fingers into his hair. He laughed because he was dead tired and already rigid with wanting her again. He wanted to go to her and pull her into his arms, to hear her tell him that everything was going to be all right as she curled herself around him. They'd go to sleep and he'd keep her in bed all morning the next day. Being with her made him feel like everything could work out. She made him feel as if there was a dawn at the end of this long stretch of night he'd been going through.

There were enough guests now that he could hear the din of their conversation from across the yard. He'd planned to go in through the back, since he was a bit dusty from riding and needed to change his clothes. But they'd already come out for the sunset, indicating that he'd probably missed supper. He was too tired to care and his arm ached. He'd go into the kitchen and find something left over.

Carolina was on the opposite side of the house from everyone, as if she'd come out from her room to look for him. He moved across the yard from the stables, hoping that he wouldn't draw any attention as he skirted the edge of the house and took the stairs leading up to the second floor balcony. His boots were quiet on the wood floor as he made his way to her. Somewhere about halfway across the veranda, he caught a hint of her lavender scent. He wanted to wrap himself in that scent.

"Carolina," he said when he was close enough that he was certain the people downstairs wouldn't hear him. She stiffened but melted into him when he put his arms around her. He had meant to wait, to stand there and talk to her, but as soon as he came close his hands reached for her and he pulled her back against him.

"Castillo," she whispered and turned her face up to him.

His fingers cupped her cheek as he leaned down to kiss her without bothering to look to see if anyone else was watching them. When he was with her, she was all he saw. It was as if he was sucked in by her flare for life, as if he only woke up when she was near. Her taste was so familiar to him now, he craved it as he drank from her lips.

Clenching her fingers in his hair, she moaned a little, deep in her throat, as she opened to him. After a moment he pulled back enough to take a breath and stare down into her pale blue eyes. "I missed you." It was the most honest thing he'd ever said to her. There was no skirting the truth or leaving anything out. He'd missed her every moment that he'd been away, starting with the moment he'd left her bed that morning.

She smiled and, though the light was faint, he noticed a blush staining her cheeks. "I missed you, too."

He kissed her again and then dragged his mouth over her cheek to her neck, unable to get enough of her. He raked his teeth across the sensitive skin below her earlobe, smiling when she gasped. He wanted to touch her all over and find every single place that made that sound fall from her lips. There was something alluring about her strength and independence, and the way he could make her beg with her need for him. And he needed her, too.

Need. How had that happened so quickly? Last week he'd been empty, but now he was filled with her warmth and craved even more of it. He wanted to hold her, to protect her and bask in the heat of her intensity. She was brave and intelligent, and possessed a fierce curiosity. All his life he'd imagined he wanted someone soft, demure and biddable. She was everything he never knew he wanted in a woman, and he couldn't get enough of her.

He kissed down her neck, breathing in her scent as he tasted her with the tip of his tongue. She was perfect. She leaned into him and he folded his arm around her, unable to resist touching her more and closing his hand around her breast. Her hand covered his to hold it there.

"I can't understand this." She didn't elaborate, but he knew she meant this pull between them. He didn't understand it, either, but it didn't matter. It was there and he simply wanted to savor it and whatever time they had together. He was a danger to her, but surely risking this little bit of time together wouldn't hurt much, as long as he didn't take more.

She curled the fingers of her other hand tighter in his hair, and pulled a little, sending a shiver of pleasure down his spine. He was hard against her already and wondering how he'd ever get through the next days of her presence without taking her innocence. If she asked him right now he'd take her into her room and this time he'd let her use her mouth or whatever else she wanted on him.

Finding her puckered nipple through the fabric of her dress and undergarments, he circled it with his thumb. She sighed and pulled his mouth to hers for another kiss. Her tongue stroked his as she took control of the kiss this time. He could only imagine how exciting getting her in bed would be. She was too strong-willed to allow him to take the lead the entire time and he loved that.

"Caroline?" Prudence called to her from somewhere inside the house, probably the hallway outside her bedroom door.

Castillo jerked his head up, aware for the first time of how far he'd allowed things to progress with the voices of the guests not very far away. His heart pounded as he realized what getting caught could mean for her. While a very large part of him wanted everyone to know that she was his, the rational part of him knew that she wasn't and that she could never be. She belonged in another life, far away from him and his sins. It took every bit of the strength of will he possessed to let her go, but he dropped his hand and stepped away.

She whirled to face him, and her eyes were wide in panic. Her expression surprised him, so he paused. "I need to talk to you. Something's happened," she said. There was a metallic click from her room, as if the door had been opened and it drew her attention.

He wanted to take her in his arms and make that look go away. His mind raced with a million different things that could've occurred while he was gone. "What's happened?"

"Caroline!" Prudence's voice was louder this time, coming from inside the bedroom.

Carolina shook her head and squeezed her eyes shut. "Go. Just go. We can talk later."

Castillo grabbed her shoulders and pulled her in to place a quick kiss on her forehead before rushing to his room. It'd be best, in his current state, if Prudence didn't find him with her.

***

Castillo bathed and dressed quickly, anxious to find Carolina again and figure out what was wrong. He took a moment to wolf down a cold plate of leftovers in the kitchen before setting out to find her. Everyone had returned to the salon, and the usual evening activities of music and conversation after dinner, so he had no choice but to join them to talk to her.

His gaze found her as soon as he stepped inside the room. She was talking to Emmy and smiling, but when she saw him he could tell that it didn't reach her eyes. She almost looked anxious, just as she had last night. What the hell was going on? Someone standing next to her shifted, blocking Castillo's view momentarily. It was a tall, thin man, a newcomer Castillo hadn't met. His hand cupped Carolina's elbow possessively before moving over to settle on her back as he leaned in and murmured something near her ear. It was a proprietary gesture that made jealousy flare to life in Castillo.

Carolina was his. He started to make his way over, but Tanner came between him and his adversary.

"Welcome home, son. I know you met him briefly last night, but I'd like to introduce you to Abner Cunningham. He's an old friend of mine from Boston and he's been thinking of investing in some of our breeding stock." Tanner smiled, unaware that he'd intercepted Castillo, and indicated a man who appeared to be in his fifties.

Clenching his jaw, Castillo tried to force his heartbeat to return to a normal pace as he turned to greet him. "Very good to meet you again." The man gave him an easy smile, his eyes crinkling at the corners. Samuel stood on his other side and gave Castillo a nod, resuming the conversation about horse breeding Castillo had interrupted.

A quick glance confirmed that the newcomer had firmly established his place at Carolina's side. Though he didn't appear to be a part of her conversation, he stood there with his hand on her. Castillo could hardly tear his gaze from that point of contact, but he did, moving it upward toward the man's face.

The newcomer turned his head, finally glancing toward Castillo. He was shocked to see it was the man from Victoria House. The man who'd looked at him so oddly that night they'd found Johnson.

Fear and anger wrestled for control of him. It was no coincidence that Castillo had seen him at the brothel. Though Castillo had no idea who the man was, Bennett's warning was fresh in his mind. This had to be the insider, and he had his hands all over Carolina.

Tanner followed Castillo's gaze and said, "You've noticed our other visitor. A Mr. Grant Miller from Boston. Caroline's mother invited him out."

Carolina's mother and aunt had just walked up to their group. Her mother smiled. "He's such a charming gentleman and from a good, strong Boston family. He'll be good for our Caroline." She glanced at her husband and got his nod of approval.

A sickening dread settled in Castillo's stomach. Had they already promised her to this stranger or had they merely arranged an introduction? The fact that Miller's hands were on her and that he'd travelled so far from Boston told Castillo it had to be more than a mere meeting. "Does Miss Hartford agree?"

Her mother's smile never changed as she said, "She will."

Not to be left out, Prudence asked, "Does it matter if she agrees?" Castillo wasn't sure if she was asking him or Carolina's parents. The look of displeasure on her face was obvious, but then she caught his eye and he realized the question had been for him. She was asking him what he planned to do about it. Castillo wondered the same thing. He wanted to go over and rip Miller's hand away from her.

"Of course she'll agree," her mother answered. "She wants to go to school in the autumn and Grant is a good man."

"He's a solid choice," her father added, perhaps because he'd noted Castillo's interest in her earlier in the week. He met Castillo's gaze and explained, "His family are third-generation foundry owners. Their family's iron was used to build the railroads. He's a good choice for her. He'll allow her to indulge her ambition while giving her stability."

"Indulge her ambition?" They spoke as if her dream was some passing fancy she would eventually outgrow.

"Castillo," Tanner began in a warning tone.

Samuel cleared his throat, looking uncomfortable for the first time. "We have to ensure her future. It's our job as her parents."

Castillo empathized with their position, but he despised their methods. Apparently Prudence did, too, because she sniffed and turned her head away. Castillo didn't know what he could do short of offering for her hand on the spot. That was out of the question with his criminal past and the mission before him. Even after Derringer was taken care of, he seriously doubted Carolina would agree to return home with him to the hacienda. There were no people for miles, and if she stuck with tending the ranch hands she'd have very few patients. That wouldn't make her any happier than Miller would.

"Excuse me," Castillo said, separating himself from the small group and making his way to her. Miller had kept a wary eye on him ever since the man had first spotted him watching them, and his shoulders stiffened as Castillo walked toward them. Tanner followed close behind him.

Carolina stopped talking midsentence when she saw him approach. The relief on her face was so obvious, Castillo wanted to pick her up and take her out of there. Rage that she'd be forced to endure this stranger's presence built up inside him with every step he took. He didn't even bother to greet the man. "May I speak with you, Miss Hartford?" He was past the point of caring how many social rules he was breaking.

Carolina nodded, and opened her mouth to speak, but the fool beside her cut her off. "Castillo Jameson, is it?" He held out his hand, and there was no mistaking the look of cool possession in his eye. Somehow, he knew that Castillo was a rival.

"It is." Because he'd caught the attention of the room, Castillo offered his hand in a brief handshake, but he kept his gaze on Carolina.

"I'm Grant Miller, Caroline's fiancé." Grant said that with such satisfaction and possessiveness that a wave of anger swelled within Castillo.

This is what she'd wanted to tell him earlier. "Is this true, Carolina?" He no longer cared to uphold the social graces that demanded he call her Miss Hartford. She was his Carolina.

"It's not been made official. It's what my parents want." The look of dejection on her face tore at his heart.

"Is it what you want?"

"You know what I want."

Miller continued before Castillo could answer that. "I've spoken at length to Mr. and Mrs. Hartford, and we've come to an understanding. We all want what's best for Caroline."

Castillo held his hand out to her and murmurs went through the people immediately around them. He meant to ask her to go walk with him. He needed to speak to her alone, to wrap her in his arms and tell her everything was going to be all right and kiss that sad look from her face. Thankfully, Tanner's logic prevailed.

"Come with me, Miller. I want to show you my collection of rifles. I believe I mentioned earlier that I have a musket that dates back to the French and Indian War." Tanner threw his arm around the surprised shoulders of Miller and walked him out of the room. It was the only time Castillo could remember ever feeling genuinely thankful for Tanner's interference.

"Walk with me?" Castillo urged her, taking her hand in his. The murmurs continued, but Castillo didn't care. He needed to talk to her.

***

Caroline allowed him to lead her out onto the veranda where an evening breeze ruffled her hair and cooled her heated skin. She was dimly aware that they'd made some sort of scene inside, but she couldn't bring herself to care. Finally she was with Castillo, and while she knew that he wouldn't be able to do anything to help her, she felt better just being in his presence with her hand in his.

"This is what you needed to tell me?" He asked as soon as they'd gone through the doorway, leading her around the side of the house away from everyone.

She nodded. "My mother brought him here with her. I meant to tell you last night, but…" Her words drifted off and she shook her head. "I don't know what to do. I've made my displeasure known, but it doesn't seem to matter. I didn't realize how desperate they were to see me married. I didn't know that I wouldn't be given a choice." Though she had suspected this was what would happen, she'd assumed she'd have this last bit of freedom before having one forced on her at home. The fact that her potential groom was here had come as quite a shock.

"How are you not given a choice?" He shook his head as if unable to understand how her parents could send her to this stranger. They came to a stop around the veranda, nearly the very same spot where he'd first kissed her. "Can't you say no and find someone else?"

"Yes, of course I can say no, but there is no one else. Could I randomly find someone back in Boston to agree to wed me? Probably, yes, the Hartford name carries enough weight there, but I don't think the outcome will be any different. I'll still be married in a couple of months." And she'd still be without

Castillo.

He squeezed her fingers gently. "Do you know this man?"

She shrugged. "I know of him. We met once. I know of his family, but I don't know him."

Castillo looked troubled, his gaze going out into the darkness of the night over her shoulder. "You can't marry him, Carolina. I don't trust him."

He took a breath and looked into her eyes. He lowered his voice a little more to tell her, "I saw Miller in town the other night. He was at a brothel, and I think he recognized me there."

Castillo had seen him in a brothel. Castillo had been in a brothel. She tried to swallow her surprise, but it refused to leave her. She knew what men did in brothels. Had Castillo been with some other woman? It was stupid of her to be jealous, because she was quite certain he hadn't led a celibate life, but to know that he'd been with a woman so recently before being intimate with her last night left her feeling bereft. She meant to focus on Grant Miller, the one man she actually did have some claim to, but instead she asked, "Why were you at a brothel?"

His eyes widened almost imperceptibly, as if he hadn't even realized what he'd told her. "Glory Winters is a madam in town and she's become an ally. A man connected to Derringer had followed Zane and I. We captured him and took him to her brothel for questioning. It was as I was leaving that I saw Miller. He seemed to recognize me."

There was so much about Castillo that she didn't know. It

brought to light once again how strange this fierce attraction was. But, then again, she didn't know much about Grant Miller and she was supposed to marry him. She should probably care that he had been at the brothel, but she couldn't find it in her. "I'm not sure what you're trying to say. I suppose he recognized you because you're a Jameson."

Castillo shook his head. "That could be it, but I have to wonder if there's more. After the shootout with Derringer's son—the man who grabbed you on the train—he said something before he died that made me think someone here knows my real identity."

"Do you think he means me? Do you think he figured out that it was me on the train and that I'm here?"

"I don't think so. It sounded more like he'd plotted with the person."

"Oh." She searched her mind for some hint of who it could be. "You think it's Grant?"

"He's the most likely suspect. He showed up here uninvited except by your parents. I'll need to talk to Hunter and Tanner, but I don't think they know him."

He was right. Grant did seem to be the most likely suspect. "How can I help you?"

He smiled at her, his hand coming up to caress her cheek before dropping it back down to his side, lest someone catch them. "Just don't let yourself be alone with him. I'll go question him and see what I can figure out."

At his smile a spark of pleasure flickered to life within her. "Are you sure that's the only reason you don't want me alone with him?" She couldn't resist teasing him.

His eyes grew heavy lidded and dark, and his gaze dipped down to her mouth. "You want me to admit I'm jealous? Fine. I'm jealous that he gets to touch you. I wanted to tear his hands off you." The gentle touch of his hand on hers belied the harshness of his words. "I want to be the only one to touch you."

Her body warmed to his words. Her nerve endings were alive and humming, eager for his touch. "I want that, too."

He closed his eyes and took a deep breath as if her words were too much of a temptation to resist. "I'm going to talk to Miller." He kissed her forehead and turned, only to come up short when Miller came around the corner.

Chapter Sixteen

M iller took in the sight of them standing close together, and even though he wouldn't have seen anything inappropriate, his eyes narrowed a little. Castillo barely suppressed the instinct to step between Carolina and the man he'd instantly disliked. She took in a quick breath, and he wanted to reassure her that everything would be fine, but he couldn't. He didn't know that any more than he knew that he'd be able to let her go when the time came.

"Would you mind giving us a moment alone, Caroline?" Miller's voice was crisp and formal. Castillo hated how he said her name, clipped and aloof, as if she was nothing to him.

"I'd rather stay." Her voice was strong and he could almost feel her drawing her shoulders back to her full height behind him.

If Miller knew more about him and was connected to Derringer, then he wouldn't want Carolina to become some sort of target for Derringer because she knew too much. Looking over his shoulder at her, he said gently, "It would be better if you're not here. Please go, Carolina."

She looked as if she wanted to argue and bit her lip as she glanced at Miller again, before nodding and walking around the corner.

"She's my fiancée, Jameson. You have no right to her. Best to forget whatever designs you had on her." Miller wasted no time in staking his claim. The worst part was that Castillo couldn't even tell him he was wrong. She didn't belong to Castillo, and he couldn't offer for her.

"You don't even know her, Miller. Why do you want her?"

Miller grinned and leaned his hip against the railing. "Why would anyone want to marry a Hartford? It's a prestigious family with money and connections. That's how we do it back in Boston. We join our families for the benefit of all. It's not quite the same as you do it out here. Ask your father. Looks like he got it right the second time."

"Keep your damned mouth shut about my family." Castillo kept his voice level.

Miller raised his hands in surrender. "It's none of my business."

"Isn't there someone else you can marry for money? Boston

Society has to be full of women willing to marry a spineless fop for money and connections."

Miller kept the smile on his face as he shook his head. "Not one with Caroline's inheritance and eager parents. I'd like to be married sooner rather than later."

"Why is that?" Castillo crossed his arms over his chest, despising this man even more with every word that came out of his mouth.

The son of a bitch smirked and said, "My reasons are my own."

"Are those reasons why you've agreed to allow her to go to medical school?"

"I don't care if she goes. Once we're married she can do as she likes. It won't matter, though. She'll be with child within a year and need to stop."

Castillo gritted his teeth and clenched his hands into fists to keep himself from lunging at the bastard. "You really are a selfish son of a..."

Miller continued to smile, unfazed by Castillo's anger. "Self-serving is a fairer description, I think."

Several sets of footsteps could be heard coming closer, accompanied by male voices. Probably Tanner and the rest of the men who'd left to view the musket collection. Miller must've left the group early to come find Carolina.

There was no damn way Castillo was allowing him anywhere close to her. The man was a lowlife. Castillo just had to figure out a way to convince her parents of that fact, and if he couldn't convince them, he'd appeal to Miller's sense of self-preservation. His fists ached to make contact with that man's smirk.

Tanner and Hunter came around the corner followed by the other men in the group—Mr. Bonham as well as Mr. Cunningham and his sons. Hunter stared at them both, correctly assessed the situation and came to stand next to Castillo in a silent display of solidarity.

"What kept you away for the day, Castillo?" Miller asked, as if they'd been having a normal conversation.

The tiny hairs on the back of Castillo's neck stood up. Miller was playing a dangerous game, leading him to believe that Miller was the man Bennett had spoken of. Castillo wanted to tell him it was none of his business, but with the guests present, he had to at least pretend to be cordial. "Out riding the perimeter of the property. We've had some coyote sightings."

The men murmured. Miller smiled and nodded, while Tanner narrowed his eyes picking up on the underlying tension. Hunter attempted to change the subject. "Why don't we all go inside, gentlemen? There's brandy waiting."

"And yesterday? Someone mentioned that you were in Helena on business, but that's not what I heard. Word is there was a shootout south of town and you were involved. Someone said you were shot. Is that why you've been favoring your arm?"

"Careful what you hear visiting brothels, Miller. Those places are full of gossip."

Miller shrugged, the corner of his mouth coming up again. "You're a curious man, Jameson. I've been asking around about you."

"Shut the hell up, Miller." This came from Hunter.

"That's enough." Tanner's authoritarian voice broke into the silence that followed, effectively shutting the conversation down for a moment.

"I thought you'd like to know that your son could be a killer. No one knows for sure, but it was reported that one body was found. There are bound to be more."

"That's enough," Tanner repeated this time in a louder voice.

"You're mistaken, Mr. Miller." All eyes turned to Carolina who'd walked around the corner with her aunt at her side. Castillo's heart stopped for a moment before slamming against his chest. His blood ran cold.

"I assure you that I am not. I have it on very good authority that that man," he pointed to Castillo, "was involved in a shootout just outside of town. He was seen—"

"Oh, well, that's where you're mistaken." Carolina smiled as if everything was all a big misunderstanding. "You see he couldn't have been seen anywhere that day. While it's true Hunter was in town on business—"

"Carolina, no. Don't do this." Castillo warned her but she kept going as if he hadn't spoken.

"Castillo was here. We spent much of the day together...in my room."

He stared at her in disbelief—everyone did. Even though he'd anticipated her saying exactly that, he couldn't quite believe she had. Her eyes were wide and afraid, and she took deep breaths as if she'd just run a mile, but she was beautiful. And he knew that no matter what happened, their lives would be interwoven from now until forever.

***

Everything went silent. No one spoke and even the night sounds of the insects seemed to still in the aftermath of what she'd said. Caroline met Castillo's gaze across the distance of the porch and saw a strange mixture of gratitude and regret, and it made her second-guess her decision to intervene. It hadn't even been a conscious decision. She'd come around the corner to hear Miller threaten him, and she'd just said the words without thinking of their consequence or even if they were believable. She'd said them to save Castillo from suspicion.

Grant Miller's face went pale, but then a blush of rage crept up his neck, mottling his skin. Everything that happened next was a bit of a blur. Miller cursed her as if she'd just ruined everything for him. Castillo rushed him, pushing him back against the railing and throwing a fist that landed on his jaw. The force knocked the man backward over the porch railing and down to the ground below. Castillo leaped the railing to follow him down, but Hunter had already rushed to the ground and grabbed Castillo before he could do any more damage to the man who was wobbly and trying to get back on his feet.

Mr. Jameson rushed forward to help him up, but it wasn't from some spirit of altruism, because when Miller looked in her direction and called her a whore, Castillo broke free of Hunter's hold and punched him again. Tanner held the man upright for the attack. Thankfully, Hunter grabbed his brother's arms and pulled them behind his back, right about the time a ranch hand came running over out of the darkness, drawn by the commotion.

In fact, everyone from the salon had been drawn by the noise. As Miller was being pulled away toward the barn with the ranch hand on one side and Tanner limping along on the other, he called her every word for whore she'd ever heard and then some that she hadn't. From the murmurs around her, she knew that word was spreading that she'd admitted to spending time alone with Castillo in her room.

Oh, dear Lord, what would her parents think of her? She'd said it on impulse to save Castillo from suspicion, but hadn't thought about the hurt she might cause her family. She whirled and found her mother standing next to Aunt Prudie. Aunt Prudie didn't look alarmed at all; in fact, she had a slight smile on her face as she grabbed Caroline's arm and rubbed her back. Her mother, however, was pale and seemed horrified.

"Mother, please understand—" But that's as far as she got before her mother shook her head and walked back into the house. Her father stood away from the group, his eyes sad and tinged with disappointment. "Father." Caroline moved toward him and he reached out and took her hand. "Please believe that I never meant to hurt you."

He nodded and gave her hand a squeeze before letting it go. "This is quite the blow, Caroline." Then he shook his head as if he couldn't quite wrap his mind around what had happened. "It's quite the blow. Come, let's go inside and discuss this in privacy."

Tears pricked her eyes as she watched him follow her mother inside, but Aunt Prudie was there to put her arm around her. "Now is not the time for tears," she whispered, so low that only Caroline could hear her. "You must finish what you started."

Caroline only noticed then that the crowd still lingered, watching and waiting to see how this thing she'd started would play out. Only she had no idea what to do next. Aunt Prudie's voice prompted her. "You made your choice and you have to see it through. Appear strong when faced with adversity."

One look at Castillo assured her that he was no better option than going to face her parents at the moment. He was livid. The intensity of his gaze ate up the distance between them and scorched her where she stood. Aunt Prudie was right, though. Caroline had set the wheels in motion when she'd defended him and she had to see it through, despite his anger and her parents' disappointment.

Aunt Prudie gave a gentle tug on her arm and she turned to follow her parents inside. Aunt Prudie took her hand and led her to Mr. Jameson's study. A few lamps flickered in the dark, but no one else was in the room other than the four of them. Her mother sat stone still on the settee, still in shock. Her father sat behind her, his hand resting on her back. He wasn't talking to her and trying to comfort her. He was probably doing his best to come to terms in his own mind with what had happened.

Caroline took in a deep breath as Aunt Prudie closed the door behind them. Her fingers shook so badly that she had to clasp them before her to keep them still. With slow, deliberate steps she made her way to her parents, taking the chair nearest them. "Please believe me when I say that I never meant to cause you any grief."

Her mother shook her head. "How could you do this to us, Caroline? How could you? I found a nice man to marry you, take care of you, and this is what you do?" Her mother didn't even meet her gaze as she spoke, but kept looking off to the distance as if the answer to her questions could be found in the cold dredges of the fireplace.

Caroline wanted to take comfort in the fact that she'd lied to save Castillo, but there was no comfort to be had there. She'd spent last night in his arms, doing things that she'd never even imagined doing with a man. Her parents didn't know about that, but she was still guilty of it. She didn't feel very guilty, though. What had happened between her and Castillo had been beautiful and tender and so full of unspoken love that it filled her heart to nearly bursting. "I didn't do anything to you. I understand that you must feel betrayed and perhaps even embarrassed by my behavior. I am sorry for that. Please believe me."

Her father nodded. "We do believe that. What we can't believe is that you'd throw away your future on a man you don't even know."

Caroline tried not to allow the brief flicker of anger she felt to catch fire. "I still have my future," she reminded them gently.

"No. No, you most certainly do not Caroline Marie Hartford." Her mother straightened her spine, finally coming back to herself as the shock began to wear off. "You just made sure of that. Grant won't marry you now. Once gossip of this spreads, I can't imagine anyone will marry you. It's not as if there was that much interest before this, but now...now there will be no one."

Her father shifted to hold her mother's hand with both of his, attempting to soothe her. To Caroline, he said, "This was uncharacteristically selfish of you. If there's one thing I could count on from you, it's that you would think things through and always do the right thing. This is not the right thing. You don't even know this man."

Caroline couldn't deny that she'd acted without thought, but only in reference to defending Castillo so publicly. She wouldn't do anything to change what had happened between them last night or the night before. It shouldn't have any bearing on her future, but she couldn't deny that it would. "I know that he's good and honorable, unlike Grant Miller."

Her mother scoffed at this. "Has he offered you marriage?"

He hadn't. They'd talked to some length about why they

were wrong for each other. "No."

Her mother tossed her head and looked away.

"Prudence?" Her father's voice held the authoritarian ring it sometimes carried during surgeries.

"Yes, Samuel?"

"Would you go and ask Mr. Jameson and his son to join us, please?"

Aunt Prudie nodded and left the room. Caroline's stomach turned at the thought of the horrible confrontation she knew was coming.

Chapter Seventeen

Castillo couldn't get over how alone and scared Carolina had looked, standing on that porch defending him to Miller. He was almost certain she'd never considered the ramifications when she'd done it. And while she had asked him to compromise her on his first night here at Jameson Ranch, he'd been certain she wouldn't see it through. She cared too much for the people around her to hurt them so badly. It was one reason he admired her so much. There was a vein of strength in this woman that he respected, but she was soft when it came to her heart. When it counted.

As he walked toward the barn to confront Miller, he admitted that he could love her so damn easily. He closed his eyes for only a second and opened them to the sound of gunfire.

His entire body tensed, but then Tanner stuck his head out of the barn and yelled, "We're all fine. Coward had a gun, but he doesn't anymore." He laughed and walked back inside, closing the door behind him.

"Maybe we should've told him about the gang," Hunter teased. "He seems to be enjoying himself."

Castillo let out a breath and hurried his steps. He kept a small frame gun strapped above his ankle at all times. He'd use it if he had to. Opening the door, he saw that Miller sat on a crate with his arms tied to a beam behind him. Aside from the blows Castillo had delivered earlier, he didn't look any worse. He glared at them when they came in and frowned, but kept his mouth shut. Tanner sat on another crate a few feet away, and the rest of the gang stood across the room, keeping watch.

"What's he told you?" Castillo asked.

"Go ahead. Tell him what you told us," Tanner prompted.

Miller gave them all a sullen glance, but must've figured the odds were against him. "I saw you at Victoria House and heard someone call you Jameson. I asked around. One of the whores said she had some information about you if I was willing to pay for it. I was."

Castillo didn't doubt that there were rumors, but Glory was the only one who knew his identity as leader of the Reyes Brothers. She wouldn't betray him to a no one like Miller. "What information did she have?"

Miller rolled his eyes. "Nothing. Gossip that you might be

tied to a criminal, and there was a shootout outside of town, and some people had seen you riding in that direction before it happened. But I didn't really need evidence to make the Hartfords see that I'd be a better choice for their daughter. It's pretty obvious who the better man is." He grinned a toothy smile. "Honestly, I never expected you to be connected to that shootout. How fortuitous that bit of information turned out to be true."

"No one ever said it was true," Hunter said, walking around Castillo to stare down at Miller. "We just don't like jackasses from back East coming out here starting trouble."

Miller laughed. "Ah, so then I guess you're really not looking for Derringer, are you?"

"What do you know about Derringer?" Hunter asked.

Miller laughed again, throwing his head back as he seemed to relish being the center of attention. "I know plenty about Derringer. More than you, I'd wager. Now there's an idea. I tell you who Derringer is, you let me go."

Castillo didn't want to believe that Miller had any information. It seemed too good to be true. "What makes you think I'm looking for Derringer?"

"The whore overheard you questioning a man in the cellar of the brothel. I almost couldn't believe we'd have the same acquaintance. You see, I knew Derringer back in Boston a few years ago. He owned a gaming house and I'm sad to admit that I lost quite a bit of money to him, primarily because he's a known cheat and thief. He's been blackmailing me ever since. Said he'd tell my father if I didn't keep paying him, knowing I'd be disinherited if he did." He paused and looked from Castillo to Hunter and back again. "Let me go and I'll give you the names of his contacts in Boston. You may be able to find him."

Hunter laughed. "We have the upper hand here, don't get cocky."

"I'm afraid you don't. I won't tell you until you let me go."

The echoes of the ugly words Miller had said to Carolina earlier still lingering in his mind, Castillo stepped forward and backhanded the man. Miller spat blood onto the straw covered floor. "Tell us what you know or you won't be walking out of here."

For the first time, a look resembling genuine fear crossed Miller's face. He looked around the barn, first to Castillo, then Hunter, then Tanner and the few ranch hands who'd gathered across the room. Perhaps all this time he'd thought he was dealing with gentlemen like the ones he knew from Boston. He probably had no idea who they really were and the things they had done. They'd questioned men before, tougher men than Miller.

Cursing under his breath, Miller sighed and told him the names of the men Derringer had done business with back in Boston. "Best I can tell he faked his death a few years ago to get out of some gambling debts. He disappeared from Boston, but he didn't stop siphoning money from me. A couple of times a year he'd demand a bank transfer or he claimed he'd contact my father. It wasn't much, at first. But then he demanded more and more. He agreed to one final payoff. I couldn't track him down to demand he stop his foolishness, so I had no choice but to find a wealthy bride." Miller sniffed, a look of downright hate crossing his features. "After that night in the whorehouse—the night I saw you—his son, Bennett, came to my hotel to meet with me. He told me he's been looking for you and asked me to help him lure you out."

Castillo steeled himself against the disappointment roiling within him. Though this was as close as they'd come to Derringer, the story felt just like all the other stories they'd heard over the years. Someone knew Derringer, but had no real way to find him. Now the hunt could take him back to Boston to find some men who possibly knew him, just to come back out West again. It was a never-ending journey, and he was tired. So damned tired. "Do you have any idea where Derringer is hiding?"

Miller shook his head. "If I did I'd have gone to find him myself."

Despite this new information, Derringer was still out of reach. Though maybe knowing his real identity would give them a better place to start with their search. Castillo sighed. "Help me find Derringer and we'll get you out of your debt. No one has to know."

Miller hesitated, glanced around the room again and nodded

his consent.

Castillo let out a breath and thought of the woman who had come to mean more to him than he'd thought was possible in such a short time. What had she done with her hasty decision to defend him? Would Derringer try to hurt her now? He didn't know, and the frustration of that was threatening to eat him up inside.

Tanner rose to his feet and grabbed his cane, leaving Hunter to deal with Miller. "Come on, Castillo. I suspect we have some people anxious to talk with us inside."

Castillo had no doubt that was true, and followed Tanner out into the night. They were halfway across the yard to the house before Tanner broke the silence between them.

"I'm disappointed you didn't come to me about this Derringer situation, son."

"I'm not in the habit of coming to you with my problems."

Tanner sighed, his shoulders slouching in a dejected manner. "I know, and I know that's my fault. But I want to be better, Castillo."

They'd just reached the porch and he turned to look at Castillo from the bottom step. The house was quiet, and Castillo hoped that meant everyone had gone to bed. Everyone except Carolina and her parents. He knew they'd be waiting up for him.

"Marisol and I grew apart. We probably never should've married in the first place."

Castillo gave him a mirthless smile. "I've done the figuring. I realize I was born six months after your wedding. You don't have to explain to me why you married her."

Tanner gave him a solemn look. "That wasn't your fault, and it's no excuse for the father I've been to you. I sent letters and money and did everything but come down there myself. I know I could've tried harder when you were younger. I should've tried harder. Part of me thought it would be better for you if you didn't have me in your life confusing everything. There wasn't a day that went by that I didn't think about you."

"It's better you didn't come. Papá had given orders you were to be shot on sight." Castillo tried to make light of the situation, because he'd actually always assumed Tanner had never thought of him. Why would he think of a little boy he'd left behind when he had all this?

Tanner laughed. "I'm not surprised. Your grandfather always hated me." Then he sobered and continued, "I want you to know that I will always support you. I don't want you putting yourself at risk when I could help you."

"It's not your problem." Castillo began, but Tanner shook his head.

"You are mine, Castillo, whether you want to be or not. My blood is in your veins. You are my son." Then he took a deep breath and glanced toward the quiet house. "We don't need to talk about the shootout and this Derringer situation right now, but I do need to know what we're planning to do about this."

He pointed toward the door. "Was Caroline lying to give you an alibi?"

Castillo hesitated before answering. "I wasn't with her...not that day."

"She'd risk her reputation for you when she wasn't even with you?" Tanner raised his brow.

Castillo knew at that moment that whatever barriers he was trying to keep between them would crumble beneath the force of her. He loved her. There was no maybe. He loved her. But he needed to keep her safe. That was the most important thing. And she wouldn't be safe with him.

Tanner cleared his throat. "What do you plan to do about this situation?"

Castillo shook his head, still no closer to an answer. "The safest place for her is far away from me."

Prudence stepped out the front door and drew up short when she saw them. "My apologies for interrupting, gentlemen. Caroline's parents have asked to speak with you."

***

Caroline couldn't sit there any longer and fidget under her parents' scrutiny. She rose and paced near the bookshelves on the opposite side of the room. It kept her parents from staring at her and for a few minutes that was enough. Then she started thinking of how angry Castillo had looked when she'd last seen him. Would he be angry when he came to the study? She didn't know what would happen and started fidgeting all over again.

The only thing she did know was that she didn't want to face him for the first time since the incident with her parents present. She wanted to talk to him alone first. With that goal in mind, she slipped out the door of the study and waited in the shadowed hallway. It was quiet and she hoped that Emmy had herded all the guests off to bed. She didn't have to wait long before she heard their boots clicking on the hardwood floor.

Squaring her shoulders, she held her breath as Mr. Jameson, Castillo and Aunt Prudie came around the corner. Mr. Jameson inclined his head and gave her a gentle smile.

"I'd like to speak with Castillo alone for a minute first." Caroline let her gaze float to each of them, briefly taking in Castillo's unreadable expression, before looking back at Mr. Jameson. "If that's all right," she added.

Mr. Jameson looked to Aunt Prudie, who nodded. "I think that'll be fine, dear. You have a lot to talk about. Don't keep them waiting too long, though." When Caroline gave her agreement, Mr. Jameson opened the door for her aunt, and then followed her inside the room.

Caroline's breath nearly squeezed from her chest when they were left alone in the hallway. She wasn't certain of what to say now, but she didn't have to wait long for Castillo to start.

"Why did you do that?" The words were low and rough, pulled from deep in his chest.

She wanted to hold him, but held herself back. "I didn't know how much he knew. I didn't want anyone to suspect you."

"That's not your concern."

She frowned up at him. "How can you think that it's not my concern? I'm not the only one who feels what's happening between us...am I?" What if she was? She didn't think that was true, given how he looked at her and touched her, but what if it was?

He stared down at her, unmoving in his anger, and she didn't know what to think. Finally, he relented, and a little bit of the tension left his shoulders. "No, you're not the only one, but it doesn't matter. This can't happen, Carolina. No matter how I feel or how you feel, we can't happen."

She nodded, a little relieved that his objection wasn't an emotional one. If it was simply an issue of logistics, then she could understand. "I know that it won't be easy. I know we're not an ideal couple, but I think we can figure it out."

He exhaled a breath and shook his head. "You don't understand."

"What is there to understand? I—"

He took her hand and laced his fingers with hers before pulling her farther down the hallway, away from the study doors. His boots thumped over the thick rug and he turned his back to the rest of the world, blocking her in against the wall.

"I'm a wanted man." He kept his voice low.

"Oh, that." She nearly laughed because she thought he was going to say something far worse. "I think, once the facts are known, that the shootout will be seen as justifiable. You were defending yourself. But as of now, no one knows about it, and I won't tell anyone you were involved."

It was too shadowed in the hallway to see his eyes clearly, but he stared down at her so intensely she was certain that she was missing some vital piece of information. His next words confirmed it. "It's not just the shootout. That's bad enough, but there have been others. I'm the leader of a gang known as the Reyes Brothers. Have you heard of us?"

She searched her memory but couldn't remember reading about them in the newspaper. "No. What do you mean by gang?"

"The hacienda was in trouble before my grandfather was murdered. There were rustlers, hired by ranchers in the area, taking our cattle and selling them across the border. I, along with some of our hands, went and took them back. Pretty soon we were being hired by other small ranches for protection, and the lines began to get blurred. Then Derringer entered the picture and I've spent the past few years looking for him. We've made enemies and sometimes we've had to kill those enemies. Sometimes self-defense looks a lot like murder."

At some point her heart had begun to pound so hard against her ribs she thought it might actually try to force its way out of her chest. He was telling her he was a bad man, but what she had seen with her own eyes was completely different. "I don't believe you're bad."

"Carolina, I'm telling you I'm a very bad, very dangerous

man. It's the truth."

She touched his cheek to keep her connected to him. No matter what he said, he was the same man who had been so tender with her. Though she couldn't see them now, every time she looked into his eyes, she saw an honest man. "I believe that you think that. But I only know what I see with my own eyes. You aren't a bad person, Castillo. You're kind and brave and honorable."

He sighed, and she sensed even more of the tension leave his body. "None of that will save you from the bad things that I've done. I can't bring you into my life. It's too dangerous." He brushed a strand of hair back from her cheek and tilted her head up a little. "If you're connected to me, Derringer could find you and use you against me. I can't allow that to happen."

"It's too late for that. I'm already connected to you." Whether anyone else knew it, she was connected to him far more deeply than she'd ever realized was possible. When he hurt, she hurt. It was why she'd opened her mouth to protect him without even thinking through the consequences.

He groaned and slanted his mouth over hers, driving his tongue into her mouth in a kiss of possession that left her breathless. Careful of his wound, she curled her arms around his shoulders and pressed closer to him. Already his body was so familiar to her, a safe place where she felt protected and loved. When he pulled back, they were both breathing hard, his hand warm on her hip, while the fingers of his other hand wrapped lightly around the nape of her neck.

Finally, he spoke. "You're right. You're already connected to me, and it's too late to change that." Taking a deep breath, he added, "Then I suppose you need to decide what you want to happen now."

She was too dazed from his kiss to think clearly. "What do you mean?"

"We have two options." He waited for her to meet his gaze before continuing, and his fingers tightened on her a little. "We walk in there and tell your parents we're getting married, or you leave here a compromised woman."

Her mouth dropped open in a silent gasp. "Married?"

Castillo nodded, the pad of his thumb running over her bottom lip. "Yes. The way I see it when the guests leave here they'll take their gossip with them and our names will be connected whether we want them to be or not. Derringer could hear about it and come for you. At least with my name—the Jameson name—I hope you can be protected."

Oh. She didn't know why, but her heart fell a little. Their marriage would be for her protection and nothing more. He must have seen her hesitation, because he hurried to continue.

"I'll make certain nothing stands in the way of your going to school."

She nodded.

"Do you think your parents will approve of me?" he asked.

She remembered his uncertainty that first night in her room, and it nearly broke her heart. "My father likes you, Castillo."

He caught her omission and prompted, "And your mother?"

"She likes you, too, but she's a traditionalist. And you're a Jameson and not Boston Society."

He nodded. "I have money for tuition. Tanner bought a silver mine in my name. I used some of the profits to pay for Miguel's tuition, and I would gladly use it for you."

She nodded and looked down, but he gently tipped her face back up with his fingers on her chin. "Carolina?"

"So it would be a marriage of convenience...as they say?" She tried to smile but was certain whatever she'd mustered fell far short.

"If that's what they name it." He nodded. "I just want you to know that you're taken care of."

She didn't know why she was hesitating. It was the perfect solution to her problems and she was already half in love with him. Pain twisted her heart and she had to admit the truth. No. She was in love with him all the way. That was why she hesitated. Could she stand to have him—but not have all of him?

Chapter Eighteen

S he was marrying Castillo. She would be his wife.

Though two days had passed since the arrangement had been made, Caroline was no closer to processing that fact. She felt anxious and excited in equal measure. Both emotions were wrapped up in a tangled mess that made her feel elated one minute and nauseated the next.

"You make a beautiful bride, Caro," Aunt Prudie said from the doorway of Caroline's bedroom.

"Thank you." Caroline had to admit she agreed. She never was one to look at herself and see beauty, but she was having trouble tearing herself away from her reflection in the looking glass. All she could think was that Castillo would approve. She couldn't wait to see his face when he saw her.

Emmy surprised her with the cream-colored dress first thing that morning. She'd had it pressed and waiting. Caroline hadn't even bothered to argue against accepting it. She had wanted the elegant confection of silk and lace the moment Emmy had brought it in. Having resigned herself to a serviceable traveling costume as a wedding gown, she was beside herself to have something of actual beauty to wear when she became Castillo's bride.

"Do you think he'll like it?" she asked.

Aunt Prudie laughed. "Of course he will, but that man would have you if you were wearing a burlap sack."

The imagery was enough to snap the spell of the looking glass. "Aunt Prudie." She turned and smiled at the woman.

"He is in love with you," she said unequivocally.

"He's not—"

"He is. Castillo Jameson is not one to give his heart easily, but he has given it to you." Aunt Prudie fussed over Caroline's curls that Mary had painstakingly pinned up so they would stay in place during the carriage ride to town where the justice of the peace would marry them. Finished adjusting, her aunt touched Caroline's chin. "Now, I presume you know all about what to expect tonight, but I'm here if you have any questions."

Caroline's face flamed. "Oh, I don't think...I mean, I do know what happens on wedding nights, but I don't think Castillo plans...it is a marriage of convenience." He hadn't made any attempt to talk with her privately since the other night. He most certainly had not come to her room, no matter how late she had waited up for him. It felt as if he'd put a boundary between them. She didn't think he had any intention of consummating their marriage.

Her aunt raised a doubtful brow. "I have seen the way he looks at you."

If it was possible, her cheeks burned hotter. "What do you mean?"

"At the wedding yesterday, he could barely keep his eyes off you, dear."

Caroline didn't think that was true, but it pleased her that it might be. Her stomach tumbled pleasantly at the idea of spending the night with him tonight.

"I assume with medical school in a couple of months that you do not intend to carry a child now?" Aunt Prudie asked.

"No, we haven't decided things, but now is not the time for a child." Her entire future seemed to be up in the air. There was medical school, but she had no idea what followed. Divorce? The idea pained her. Castillo injured by his nemesis, or worse?

Her aunt nodded. "Then you must take precautions."

"I don't think precautions are necessary, but in the event that…" That Castillo wanted to. "I do have a tin…in my medical bag." She couldn't say the word to her aunt.

"Good. Good. Then we should head downstairs. I believe everyone is gathered on the veranda."

A soft knock sounded at the door. Aunt Prudie raised her

brow again and gave Caroline a kiss on the cheek before going to answer it. Anticipation shimmered down her spine when she heard Castillo's voice.

"Could I have a moment with Carolina?" he asked.

"Of course, I'll await you both downstairs with the others." Her aunt swept out of the room and Caroline met her groom at the door.

His eyes widened in appreciation when he saw her and he took the length of her in, all the way down to her toes and back up again. "You're beautiful."

"You look very handsome in a suit." She hadn't been able to tell him that yesterday at the wedding. Somehow she had lost her words in between their engagement and now. But it was true. His shoulders seemed impossibly broad and the fine fabric brought out the green in his eyes and the olive tone of his skin.

He grinned, revealing a flash of white teeth, but it was gone almost as quickly as it had appeared. "I've come to make certain that this is what you want. It's not too late, if you aren't sure."

That was the last thing she wanted. Her claim on him was tenuous at best, but she wanted him in her life. Needed him, if she was honest. She loved him now and there was no turning back on that. "I am certain. But if you—"

He was smiling before she could finish asking if he wanted to call off the wedding. Reaching up, he stroked her cheekbone with his thumb, sending a flutter through her belly. "This is what I want."

He wanted her. He hadn't said it, but that's what that statement meant.

Before she could answer him, he said, "I have a ring, so don't concern yourself with that. I am more than ready to make you my wife. Let's go."

He offered her his arm and she took it, allowing him to lead her into this brand new start.

***

No one had been more surprised than Castillo when he'd offered to marry her. In that startling moment of clarity, he'd realized that the only way to really keep her safe—from scandal and her family interfering in her education—was to keep her under his protection. The meeting with her parents had been very brief and to the point. Her parents had agreed to the marriage as an inevitable consequence of her admission, but they weren't happy about it. Castillo suspected her mother wanted someone more socially acceptable, but her father seemed content as soon as Castillo had voiced his opinion about Carolina's education.

Hunter and Emmy had offered a double wedding, but Castillo had refused. He told them that he didn't want to take away from their ceremony. The truth was, he wanted Carolina all to himself. Despite the fact that his marriage to her was supposed to be little more than an arrangement, he'd wanted the moment they took their vows to be for her alone and not shared with another couple.

He'd barely seen her since the night in Tanner's study. Hunter's wedding had been the day before, and Carolina had sat with her parents while Castillo and Zane had stood at Hunter's side. Then he'd had to go back out and ride the property, ever vigilant to the possibility that Derringer could make an appearance. The few times he'd made eye contact with her, she'd smiled but looked away as if unsure of herself.

This morning was the first time they had really spoken. It had taken all he could do not to pull her into his arms and kiss her in the doorway of her bedroom. Instead, he escorted her outside and to the carriage where her family waited and then ridden outside to keep watch for Derringer.

Derringer. It always came back to him. Castillo had to get her safely to Boston as soon as possible, but he couldn't think about not seeing her again. Not yet. Not when they had the rest of the day and tonight.

Already apprised of their arrival, the justice of the peace ushered them into his office, a small, stuffy room that everyone barely fit inside. "Welcome, welcome," he greeted them.

Carolina found her way to Castillo's side and slid her hand in his. He gave it a squeeze. Though his heart was beating faster than the hooves of a galloping horse, he was certain that this was right. He wanted her in every way a man could want a woman and for more than he'd let on. More than the years it would take her to get through school.

"Let's get started," the man said a moment later when the

door closed and took his place standing behind his desk. "We are gathered today to join Castillo Jameson and Caroline Hartford in marriage."

Minutes later, Castillo was sliding his mother's ring onto her finger. The room was silent after he'd voiced his vows. Giving her hand a gentle squeeze, he stared into her eyes, hoping that she knew that he meant them. He would love her and honor her even though he still hadn't the slightest idea how to actually be with her. He searched her eyes for some hint of regret or sorrow—this couldn't possibly be the wedding she'd imagined for herself—but all he saw was hope and an emotion he couldn't identify shining out at him. Part of him wanted to call it love, but—

"I now pronounce you man and wife." The words penetrated Castillo's thoughts, bringing with them a well of emotion that swelled in his chest and made it ache.

Carolina smiled up at him. Shyness and nervousness was evident in that smile, but she wasn't uncertain. She tightened her hold on his hand until her father shoved in between them to shake his hand. She stepped back out of the way, but her gaze didn't leave Castillo's until her aunt pulled her into an embrace, blocking her view of him. Castillo mumbled words to Hunter, Zane, Tanner and her father, but he couldn't stop looking at her. He couldn't believe that she was his—that this amazing woman had agreed to become his wife.

Wife. He knew he shouldn't get too attached to the word

because this was only a marriage of convenience, but he liked it. He liked it a lot.

They were back on the boardwalk outside the office in the late afternoon sun a few minutes later. Castillo found he didn't quite know what to say to her and suspected that she felt the same. Instead of speaking, he offered her his arm and they followed their families to the Baroness. Tanner had booked rooms for the group since Carolina and her family would leave for Boston the next morning.

They had a meal together in the hotel's dining room. Tanner ordered champagne and made a big fuss about toasts and the importance of families, and for a brief moment Castillo found himself believing him. If he forgot the past and the future, he could believe that Carolina was his wife in every way.

Caught up in the moment, Hunter swigged his champagne and pulled Emmy in for a kiss, and everyone laughed. Their joy and obvious love for each other was easy to see. Castillo laughed, too, and for the first time didn't feel that pang of envy. When he glanced at Carolina she was smiling, but she'd been watching him. Her gaze dipped down to his mouth and a spark of heat leaped between them. He wanted to pull her into his arms, but he didn't know if that was what she wanted.

When the meal came to an end, Tanner not-so-subtly suggested they retire for the evening. Castillo agreed because he was greedy to spend time alone with her before she left, no matter what the night would bring. Castillo pushed the door of their suite open and followed her inside. She was beautiful in a cream dress that hugged her figure and flared out softly in the back. Its skirt was pulled up to reveal a matching underskirt that swished past her ankles. Her back was straight and her shoulders squared, as if she, too, was suddenly uncertain and doing everything she could to hold that uncertainty at bay. She looked feminine and strong.

This was the first time they'd been alone since his proposal in the hallway and he didn't quite know what to say to her. She was his wife. The weight of that settled over him again, but it wasn't suffocating. It was warm and strangely comforting. He tried not to examine it too much. After all, this wasn't real. His life was finding Derringer, and then his life would be at the hacienda. Hers was in Boston, somewhere there was no place for him. They hadn't spoken of what would happen after she graduated, but he had no right to expect her to come live with him.

Her trunk had been delivered earlier and she walked over to it as if to change her clothes, but stopped once she reached it, uncertainty had crept in.

"I'll give you some time alone," he said awkwardly, walking into the connected washroom and closing the door behind him. The room was small, but serviceable, with gleaming white tile. It was hot, so he shrugged out of his coat and waistcoat, and hung them on the hook on the back of the door. As soon as he did, the weight he hadn't realized he'd been carrying around left him and he leaned his palms on the cool porcelain of the sink. This marriage felt real. Staring at his reflection in the small shaving mirror, he saw that his eyes were wide and unsure. He'd stared down men holding him at gunpoint, but this woman who was now his wife scared him.

His wife. Something tightened deep in his gut as a vivid memory of her spread out on her bed flashed behind his eyes. He could have her now, because she was his. His stomach dipped at the thought of the night ahead. Should he have offered her a room of her own? Mierda. Turning the knob of the faucet, he splashed cold water on his face. He had no right to expect anything to happen, and he didn't. He should've asked her if she wanted her own room. Grabbing a towel from the stand, he dried his face and turned to go back to her. He'd tell her she could stay and he'd go find another room.

Grabbing his clothes from the hook, he slung them over his arm and opened the door. She sat on the velvet upholstered bench under the window, staring down at the ring he'd given her. He paused to admire her, his gaze lingering on the delicate slope of her neck, but she looked up and caught him. The soft light of dusk painted her in a warm glow. She still wore the simple but beautiful cream dress she'd said had come from Emmy.

"I didn't expect anything like this." She smiled, holding up her hand so he could see the ring. "It's too much."

It was a delicate gold band with a ruby surrounded by small diamonds. "My grandfather gave that to my grandmother on their wedding day nearly fifty years ago, and then it became my mother's. Now it's yours." He'd carried it around since his mother died, with the expectation that one day he'd find a woman to give it to. But with everything that had happened with his grandfather, he'd begun to doubt that day would come.

"Oh." She turned her hand around so she could look at it again. "I didn't expect to get anything so precious from you. I hope you don't feel obligated—"

"It's not obligation, mi corazón. I want you to have it." He walked toward her, dropping his coat and waistcoat on the foot of the bed as he passed by. Coming to a stop before her, he dropped down on his haunches and took her hand. The ring looked perfect on her finger, and he couldn't help the pride that welled up within him when he saw it. "It's beautiful on you."

"I'll treasure it." She gave him a shy smile and closed her fingers around his. "But...I want you to know that..." Her gaze skittered off to the side and she took a breath. "If you want it back some day, I'll understand."

Her words hit him like a knife in the chest, reminding him anew that this was just an arrangement. They'd spoken the vows, but they hadn't meant for them to be real. He rose to his feet, but she didn't release his hand. His leather satchel with a change of clothes sat next to her trunk, mocking him. "I wasn't thinking clearly when we checked in downstairs, but the room is yours. I can go and see if they have another room."

"No, Castillo, that's not what I meant." She tightened her

grip on his hand. "Forgive me, I don't know the rules. I only meant that if..." She laughed, releasing the tension that held her back rigid. "I don't know what I mean. I'm nervous."

Something about her anxiety relaxed him. Brushing a strand of golden hair from her cheek, he smiled back at her. "You don't want your own room?" But he knew the answer without her even saying it. She sobered and her eyes darkened as her gaze dropped to his mouth.

His entire body tightened in response, heat prickled down his spine.

"No, I don't want my own room." She licked her lips and her gaze flicked to the bed and back. "I'd hoped that since we're married now you'd want to...."

Chapter Nineteen

Desire flared to life inside Castillo, fierce and raw and undeniable. His blood thickened and rushed downward, tightening his trousers. Still, he stopped himself from touching her because he had to ask, "Are you certain?"

"Yes." Her eyes were so vivid and earnest they pierced his soul. "I've never been more certain of anything in my entire life."

His heart slammed against his ribcage as he leaned forward and finally took her mouth the way he'd wanted to ever since she'd said "I do." Cupping her face in his hands, he tasted her sweetness, drawing a tiny moan from her lips when he pulled away to look at her. She was so beautiful, so sweet, so strong and perfect he could hardly believe she was his. He ignored the little voice in his head reminding him that she wasn't really his, that he hurt everyone close to him, and kissed her again. Now that he knew he could take her, that nothing was stopping him from being inside her, he couldn't stop kissing her.

His mouth drank from hers as his fingers went for the tiny buttons on the back of her dress. She flattened herself against his front, her palm moving down to find him hard and throbbing in his trousers. A groan escaped him before he could call it back. She squeezed him, moving her fingers along his length from root to tip. He remembered the last time she'd touched him and the innocently wicked things she'd said to him as she'd explored.

One night wouldn't be enough. He dragged his mouth from hers only so he could turn her around and attack the damn row of buttons. With each one he unfastened, he placed a kiss on the bare skin he revealed until her undergarments obstructed him. Finally, he pulled the bodice down her shoulders and she shrugged her arms out of it, pushing it over her hips. His fingers shook as he unlaced her corset. He'd never wanted a woman this much before, and it had nothing to do with the fact that she was innocent or that he hadn't had her yet. It was because this was his Carolina.

He was breathing like he'd just run a mile, but he forced himself to go slowly and pulled the laces with gentle strength, not the brute force he wanted to use. When he'd finished, she pulled it off and he grabbed her shift, pulling it over her head. She turned, her arms going up to cover her breasts, but he pulled her against his chest and her arms went around him instead. He could feel her hard nipples pressing into him through his shirt. His hands roved down the silken skin of her back and cupped her buttocks through the thin cotton of her drawers, squeezing her and pulling her toward him. His erection throbbed and he couldn't resist grinding against her to ease the ache.

She gasped against his mouth, breaking the kiss, and he picked her up in his arms and walked over to the bed. Grabbing the edge of the counterpane, he pulled it back before dropping her onto the downy sheets. Toeing off his shoes, he shrugged out of his suspenders and unbuttoned his shirt. Her eyes were ravenous as she watched him, and he loved that she wanted to see him. His left arm still hurt, and she must've known, because she rose to her knees and helped him slip his shirt off his shoulders and tugged it free of his hands to toss it aside.

He couldn't resist another kiss, dragging his tongue along her plump bottom lip. She surprised him by nipping at him and smiling when he pulled back. God, he loved her. She was such a contradiction, and she'd keep him guessing for the rest of his life, if they got that much time. His fingers went to the tie on her drawers, yanking it free before pushing the fabric down her hips, desperate to see her. A blush stained her cheeks pink, but she sat back and allowed him to pull them off her, and then she made quick work of her stockings.

Castillo unfastened his pants but paused before pushing them down. Making his way to his satchel, he rummaged for the tin he'd brought. He hadn't been certain that anything would happen tonight, but he'd hoped—he'd hoped—and he'd wanted to be prepared. Coming back to stand beside the bed, he dropped the tin on the nightstand beside her spectacles.

She saw it and her eyes widened in surprise. "You brought prophylactics?"

He nodded, a little unsure if her surprise was because she hadn't expected him to bring them or because she didn't want to use them. "I hope that's okay. I know neither of us wants this to result in a child."

She grinned and rose to her knees. "Thank you for thinking of that. I have some in my medical bag, too."

Then he couldn't think anymore because her palms were running over his chest and down over his flat stomach to the open fastening of his pants. He sucked in a breath when she reached in and gripped him. Her hand was so small and tight around him that his eyes nearly rolled back in his head from the pleasure. "Carolina," he whispered.

"I think it's time to open the tin." Her voice was husky and soft as she stroked him.

"Are you certain? Are you ready?"

She nodded, and he yanked the lid off and grabbed one. She pushed his trousers down over his buttocks and her eyes widened as she saw him fully erect. Her fingertips trailed down his length almost reverently, making him shudder in pleasure. "I'll go slowly," he assured her.

She smiled at him, and though it was a shy smile, she moved

back to lie against the pillows. "Hurry."

He gritted his teeth against the need to have her and forced himself to look away from her as he rolled it down his length. Then he moved over her, fitting himself between her thighs. Catching himself to keep the bulk of his weight from her, he stroked her with his other hand. She was so hot and wet he could barely contain the tremor that moved through him. He pushed a finger inside her, gently stretching her before adding another. She moaned softly and rolled her hips, making his fingers move in and out of her. She felt ready, but he'd never taken a virgin before and wanted to make sure he didn't hurt her any more than necessary. Leaning down, he took her nipple into his mouth, alternating between rolling it with his tongue and sucking it deep into his mouth.

When she yanked his hair and called his name again and again, he knew she was close. Moving over her, he held her knees wide and notched the head of his shaft at her slick opening. She stared up at him with heavy-lidded eyes and arched her hips up toward him. He pressed forward, moving deeper inch by excruciating inch so he wouldn't hurt her, when all he wanted to do was sheath himself inside her. She groaned, a soft cry of pleasure deep in her throat that turned into something more intense when he hit the barrier of her innocence. His throat ached with an emotion he was too overwhelmed to examine. This amazing woman was his. An instinct both sacred and primal roared through his blood.

He fell over her, catching himself on his uninjured arm as he kissed her deeply and then trailed his lips across her cheek. When he reached her ear, he scraped his teeth against the soft lobe and whispered, "Are you ready for me, Carolina?"

"Yes." It was a barely coherent gasp as she clutched him, her fingernails raking down his back. But he couldn't hold back anymore and thrust forward, driving deep in one stroke. She cried out softly against his neck, and he stilled, holding her against him.

"I won't move until you're ready," he assured her. He closed his eyes to fight against the pleasure of her body gripping him so tightly. She felt perfect beneath him. When he regained a little control, he reached between them to stroke her just above where they were joined. Soon she was shifting against him, anxious for more friction.

"Castillo," she whispered against his ear.

Finally, he moved inside her. First in a gentle rhythm and then with deeper thrusts that had her writhing beneath him. She cried out when the first wave of her release came over her. Her fingernails bit into his back, but he welcomed the sting and held her tighter as he gave himself over to his own pleasure. Just moments later, he found his release within her.

**

Hours later the huge bed was littered with the remnants of a meal they'd ordered and fed each other, and she slept at his side. Castillo couldn't remember ever enjoying a night the way he'd enjoyed this one. It wasn't just the sex, though that had been better than any he could recall. It was the way she'd felt in his arms, like he was home. It was the way she'd smiled at him as she'd fed him a slice of apple, while telling him a story about sneaking into the kitchen as a child and eating two whole pies and making herself sick. Being with her was natural.

There were still hours until dawn, but he couldn't stop looking at her. He didn't want to sleep because he knew it'd be a long time before he saw her again. If he saw her again. The plan had been to part in the morning, and they'd thought no further. But how could he not see her again? How could he not have her in his life?

The thoughts bothered him, but he had no answers. Absently twirling a strand of her golden hair around his finger, he reasoned that he had plenty of time to sleep after she was gone.

She stirred, rolling forward so she lay on her tummy, and tucked herself against him. Pulling the blanket up over her back, he leaned forward and placed a kiss on her temple.

"You're not sleeping," she whispered without opening her eyes.

"I don't want to miss anything."

"Neither do I," she replied, opening her eyes to look at him. Only a sliver of moonlight came through the window to light the room.

"Go back to sleep. You're tired."

She laughed and kissed his hand. "So are you. That was an

excellent performance earlier."

He couldn't help but touch her and stroked a hand down her back to settle over one of the plump cheeks of her bottom. "Glad you approve."

"Of course I approve. I've married an amazing lover."

He laughed and kissed her nose, her mouth, her chin. He couldn't stop kissing her. He loved her. The idea of waking up without her by his side was abhorrent, but it was also unavoidable.

Maybe it was the dark mood of his thoughts, but they drifted into silence, their hands clasped beneath the blanket. Finally, she broke the silence. "What will we do, Castillo? I don't want to leave you tomorrow."

"Boston is safer than here." He took a deep breath and tucked his arm beneath her, pulling her onto his chest. "And you have school in September…"

"And you still have to find Derringer." She finished the thought for him.

He nodded once and kissed her head. "I do."

She didn't say anything for a moment but he could practically hear her thoughts churning. "What about after you find him? What will you do then?"

"Go back to Texas and work on restoring the house. Miguel needs something to come home to." The thought of his home didn't evoke the same pride and conviction that it used to. He thought of it and he thought of a place cold and distant. A place she would never call home because she had much grander plans than to be the mistress in charge of feeding the small army of ranch hands they'd need when he got the place back to what it had been. He couldn't blame her for that. With her talent and education, she'd be far more useful as a physician, but tonight he'd found himself hoping that things could be different.

"What..." Her fingers splayed over his heart, and she subtly rubbed her cheek against his chest. "What about after?"

He gave a grim smile though she couldn't see it. "There is no after. Once the house is restored, I'll need to get new cattle and new equipment, and work toward earning a profit."

She took in a breath, but it was shaky, and he thought she might be fighting back tears. Tightening his arms around her, he swallowed against the sudden ache in his throat. The future he described was bleak and gray. It was nothing without her in it.

"Do you think you might ever come and see me in Boston?"

The ache swelled, expanding into an unbearable pressure behind his eyes and deep in his chest. "I don't know, Carolina. I can't make any plans past finding Derringer."

She nodded as if she understood, but he felt the warm wetness of her tears against his chest. Abruptly she sat up, surprising him by leaning over him. "I don't know what will happen, but I want you to know that I love you. No, don't say anything. Don't tell me I shouldn't. It's too late for that." She covered his mouth with her fingertips. "I love how brave and honorable you are. I

275

love that you love your grandfather enough to sacrifice years of your life to this, but I hate that it's keeping us apart."

His heart swelled two sizes in his chest. Taking her hand in his, he sat up and settled her onto his lap and put his arms around her. "That's not all that's keeping us apart. I told you I've done bad things. Besides that, you belong in Boston and I belong out here. No matter how I wish that weren't true, it is. We can't change it."

She stared at him as if it pained her. "But can't we...if we really wanted to?"

Castillo closed his eyes against the pain he saw in hers. He loved her. He loved her with all his heart, which was why he knew that sending her away from him was the best thing to do. She had dreams in Boston. There was nothing for her out here, and the only thing for him in Boston was her. His dreams were in Texas. "I care for you, but our lives are too different, mi corazón. It wouldn't work."

"If you think that, then you couldn't possibly love me the way I love you."

"Shh...don't say that." He drew her into his arms and held her. The problem was that he was very much afraid that he did love her that much. He loved her enough that he didn't know how he was going to say goodbye to her in the morning. He loved her enough that he knew he had to.

Chapter Twenty

Castillo woke her up the next morning with kisses and murmured love words in Spanish. She opened her eyes to his tousled head and smiling eyes.

"I need you again," he mumbled against her neck as his fingers skimmed up and down her body.

She needed him, too, and held him against her. Carolina had laid her heart before him last night, and he'd not taken it. She refused to let the bitterness of that come between them. How could she be bitter about his refusal to give up his dream when she wasn't able to give up hers? Maybe Aunt Prudie was right. Maybe this was the point where she had to have faith that it would work out. Somehow.

"I need you, too," she whispered and savored his groan as he moved between her thighs.

Blindly, she reached for the tin on the bedside table and pulled out the last prophylactic. He raised up enough so that she could reach between them and help him slide it on, and then he fell over her. They made love gently and slowly. He lingered over her, careful of the tenderness of her untried body. Neither one of them were willing to deny themselves the pleasure of just one more time before she left. Once it was over, they held each other, barely speaking lest something break the spell of their love. Finally when it was time, they helped each other dress.

As they left the hotel and walked the few blocks to the train station, he slipped his hand into hers and gave it a squeeze. She smiled as the warm comfort of his presence filled in all the hollows in her body. Gazing up at his profile, she noted his strong jaw with the bit of scruff he hadn't bothered to shave that morning. The memory of how it had rasped the skin of her breasts as he'd moved over her made her blush. It didn't seem fair that this beautiful man was her husband and she'd only have the one night with him. It didn't seem fair that he was hers, but not as much as she was his.

He felt her watching and looked down at her, giving her a half smile. "You know, I've been thinking." His boots thudded on the wooden planks of the boardwalk with each step. She thought she'd remember the cadence of his step for as long as she lived.

"About what?" she asked when he paused.

"I spent so much time worried about your virginity...and here we are, married with a proper deflowering on our wedding night." The smile stayed intact while his heavy gaze raked down to her lips.

She knew she was blushing at his crude words even as they pulled a laugh from her. She couldn't seem to stop blushing around him. "Maybe next time you'll listen to me," she quipped.

He threw back his head and laughed. When his eyes met hers again, they were filled with so much emotion that a lump welled in her throat. The train's sharp whistle cut through the air with the quarter-hour warning. The hotel had sent her trunk ahead hours ago, but only now did leaving feel real to her. She hadn't even realized they'd come to a stop on the boardwalk until his fingertips touched her face and ran across her bottom lip. His touch was heated, awakening all the nerve endings that had been slumbering, sated from their night together.

"Oh, Carolina," he whispered, his eyes heavy lidded and dark.

Someone jostled past them, prompting him to take her arm and lead her to an abandoned storefront, set into the corner of the brick building. They were only a block from the station now, where her parents and Aunt Prudie were waiting for her. Pushing her back against the paper-covered glass window, he kissed her. It was a proper goodbye kiss filled with passion and longing, a tender reminder of how they'd passed their wedding night.

"Come with me," she whispered when they broke apart to catch their breaths. "We have the money my father settled on me. We can find a little house near the university." She wasn't certain Castillo had even read the paperwork he'd signed yesterday. Her father had settled a healthy amount of money on them with their marriage. It wouldn't last indefinitely, but it'd be enough to last them for a few years. She knew how he felt about his father and the silver mine. He wouldn't have to touch that if he didn't want to. She pressed her hands against his chest, trying her best to memorize how he felt against her. The memories would have to last.

"I cannot." His voice was low and he'd closed his eyes, pressing his forehead against hers. "My life is here, and your life will be better without me in it." When he opened his eyes, she saw that he truly thought that.

Despite her resolve to not allow bitterness to overtake the morning, a shard of anger tore through her. "You're too stubborn to see how things could be so much better for us."

"I'm not stubborn, Carolina." He kept his voice calm and stroked her cheek. "I'm realistic."

The sting of tears prickled the backs of her eyes, but she refused to give in to them. They were little more than self-pity. The simple truth was that he didn't love her as much as she loved him. She shoved him away, intent on making her way to the train station alone. Better to get used to being without him now.

Before she'd gotten two steps past him, he grabbed her wrist and pulled her around so she fell into his chest, and he supported her with his back to the window, much the same as he had held her on the train. Only, this time, he was searching her face, looking for some answer when she didn't even know the question. He whispered her name again and kissed her, gripping her face gently with his hands.

She didn't see the man approach or sense his presence until it was too late.

**

Castillo opened his eyes to a world that had changed. Or maybe he was the one who'd changed. One moment he was holding Carolina in his arms and the next she'd been pulled away from him. He grabbed at her but was a second too late. Her eyes were wide with fear as she was whisked around the corner and into the alley, a large arm wrapped around her shoulders and pulling her away. He only got a glimpse of a dark shadow as she disappeared.

Pulling his gun from its holster, he bolted after her, rushing around the corner and into the alley. Derringer stood there, looking dirty and disheveled, his hair a bright beacon of white in the shadows, with her in his arms, the muzzle of his Colt .45 held against her temple. She gripped his forearm, her knuckles white as she tried to loosen his hold, but he only tightened his grip. Castillo's blood ran cold. He'd faced down enemies before and always managed to find a cold focus as he did it. It allowed him to stay calm and measure the outcomes of his choices before he acted.

Not this time. This time he couldn't see past the one outcome that scared the life out of him. Carolina's lifeless body lying on the dirty ground. Just thinking of it made his fingers numb.

"Stop where you are, Reyes." Derringer's voice was cultured, calm despite the fact that they were in an alley holding guns.

Castillo stopped, but he took in their surroundings, looking for a place someone could hide. The alley was littered with debris, a broken chair, a forgotten weather-beaten sign advertising an apothecary leaning against the brick wall, but there was nothing large enough to hide a man. He couldn't see the roof, though, so he figured that'd be the most likely spot for someone to be hiding, ready to unleash a hail of bullets. Derringer had probably been staked out all night waiting for his chance.

Damn, Castillo should've been more prepared instead of being so infatuated with his wife. He'd put her at risk because he couldn't keep his hands off her. She would die in an alley because of him.

"Put the gun down nice and slow." Derringer's tone was that of a man meeting a long-lost friend in a saloon. It didn't seem right. Something about this was very, very wrong.

"I can't do that, Buck. You need to let her go." Castillo gauged the distance between them to be about nine feet, give or take. He'd be able to reach Derringer quickly, but not before the man had a chance to pull the trigger.

"Put that gun down or I'll shoot her right now."

Derringer didn't betray impatience in his voice or demeanor. Castillo's only clue was the subtle tightening of the man's finger on the trigger. In the split second it took for Castillo to make that assessment, he realized that Derringer held everything that had ever mattered to Castillo in his arms—his hopes and dreams for a better future. Because if Castillo walked out of that alley without her, he wouldn't care about the hacienda or restoring the ranch to a profit. He only cared about Carolina. He wanted to know that she walked the Earth, that she was happy and cared for. In that moment, his quest for vengeance became a thing of the past.

"Don't hurt her, Buck. Please." His voice shook a little and he sent up a silent prayer. Take me, not her. Please, God, not her.

Derringer smiled, and then he laughed a little as if the joke was too funny not to. "Oh, I'm going to hurt her, Castillo. I'm going to hurt her so badly that she'll wish she was dead long before I get to that part." His eyes were cold under the brim of his bowler hat. He looked like madness. The wind picked up as if prompted by his words and blew through his shoulder-length, bright white hair.

Castillo's mouth went dry, but he knew if he dropped his gun he'd lose any chance he had to free her. "If you plan to kill her anyway, I'll keep my gun."

Derringer glanced down at Castillo's gun and back up before

cocking his own gun. The metallic click sent a cold chill down Castillo's spine.

"Figured you'd prefer the fast way." Derringer grinned and the muscle in his hand flexed.

Castillo couldn't get a clear shot, but that didn't matter. He only had a second to act, so he launched himself forward, planning to plow into them. The bang of a gun firing sounded loud in his ears as he fell forward. Carolina screamed.

Castillo landed hard on his knees, stunned that he couldn't move forward and uncertain about what had happened. Derringer crouched before him, blood spewing from behind the hand that cradled his nose. He groaned like an old man in the throes of death, but Castillo couldn't figure out how that had happened. Castillo hadn't shot the man. Derringer had shot. He'd seen the flash of Derringer's gun firing. The man still held that gun loosely as he cradled his nose.

The ringing in his ears faded enough that he could hear Carolina calling his name. "Castillo!" She landed on her knees beside him. He tightened his grip on his gun and put his other arm around her, trying to get her behind him. A searing pain shot through his side, like he'd been stabbed with a hot branding iron.

But he couldn't pay attention to that. Derringer was coming back to his senses, lowering his hands to show a nose that was slightly askew and spewing blood. Castillo realized that Carolina must have hit Derringer in the nose as he'd fired, likely breaking it from the amount of blood that poured out. The man raised his gun, but Castillo raised his first and fired three shots to Derringer's chest.

Then it was over. Dear God, all these years his life had been put on hold as he searched for this man...and it was over. Derringer fell backward, his arms splayed out wide. Castillo could only stare at him and wait for the triumph to find him. It didn't. It was over, and he felt relief, but there was no feeling of victory. Just a grim certainty that he'd accomplished his goal and a glimmer of satisfaction that Derringer would never hurt anyone else.

Dimly, he became aware of the strength leaving his body, but he couldn't focus on it. Carolina was at his side and her arms went around his shoulders. "Carolina," he said her name over and over as he gathered her in his arms. "Forgive me. I didn't know what was important until I saw him put that gun to your head. Please forgive me."

She clutched him back briefly and then tugged away to look down at his stomach. "We need to get you inside." She looked down the alley toward the street and then the other way.

"Carolina," he said again, reaching for her face. His arms felt like lead weights and he didn't understand why, but he needed to hear her forgive him. "Forgive me, please."

Her eyes shone with absolute terror when she looked at him. "Yes, yes, of course I forgive you."

He smiled and noticed how soft her skin was beneath his palms. "I love you." Suddenly, his knees wouldn't hold him anymore and he fell forward. She moved with him to brace his fall. The horrible pain shot through him again, twisting him up on the inside.

"Cas!" Zane called to him, but his voice sounded far away.

"Down here!" Carolina called back. She was hovering over him now, worried lines across her forehead. "Keep your eyes open. It'll be fine, but keep your eyes open."

"What's happening?" He should know. His ears still rang with the gunshot. Dammit. He'd been shot. The knowledge had been there all along, but he'd only just now allowed himself to recognize it.

Panic overtook him that her train was due to leave soon and he might not see her again. "Don't go, Carolina. Don't get on the train."

"I won't," she assured him as she tore off a length of her skirt and wadded it up. "I'm staying here to take care of you." She pressed it against the wound and he nearly came out of his skin from the pain.

Zane ran up beside them followed by Hunter. "Let's get him to Glory's. She has a room, and it beats that damn butcher they call a doctor at the hospital."

Castillo nearly blacked out when they picked him up.

***

Castillo awoke to a room full of his family. Hunter and Emmy sat in a chair in a corner consoling each other, while Zane stared out the dark window and Tanner sat on a chair right beside the bed. But the most important person was Carolina and she was nowhere to be seen.

"He's awake." Tanner's proclamation alerted them all so that four sets of eyes turned to him.

The room was sparsely furnished and clean, but he couldn't place it. "Where am I?" he asked through a throat that felt like sandpaper.

"Get him some water," Tanner called to no one in particular, but Zane moved first, crossing the room to a table with a pitcher. "We're at Victoria House."

Castillo laughed, but it hurt so he groaned instead. "I nearly die getting shot and you bring me to a brothel?"

"Take it easy." Hunter had walked to stand on his other side, opposite Tanner, and put his hand on Castillo's shoulder to gently hold him still. "We brought you here so you could have a better doctor."

"Caroline patched you up, with the help of her father." Tanner grinned like he was proud of her. "We didn't know what to do...you lost so much blood, but she came in and had us all following orders. The bullet passed right through you, and she had you stitched up before your head hit the pillow."

"Where is she? Did she take the train to Boston?" He'd been so stupid to ever think his revenge was more important than her.

"I'm right here, Castillo." She stood inside the open door of the room. She was beautiful, her face beaming in the gentle glow of the light, but he immediately saw the blue shadows under her eyes. She was tired, and her hair was a mess, pinned up with tendrils falling down around her face.

She was beautiful.

"Carolina. You stayed."

She smiled as she walked over to him, taking Hunter's place at his side and holding his hand. "You got yourself shot. Someone had to fix you."

"You stayed and you saved me." He could hardly believe it.

With her other hand, she touched his forehead, her fingers stroking his hair. "My father helped."

He brought her hand to his mouth and placed a kiss on her palm. "I was so stupid to let you go. When I saw him grab you, it became clear to me everything that I had to lose. I don't want to lose you. I want to go to bed with you every night and wake up to you every morning. I want to live my life with you. Say it's not too late. I know I don't deserve it after putting you in danger, but I swear I'll live my life making it up to you."

Her smile widened and tears formed in her eyes as she leaned over him. "It's not too late. I want that too. I want to spend my life with you, Castillo."

Despite the pain, he pulled her forward until he could tangle his fingers in hair and take her mouth in a kiss again. She laughed but kissed him back.

"I love you, Carolina."

Epilogue

Caroline came to a stop at the open doorway of the study and took a moment to watch the man within. Castillo sat at his cherrywood desk with a single lamp switched on as he poured over the leather-bound ledger in his lap. Sitting with one ankle propped on his knee, he held it loosely in his grasp and mumbled something to himself as he made a notation on the paper. A strand of dark hair had fallen down across his forehead, but he brushed it back with his fingers.

Her own desk sat adjacent to his, nearly unused since she'd finished her studies back in the spring. Textbooks were stacked on one side with a few patient files taking up the rest of the surface. She was generally able to finish her work before she came home from working at her father's practice.

"Did you miss me?" she asked, finally walking into the room.

Castillo looked up immediately and closed the ledger when he saw her. "I didn't hear you come in." A smile softened his features, and he stood to pull her into his arms.

Her arms went around him as she lifted her face for his kiss. She was usually home by dark, but as Caroline had been about to go home a father had brought his daughter in. The girl had taken his bicycle for a ride and without knowing how to properly operate it had fallen and fractured her wrist. Caroline had only just been dropped off at the house she and Castillo rented.

"I'm sorry I'm late," she said when he pulled back to look down at her.

"You can make it up to me later." He smiled suggestively.

Caroline laughed, but his insinuations never failed to make her body come alive. She was already anticipating when they could go upstairs to bed. "Anything interesting happen today?" She nodded toward the ledger.

His grin widened. "I've sold all the foals. There isn't one left that hasn't been accounted for."

While she'd been attending classes, Castillo had spent the past three years helping Hunter bring his prime horse stock to market here in Boston. Because of their superior performance in a few of the better-known races, Jameson horses had become something of a status symbol among the gentlemen in the highest social circles. "All of them?"

"All of them," he confirmed. "There's a waiting list and deposits for the foals that'll be born in the spring."

"That's wonderful. I'm so proud of you." He'd been at loose ends a bit when they'd first come to Boston, reluctantly accepting the money her father had settled on Caroline to help them make it through that first year. But by the second year, they'd been able to afford a modest lifestyle with his income.

He let out a little whoop and tightened his arms around her waist to lift her off her feet and twirl around with her. "If you're proud of me now, just wait until we break ground on your new office come spring," he teased, nipping at her bottom lip.

She laughed and wondered how it was possible that she could be so deliriously happy. How had she been lucky enough to find him? He didn't want to use her father's money to pay for their living expenses, but he'd had no problem suggesting they dip into his mining income to build her a respectable clinic in Helena. Of course, his relationship with his father had improved a bit over the past three years. Tanner had come to visit them a couple of times and had welcomed Miguel at Jameson Ranch when he'd graduated and shown an interest in the business.

As much as she loved her parents and was sad about leaving them behind in Boston, their family was in Helena and Caroline wanted to be there with them more than anywhere else in the world. Aunt Prudie had even indicated she'd be a frequent visitor when they moved and Caroline hoped her parents would follow suit. Her mother had come to like Castillo very much, and her father spoke often of retiring. Besides, there were few qualified physicians in Helena, and Caroline felt she could make a bigger impact there than in Boston.

She had Glory on her side, too. Since the tragedy with Victoria House...well, Glory and Zane hadn't looked back and Glory had committed her considerable resources to helping the women of Montana with Zane at her side. With so many people committed to helping Caroline succeed, she was looking forward to embracing her new family in Helena.

"I can best your new office," she teased.

His brow furrowed. "Impossible. You saw the sketches. It's as fine as anything you can find here in Boston."

"That's not what I mean." She shook her head for emphasis. She had no doubt the clinic would be the best in the state. They'd made sure it would be outfitted with the best equipment needed to cater to the medical needs of the women of Helena, along with the few brave men who might come to her for treatment. "I'll have something even more amazing for you in the spring."

"What?" He clearly had no clue what she meant, so she decided to put him out of his misery.

"A baby." She couldn't stop a gigantic smile from taking over her face.

His face went completely blank, and then a small smile tugged the corner of his mouth. His hands came up to cup her face. "A baby?"

She nodded.

"You're certain?"

She nodded again. "Positive. I waited to tell you until I was sure."

He stroked a strand of hair back from her face, and stared down at her as if she was the most precious thing in his world. Then that hand went down to her belly as if to check and make sure she hadn't changed somehow since morning. She was only two months pregnant, so it'd be a little longer before he could feel it. He didn't move his hand, though, and she covered it with hers.

"A baby," he whispered, his voice husky and reverent. "I can't think of a better way to start our new life together."

She kissed him again, thinking that Aunt Prudie had been right all along. Her hope that things would work out had seen them through to this amazing life they'd created.

Keep reading for an excerpt from The Gilded Lady the next book in The Gilded West series by Harper St. George...

The Gilded Lady

The Gilded West (book 3)

Being the madam of the most notorious brothel in Montana Territory came with certain privileges. Financial security and independence rode high at the top of that list for Glory Winters. In fact, she would go so far as to say that those were the only benefits that really mattered. For they allowed the other freedoms to exist. Without them, she'd never have been able to open her home to women running away from unfortunate situations. Nor would she have had the resources to purchase nearly an eighth of the town of Helena, making her the single most prosperous female landholder.

Unfortunately, those very same privileges that she so enjoyed came with some definite negatives. One of those negatives sat across the table from her now. He grinned, giving her a flash of the gold crown capping his left bicuspid as he tossed back the remainder of his brandy. Glory suppressed a shudder as he swallowed, making the beginnings of what would soon be a double chin wobble as he did so. He brought his handkerchief up and pressed it to his mouth before wiping it across his sweaty forehead.

"Excellent beefsteak as usual, Miss Winters."

Drawing on the impeccable manners she'd been taught at her mother's knee, Glory offered him a dazzling smile. He was a guest and she wouldn't insult him, but making conversation with him made her skin crawl. "Thank you, Mr. Harvey. I'm so pleased you enjoyed your meal." She intentionally drew out the vowels to make her Southern drawl more pronounced. It never failed to charm even the most cantankerous gentleman. Though she used the term gentleman loosely in the case of William Harvey. The only thing noble about him was his dress. He was a snake in the trimmings of probably the most expensive suit she'd ever seen on a man. For a town that had made millionaires out of humble miners, that was saying a lot.

"You've done quite well for yourself here." He sat back in the chair, leather creaking as he laced his hands over his lap.

Glory kept her smile in place. The words hung heavy in the air between them, filling it with silent tension broken only by the hushed conversation at one of the other tables across the dining room. Harvey always had something up his sleeve. She recognized this as the moment before he would strike and she tried to prepare herself for how bad the bite would be. One thing she had learned in her years here was to never underestimate the greed of men, especially when they saw a woman who had something they wanted.

Harvey wasn't the first to want a stake in her business. He wouldn't be the last.

"You're too kind," she said.

"And you're too humble. I remember when this place was little more than bare floorboards and straw mattresses."

She tried not to wince. Victoria House had never been quite that shoddy. When she'd arrived with her dear friend Able, the place had been a neglected mansion that had seen better days, but it certainly hadn't been a hovel. They had slowly transformed it into the grand club it was today. She'd hired a proper chef, and they had several dining rooms and parlors where gentlemen could come to relax surrounded by opulence. There were plenty of saloons down the road where they could go to get a whiskey for half the cost with cheaper buy-ins for poker and faro, but they came to Victoria House because they liked the atmosphere. The dust of sophistication that coated the mansion fed their need for luxury.

These men had pulled gold, silver, and copper from the earth to make themselves wealthier than they'd ever dreamed possible. The social salons of New York and London might not welcome their new money, but Glory was happy to give them a taste of that same opulence right here in Helena. Even her gowns came straight from Paris. The men were more than willing to hand over a portion of their riches for a taste of that life.

"Well, I've always known the value of a little hard work. As do you." She wasn't above pouring on a little flattery.

He inclined his head as if it were quite the task to lord over the men who did the back-breaking work of maintaining his gold mines. "It'd be a shame to see all of this hard work go to waste." He raised a hand and indicated the room with its silk wall coverings, Persian rugs and brass finishings.

Ah, and there it was. He was after her wealth. Now to figure out his game before he could lower the trap. She'd perfected her poker face years ago, so she managed not to reveal so much as a flicker of her lashes. "Hard work rarely goes to waste."

His smile faded, replaced by cold calculation. "You are aware that statehood is just around the corner for our humble little territory? Helena is in the running for state capital. Thanks to the railroad, nice Christian folks are moving here and they don't want to see an establishment such as this in our midst. Surely you can see the benefit of having a friend like me."

Rumors were that Harvey would be elected to the legislature; it was the main reason she tolerated his odious presence. She couldn't afford to alienate anyone with political clout. "But I thought we were friends." She countered.

He shrugged, his cold gaze sliding over her exposed shoulders and down further in a slow glide that made her want to scrub away the filth he'd left behind. "We could be closer, Miss

Winters. Much closer. I could help you keep everything you've worked for, and you could help me."

She didn't even want to entertain the thought of what helping him would entail. "I think the fine people of Helena will come to understand how much good I do for the town. My taxes and personal donations have contributed to the school that was recently built."

He laughed. "Money only goes so far. The reputation and honor of our fair city is at stake, particularly when it comes time to vote for statehood. Why, a notorious place such as this might not be able to exist in a law-abiding state."

"Then the fate of Victoria House is sealed either way," she said with a shrug of her shoulder.

"Ah, but I have friends, Miss Winters. And soon I'll have influence. If we were...friends...I could extend that influence to you." He licked his lips, leaving them wet and shining in the light of the candle flickering on the table between them.

She swallowed past the bile that threatened to rise in the back of her throat, and opened her mouth to tell him in her sweetest voice that no way in hell would she ever be that sort of friend to him. Because she was a madam, men often assumed incorrectly that she was also for sale and she had to set them straight. Thankfully, Able intervened before she said something foolish and made an enemy they didn't need.

"Miss Winters." His large frame took up nearly the entire doorway of the dining room. "You're needed upstairs."

He had a sixth sense when it came to saving her. It had been that way ever since they escaped together twelve years earlier. She simply wouldn't have made it out of that house in the South Carolina low country all the way to Helena had he not almost literally carried her the entire way.

"Excuse me, Mr. Harvey. Duty calls. It's been a pleasure." She rose and nearly gasped audibly when the man leaned forward and grabbed her wrist. No one ever touched her. From the corner of her eye, she saw Able step into the room, ready if he was needed.

"Think about what I've said, Glory. You may not have that long to make up your mind," Harvey said. His eyes flashed with cruelty as he let her go just as Able came to a stop next to his chair.

"Is that a threat?" She bit the words out through clenched teeth.

"Not at all." He grinned, but it wasn't the least bit friendly. "Merely an observation of things to come."

"Good evening, Mr. Harvey." Without another word—as much as she hated him and all he stood for, she wasn't willing to make Harvey an enemy—she strode out of the room with Able close behind her.

"Thank you for intervening," she whispered once they'd walked far enough down the hallway to not be overheard.

Able made a grumbling noise in the back of his throat. "I've never liked that man. Don't trust him."

"You and me both." She opened the door leading to the servants' quarters in the back of the house and paused to make sure no one followed them. Closing the door behind them after Able had stepped inside, she said, "He wants Victoria House."

Able drew in a sharp breath through his nose. "He won't get it." The light of the electric wall sconce reflected off his medium-brown skin revealing a brow that was smooth and not furrowed in worry. His dark eyes were calm. Quiet and sensible, he'd become the barometer against which she measured the scope of their problems. There wouldn't be reason to worry until he was worried.

Nodding her agreement, she said, "It's nothing we haven't faced before." A couple of years ago they'd faced a similar threat only this one had been a group of investors looking to purchase the place from her at a value far below market. Little had they known that Able was part owner and any decision she made would have to be corroborated by him. Once they'd found out they'd resorted to force instead of seduction. In the end, they'd dealt with those men and she had confidence that Harvey could be handled as well.

"Is everything else going well?" she asked.

"Fine. We're a little busier because of the faro tournament across the road, but everyone is behaving themselves."

"In that case, I'll go get a little work done in my study and give Harvey some time to leave. Let me know if I'm needed." Able agreed, and Glory took the back stairs up to her study on the mansion's third floor. The top floor was private. Her apartment was attached to her study and the other ladies who lived at Victoria House full time had rooms there. It wasn't decorated quite as ostentatiously as the rest of the house. The wall color was a soft cream with a blue-and-gold runner softening her steps in the hallway. Each door boasted a wreath or some other decorative trinket that reflected the resident's personality. In short, this floor felt like home and was a respite from the bustle of the rest of the house.

Up here the William Harveys of the world felt far away. Glory let out a breath, already anticipating the nice long soak in her bathtub she'd take when the evening was over. It seemed like the nights were getting longer, or maybe she was simply getting older. She'd be thirty in a couple of years, which didn't seem particularly old, but this wasn't where she'd imagined herself at this point. Life was strange in that way. Nothing ever seemed to happen the way she meant for it to happen, but she'd learned that it could still be good. She had about a million things to be thankful for, not the least of which were security and independence. It was more than she'd had a decade ago.

She was smiling when she approached her study, but the smile faltered when she realized that the door wasn't latched. A gentle nudge revealed that her assistant's desk sat empty. Glory turned on the wall sconce to reveal that no one was in the antechamber at all. How odd. Charlotte, her assistant, always closed up when she finished her work for the evening. A stack of correspondence ready to post the next morning sat on the corner of Charlotte's small desk, exactly as she'd left them. It was possible that Charlotte had forgotten to lock up, but a strange sense of foreboding made her stomach tumble.

Glory took in a deep breath, consciously avoiding looking across the room at the door that led to her study. Glory was the only person with a key to that door. If it was open then it meant that someone had broken in and she'd have to face that her sanctuary wasn't really a sanctuary at all. But she was being silly. Of course, it was locked. To prove it to herself she put her hand into the hidden pocket of her skirt and wrapped her fingers around the warm metal of the key. It was still safely with her. Charlotte had simply forgotten to close the door to the hallway.

Her heart pounding, she turned toward her door. It was mercifully closed. An exhale of relief left her feeling deflated and weak. She put a hand on the corner of Charlotte's desk to keep her balance. Even after all these years she was wary of any irregularity. She knew all too well how quickly life could come crashing down with very little warning.

There was no light coming from beneath her door and no sound came from within her study. No one had been inside. She knew that, but her heart resumed its pounding as she approached the door with her key in hand. The cool metal of the latch chilled her palm and she gave it a quick turn to test the lock. Her key held useless in her other hand, the door latch made a clicking sound as it unlatched. She gave a little push and the door creaked, swinging open to reveal the interior of her office. Moonlight flooded in through the windows facing the street, spilling onto the carpeted floor. No one was inside, but nevertheless she moved forward cautiously.

As soon as her feet crossed the threshold she saw it. It was a square piece of parchment sitting in the middle of her tidy desk, and it seemed to have a nearly ethereal glow in the moonlight. It had not been there when she'd left earlier in the evening.

Turning on the electric sconce on the wall didn't help. The white parchment lost its glow, but it didn't seem any less dangerous. It hadn't been sent by post. There was no envelope, no markings at all. She crossed to her desk, watching the note as if it were a living thing that could jump out and grab her at any moment. Blood pounded through her head, filling her ears with its roar. Somehow her life would change when she read that letter. She just knew it. Good things rarely came along unexpectedly.

Her fingers trembled when she reached for it. The stiff paper was cool under her touch, barely crinkling as she sucked in a deep breath and flipped it open. The first five words on the page jumped out at her, sending a shard of terror straight through her heart.

I know who you are.

Get your copy of *The Gilded Lady* by Harper St. George

Also by Harper St. George

The Gilded West

The Runaway Heiress (novella)
The Copper Heir
The Bastard Heir
The Gilded Lady

The Doves of New York

The Stranger I Wed
Eliza and the Duke

The Gilded Age Heiresses

HARPER ST. GEORGE

The Heiress Gets a Duke
The Devil and the Heiress
The Lady Tempts an Heir
The Duchess Takes a Husband

Sons of Sigurd

Falling for Her Viking Captive

To Wed a Viking

Marrying Her Viking Enemy
Longing for Her Forbidden Viking

Viking Warriors

Enslaved by the Viking
One Night with the Viking
In Bed with the Viking Warrior
The Viking Warrior's Bride

Blood and Glory

Dirty Boxing
Take Down
No Contest

About the author

Harper St. George was raised in the rural backwoods of Alabama and along the tranquil coast of northwest Florida. It was a setting filled with stories of the old days that instilled in her a love of history, romance, and adventure. By high school, she had discovered the historical romance novel which combined all of those elements into one perfect package. She has been hooked ever since.

She lives in the Atlanta area with her family. She would love to hear from you. Visit her website to sign up for her newsletter at www.harperstgeorge.com/newsletter and connect with her on social media.